DEADFALL

A RAINE STOCKTON DOG MYSTERY #12

Donna Ball

CHAPTER ONE

I have been told that I need to learn to mind my own business. On occasion I've been told that by people who were pointing a gun at my face. But most of the time I hear it from those who actually have my welfare in mind: my aunt, my ex-husband, my current boyfriend, and even, now and then, an exasperated officer of the law. But I would like to point out in my own defense that in this particular instance I *was* minding my own business...or trying to, anyway.

My local tracking club was hosting an AKC tracking test and a just-for-fun wilderness tracking event in December, and my job was to scout the location. I'd decided to make a holiday of it for my three dogs, who love to explore new places. So Mischief and Magic, the Aussies, were crated in the back of my SUV while Cisco, my intractable Golden Retriever, was buckled into the bench seat, grinning happily as he swung his gaze from one window to the next, trying not to miss a thing. Come to think of it, that kind of lively curiosity—which might sometimes be misinterpreted as an inability to mind our own business—is one of the things Cisco and I have in common.

I was halfway up the rocky, switchback dirt road that led to Overlook Falls when my cell phone rang. Actually, it didn't ring so much as it *blared* through the car speakers, startling me so much that my foot hit the brake and gravel spattered from the back tires. So much for the safety features like the integrated Bluetooth hands-free telephone that the salesman had touted so enthusiastically. I had only owned the car for a few weeks (love the sporty red color; hate the payments), my former vehicle having met with a misfortune I'd rather not think about. It wasn't new, but it was definitely new to me, and I admit I was baffled by the technological advances that had overtaken the auto industry in the nine years since I'd purchased a car. It took me a minute to remember how to answer the phone. The speakers blared three more times before I found the right button. My friend Sonny was on the other end, and she got right to the point.

"I need a favor," she said through the car speakers. "So hear me out before you say no."

I knew from experience that that kind of admonishment usually precedes a request I'd really regret *not* saying no to, but Sonny was not the kind of person who asked for favors very often; in fact, it was usually the other way around. She was an environmental lawyer who'd moved here a few years back and bought a big spread on top of one of the nearby mountains which she was slowly turning into an animal sanctuary. She had goats and chickens, sheep, cats, a donkey, and two cows, all of whom had for one reason or another been unwanted by their owners. She also had two amazing dogs: Mystery, a border collie, and her service dog, Hero, a yellow Lab. So animal welfare was one thing that had brought us together; environmental protection was another. And the truth was that she had done me enough favors over the past couple of years to earn a few minutes of my attention, at the very least. So I geared down to continue the climb up the road and said cautiously, "Okay."

"Do you remember over the summer, that case of the service dog biting the little boy at the baseball game? Or, I should say, the alleged service dog allegedly biting the child, even though there were fourteen sworn witnesses to the event."

It had been a busy summer for me, and an even busier fall, but it wasn't likely I would forget something like that. For one thing, it involved a dog. For another thing, Hanover County, North Carolina, is a small community in the heart of the Smoky Mountains where hometown gossip is a tradition as old as moonshine. It's hard not to know every detail of pretty much everything that goes on around here. For another thing…well, it involved a dog, and dogs are, in fact, my business.

My name is Raine Stockton and I own Dog Daze Boarding and Training, which is the only full-service canine care facility for seventy-five miles in any direction. I'm also secretary of my local agility club, three-time past president of the Humane Society, sole representative of the local chapter of Purebred Rescue and Golden Retriever Rescue, and Vice President of the Western Carolina Wilderness Tracking Association. I'm also a member in good standing of the Golden Retriever Club of America, both local and national, the AKC, Blue Ridge Search and Rescue, and the Smoky Mountain Canine Obedience Club. When people hear the word "dog" they think of me. And at least half a dozen of those people had called to make sure I knew about the dog bite at the softball game before the parking lot had even cleared.

I said, "I remember it, sure."

"Well, the case is going to trial in a few weeks, and the family of the little boy has asked me to represent them." She sounded both pained and uncertain. "I don't usually do this kind of thing—heaven knows I haven't done a personal injury case in twenty-five years—but they lost their counsel at the last minute—Tucker Williams, dropped dead of a heart attack, horrible thing—and they were referred to me because I have a service dog, I guess..." She sighed. "At any rate, I've looked over the paperwork and I think they've got a good chance of getting a jury judgment far bigger than the one the insurance company is offering. But before I commit to anything, I'd like to talk to you."

"Me?" I said, surprised. "I don't know anything except what I read in the paper."

"I'll buy you lunch," she suggested. "Miss Meg's, about 1:00?"

4

The digital clock on my dashboard informed me it was 10:30. Plenty of time to scout the site, take the dogs for a nice romp, and be back in town by 1:00. I was teaching a nose work class at 4:00, but we only had six boarders at the kennel, which my assistant, Corny, could handle perfectly well on his own, and no grooming appointments until tomorrow. All that aside, it was Wednesday, and on Wednesdays Meg made her famous banana pudding. The thought made my mouth water.

So I replied, "I'm not about to turn down a free lunch. But I still don't see what I can do to help."

"One o'clock," she confirmed. "See you then."

I pictured her making a note on her phone calendar as she disconnected, despite the fact that our meeting was less than four hours away. She was still big-city enough to do things like that, even though she had once confessed to me that the main reason she had moved here was so that she could get rid of her appointment calendar.

The place I was headed was called Little Man Ridge, and I had taken the long way around specifically to hike the terrain—and to enjoy the falls, of course. On the other side of the ridge there was a hard-packed gravel road leading to the remnants of an old hunting lodge, which was perfect for the tracking club event. The lodge itself was nothing but a tumbled chimney and a pile of foundation stones, but the wide, flat area surrounding it could easily park a dozen RVs and twice as many cars, with plenty of room left over to accommodate a hospitality tent for registration, coffee, and snacks. Spreading out around the lodge were a couple of partially wooded, rolling acres of scrub grass and rock, perfect for laying tracks. Beyond the lodge, the gravel road narrowed and began to climb steeply, eventually ending at the scenic hiking trail to Overlook Falls where we'd hold the wilderness tracking event.

The AKC only offers three tracking titles, which basically acknowledge a dog's ability to pass a tracking test in field terrain, urban terrain, and both. However, most serious canine search and rescue groups in this part of the country require their dogs to pass a rigorous wilderness certification test as well, which was why our club always offered a wilderness track when we hosted a tracking test. I think that's one reason we always got such a good turn-out, and the entry fees from the wilderness event pretty much paid for the whole weekend.

It was a gorgeous, bright blue November morning, crisp enough to make me glad of my down vest and flannel shirt, but minus the bitter winds that can make even the prettiest autumn day miserable in the mountains. There were even a few colorful leaves left on the trees, showing off in bright patches of crimson and yellow that peeked from the woods and decorated the distant vistas. The dogs love nothing better than an autumn morning in the woods, and they tumbled out of the car like prisoners seeing sky for the first time in twenty years, spinning in circles, bouncing away, sniffing the scrub grass and plowing through fallen leaves, bouncing back again. The

Aussies were perfectly reliable off leash, but Cisco had a tendency to get distracted, so I hooked his collar to a retractable leash before letting him out to explore. I let him romp to the end of the twenty-foot leash and watched the three dogs for a minute, grinning, while they play-bowed and teased and sprang at each other. Cisco, who believed himself to be the most important dog in the vicinity no matter what the circumstance, was not in the least inhibited by the fact that he was leashed and the two girls were not, and he gave as good as he got until I called them all to heel and started up the path toward the waterfall.

For the real tracking test, we would start the dogs at the lodge ruins, pick up the trail to Overlook Falls, cross the stream and circle back down to the access road where I had left my car. I was hiking it backwards, getting the steepest part of the trail out of the way while I was still fresh. I'd end up in the lodge parking lot, and it would be a mostly downhill hike when I returned to my car. It was only a twenty-minute hike to the waterfall, slightly less if you have an impatient golden retriever pulling you up the steep parts. Mischief and Magic did their usual herding-dog thing, cutting back and forth across the trail, sniffing the ground with tailless butts wagging, racing ahead and circling back to check on Cisco and me, their flock of two. I kept an eye out for deadfalls, downed trees, and earth caves that we could use to hide "victims" for the wilderness search. But mostly, I admit, I was just enjoying a hike in the woods on a crisp autumn day with three happy dogs.

We approached the falls from the back side, which is not the safest way to do it, and which is why tourists and casual hikers are directed up the path from the lodge. I had been roaming these woods since I was old enough to walk, and considered myself more than a little trail-savvy, so I called the Aussies to heel and reeled in Cisco's long leash as soon as we started to hear the roar and tumble of water in the distance. Dogs are pretty smart, but they make mistakes just like humans do. It would be far too easy for one of them—Cisco, in particular, leaps to mind—to go splashing through the stream and fail to stop in time to avoid the steep, slippery cliff that preceded the hundred-foot drop of rushing water.

There are thousands of waterfalls in and around the Nantahala National Forest, some of them smaller than a backyard landscaping feature, some of them wide enough and shallow enough to climb like a staircase. Many are part of the river rapids that make for some of the best whitewater rafting in the country, and a few even form pools at the bottom deep enough for swimming. Very few are suitable for diving, although I'll admit that as a reckless teenager I tested that theory more often than I should have. Overlook Falls is suitable for neither climbing nor diving, which is why the Forest Service put up warning signs at the end of the trail approaching the falls: *Danger. Falls Ahead. Stay Back.* Since I was the one who had actually installed those signs, back when I worked for the forest service, I felt free to ignore them and guided the dogs up the hill through a short stretch of woods that would take us to a breathtaking view of the waterfall before we picked up the trail that led back down the mountain to the lodge.

There is something utterly magical about these woods in autumn, or anytime really. I could actually smell the mist in the air as we pushed our way through a rhododendron thicket and feel the temperature drop a good five degrees. The sound of tumbling waters sounded like a distant ocean, and there was a subtle charge to the atmosphere that felt electric. Someone once had told me that had to do with the positive ions around the waterfall, and that, because of them, the Creek Nation had designated this area a sacred site. I'm not sure how much of that is true, but I do know that if it hadn't been for the sound of the falls I might have heard the voices, I might have had a warning about what was going on, and things might have gone very differently that day.

We came out of the woods abruptly onto a flat rocky expanse of pine straw-strewn ground with a wide, shallow creek dancing and gurgling through the center of it. About twenty-five feet away the creek took an abrupt downward turn, spilling over the edge of the cliff onto the boulders a hundred feet below. At the edge of that cliff, up to their ankles in the flow of the stream, stood a man and a woman. He had his hands on her shoulders and she appeared to be struggling against him. There was shouting, but I couldn't hear what was said. Cisco barked, and I cried, "Hey!" and lunged forward. The man whirled around, looking startled. I took a few more running steps toward the couple, with Cisco barking at my side and the two Aussies joining in the chorus. I cried again, "Hey! Stop that! Be careful!"

And that was when the woman flailed her arms, her feet slipping dangerously on the wet rocks, and before I could draw another breath for a scream, she went over the cliff.

Chapter Two

I raced forward, my heart tearing from my chest to my throat, and Cisco loped beside me, dragging his retractable leash. Abruptly he stopped, spun and started barking madly at something that was so out of place in this idyllic glen that it might as well have been a prehistoric monster, its one giant leg planted firmly on the leaf-covered surface, its misshapen head looking down on us from the tree line. I stumbled and stared as Cisco continued to bark, and just then someone splashed across the shallows of the stream toward us, exclaiming, "Lady, what the hell—"

He tried to grab my arm but Cisco, distracted by this new game, slammed his front paws onto the stranger's chest in a happy, tongue-lolling greeting. The startled man almost dropped the walkie-talkie he was carrying, but not before I heard another voice crackle through it, "Cut! Cut, for God's sake! Dallas, are you okay?"

Cisco bounced away and, somewhat belatedly, I snatched up his leash from the ground, halting his forward motion. I heard a distant female voice calling, "I'm okay!" I swiveled around in time to see a woman climbing back over the edge of the cliff from which she had just fallen. My jaw dropped.

To be fair, it had all happened so quickly, and so unexpectedly, that my startled brain hadn't had a chance to put it all together. It wasn't until I saw the woman's ascent over the edge of the cliff was assisted, not only by the hand of the man with whom she had been struggling only moments ago, but by nearly invisible guy wires attached to a harness beneath her outer clothing, that I began to suspect all might not be exactly as it appeared. And it was about that time that I realized the mechanical dinosaur that had so startled Cisco—and me—was in fact a kind of crane with a chair at the end of its long arm. And on that chair, high above us all, was a camera operator.

The woman pulled herself upright and started to unbutton her water- splotched suede jacket. Two more people splashed across the stream to help her unfasten the wires and strip out of the harness as she called, "How did that look? I tried to improvise. Can you use any of it?"

An agitated-looking man with curly dark hair, amber tinted glasses, and a plaid flannel shirt came striding up the path that led to the lodge. He spoke tersely into a walkie-talkie. "T.J., did you get any of that?"

Across the stream, tucked to one side and mostly out of view, were two pop-up canopies, one of which sheltered a long table filled with pastries, coffee carafes, and an assortment of bottled juices. Cisco must have caught the scent of pastries because his tail started swishing as he wandered nonchalantly in that direction. I hit the brake on his retractable leash and reeled him in. The Aussies had noticed the crane and were sniffing far too close to the expensive equipment for my liking, so I called them over to me with a sharp, "Mischief! Magic! Heel!" The two girls dashed to my side, executed twin flip-finishes that would have earned them a perfect score in an obedience trial, and sat on either side of me. Cisco, once I pulled him close, sat sloppily in front of my toes, tongue lolling, bright eyes taking in every detail and calculating the odds that I would release him to go exploring again.

A couple more people trotted up the path on the other side of the stream, and one of them grinned and paused long enough to take out his phone to snap a picture of the dogs. The man in the plaid shirt said into the radio, "Yeah, we had a little distraction up here." He glared at me as he said it. "We've got time for maybe one more take before the sun hits the trees." He thrust the radio at one of the eager young people who had raced up the path after him and shouted, "Wardrobe! Makeup!"

"Ah, man!" The woman who'd fallen off the cliff strode toward us, jerking off her stocking hat, and with it, a damp blond wig. "That water is freezing!"

Without all the extraneous gear she proved to be a slim, athletic woman in her thirties with caramel-colored hair pulled back in a short braid and pinned against her neck. She had an easy gait and a relaxed manner, despite her scrunched-up expression when she remarked on the temperature of the water. Her jeans were wet to the knees and her leather hiking boots soaked. Black mud smeared her hands and the cuffs of her thermal knit shirt, but despite the fact that she had just fallen over a waterfall—and climbed back up—she seemed to be the most comfortable person here.

She glanced at me as she passed and said, "Cool dogs." Cisco wiggled his appreciation and tried to nudge his way toward her. I tightened my grip on the handle of his leash, speechless.

"Five minutes, Dallas, I'm not kidding," replied the plaid-shirted man shortly. "We're losing the light and it'll take you that long to get strapped in. Get into wardrobe and make like a quick-change artist."

"My best thing," she assured him with a grin and hurried toward the tent that was set up at the edge of the woods. Halfway there she turned back and called to me, grinning, "Hey! Thanks for trying to save my life!"

At least someone had noticed.

The man shouted at her, "Dallas!"

"Going!" She broke into a lope.

The man raised his voice another notch and shouted to the world at large, "Five minutes!" Then he turned on me, dark eyes snapping. "Who are you and how in the *hell* did you get on my set?" he demanded. "The trail is closed. Didn't you see the signs? Jeez, where is security?" He swung around and shouted, "Lonzo, who's in charge of security? Don't tell me it's one of those local yokels we had up here yesterday. Will somebody for the love of God find Lonzo?" He pivoted back to me. "Who *are* you?" he demanded again.

By this time I had figured out what was going on. I would have had to be a fool not to, especially since the town had been talking about little else all month other than the fact that our little corner of paradise had been chosen for the making of a major motion picture. Some pretty big names were attached, too, although my sources—consisting mainly of ten-year-old Melanie, my boyfriend's daughter—informed me that none of them were likely to show their faces around here, since they had doubles for that kind of thing. The paper said the local economy was likely to benefit by as much as a million dollars during the time the crew was here, but our local paper has been known to exaggerate. There were notices posted all over town about street closings and business closings to accommodate the filming, but I hadn't heard anything about waterfall closings. I was about to point this out when another man came jogging up, wearing a pink and purple striped wool scarf knotted at his throat and a harried expression.

"I'm sorry, Mr. Rosenstein," he exclaimed breathlessly, "my fault! My fault entirely!" He whirled on me and demanded, "Are you the dog wrangler? What are you doing here? Didn't you get the call? You're not due on set until Friday! Can't you people learn to read a schedule?" He turned back to the man he'd addressed as Mr. Rosenstein. "I'll take care of it, sir. I'm terribly sorry."

"It's not your fault," I said. I turned to Mr. Rosenstein and repeated, "It's not his fault. There's a back trail up here, and I'm guessing you only closed off the main trail up from the lodge. By the way," I added, "I'm not the dog wrangler, whatever that is, I'm just a hiker. My name is Raine Stockton."

I thrust out my hand, but Rosenstein ignored it. "Oh, for God's sake, Lonzo, just take care of it, will you? And get me another coffee, black this time, no sugar. I hate shooting on location," he muttered as he strode away. "*Hate* it."

"Yes, sir," Lonzo called after him. "I'm on it! No problem!"

He turned back to me with an edge of panic in his eyes and said, "You've got to get out of here. Seriously. This is a closed set. How did those dogs get here?"

Cisco gave a happy bark of greeting when the stranger looked at him, and I pulled him closer to me protectively. The Aussie girls, the little-show-offs, didn't move a muscle in their perfect sits. "They came with me," I answered. "We walked up through the woods." I glanced around. "So wow. You're shooting a scene here, huh? I sure thought it took more equipment and people than this. I never would've known if it hadn't been for…" I gestured toward the camera crane, uncertain of the term.

"Boom," he replied distractedly. "We're shooting the master shot, all we use is the boom. Really, we're on a tight shooting schedule here, so..." He stopped suddenly and stared at me. "You're not the dog wrangler?"

I shook my head, still looking around. "Are you all going to be here very long?" I asked. "I came up here to scout the trail back to the lodge. Do you think it would be okay if I—"

"No!" He looked at me as though I had lost my mind. "No, no, absolutely not! You're not even the dog wrangler, you are not authorized to be here! You have to leave, you have to leave right this minute!" He made as though to grab my arm, glanced at the dogs, and stepped back, making shooing motions at me with his hand. He cast an anxious glance over his shoulder and turned back to me, distressed. "Please? This is my first shoot with Mr. Rosenstein, and I can't screw it up!"

Well, of course I didn't want anyone to lose his job, even though I really didn't see what the harm would be in letting me hang around a while, and I was a little annoyed at having driven all the way out here for nothing. But just in case I had any doubts about the seriousness of the situation, Rosenstein bellowed behind me, "Places! Places *now!* Lonzo, where's my damn coffee!"

"Coming, Mr. Rosenstein!"

Lonzo gave me another pleading look, this one even more desperate than the one before, and I said, "Okay, okay, I'm going." I clucked my tongue to the dogs as I turned back toward the trail from which I had come. "Mischief, Magic, let's go." They fell into step beside me, and I would have puffed out my chest with pride had it not been for the fact that I was using all my strength and both hands to tug Cisco into something resembling a heel position at my side.

Lonzo scurried off for coffee, and Rosenstein shouted again, "Dallas, I swear to God if you're not in gear in thirty seconds you're fired!"

Dallas came out of the tent just as we were passing it, adjusting her blond wig and buttoning up her now miraculously dry suede coat. "Yeah, well, good luck replacing me in the middle of nowhere!" she called back and paused to swoop down and cluck Cisco under the chin as she passed. "Besides," she added under her breath with a wink to me, "I'm union. Really cool dogs," she added, and when her name was shouted again she shouted back, "I'm here, already!" And she hurried off.

Of course, my first inclination was to ease off to the side and watch the scene play out again—after all, I deserved something for my trouble—But when Mr. Rosenstein looked straight at me and shouted, "*Clear the set!*" I thought better of it. Reluctantly, I pulled Cisco close, clucked my tongue to the Aussies, and started back down the trail toward the car. That, as they say, should have been that.

But it wasn't.

CHAPTER THREE

I live in the most beautiful place in the world; it's no wonder they wanted to make a movie here. My century-old farmhouse is nestled at the base of Hawk Mountain and bordered by one of those crystal-clear streams that the mountains are so famous for. In mild weather, when I leave my windows open at night, I can hear the water bubbling and gurgling as it dances over stones made smooth by its passage, and the sound really is like music. When the leaves are off the trees in the winter, I can look through my second-story window and see layers of lavender blue mountains where drifting pillars of clouds rise like ancient smoke signals from the coves and eddies of our own Smoky Mountain rain forest.

Of course, there are a couple of things I could have done without, most of them related to the construction that had been going on pretty much nonstop since a millionaire developer by the name of Miles Young had purchased most of my mountain for a fly-in resort community he called Eagle's Landing. On the other hand, Miles had brought a few good things into my life, too: broadband Internet, a great jogging trail through the woods that connected my house to his, a bone-shaped swimming pool that my dogs were welcome to use any time, and his ten-year-old daughter, Melanie.

Then there was Miles himself: sexy, funny, bossy, stubborn, tender, generous, opinionated, and on the wrong side of every argument we'd ever had, and we'd had a few. He was an amazing cook, and the smartest man I'd ever known. Most importantly— believe it or not—he was wild about me, and I have to admit, the feeling was mutual. Most of the time.

But it was Melanie who was on my mind as I swung the SUV into the driveway that separated my house from the Dog Daze building and released my three canines from their various restraints. Melanie's bicycle was propped up against the picket fence that enclosed the front entrance of the building, and by the way Cisco made a beeline for the gate, I guessed she'd brought Pepper, her own golden retriever, with her. Of course, that didn't take much guessing skill. I don't think she'd ever been to my house without Pepper at her side.

"Hey, Raine!" she called from the grooming room when I opened the front door of Dog Daze.

There was no need to wonder how she knew it was me. Cisco's claws were scrabbling on the tile before the door chime that announced my arrival had ceased its second note, and he flung himself on the Dutch door that separated the office from the grooming room with enough enthusiasm to make it creak. Only the bottom half of the door was closed, so by the time I ran to the rescue, he was elbows and torso over the door, back feet clawing for purchase as he attempted to heave himself the rest of the way over.

Before I could draw a breath for a command, Corny turned from the tub where he was sudsing up Pepper and exclaimed, "Mister Cisco! Where are your manners? Act like a gentleman."

That was all it took. Cisco dropped all four paws to the floor—on the proper side of the door—and wagged his tail apologetically. I couldn't have achieved that kind of cooperation with a pocketful of liver treats and a professional grade clicker, and I've been training dogs for ten years.

Corny is a flamboyant young man with a fuzzy aurora of orange-red hair, oversized Coco Chanel-type glasses, and a tendency to dress in bright stripes and polka dots. He showed up at my doorstep virtually homeless in August, and almost immediately gave new meaning to the term "heaven-sent." I could no longer imagine running the kennel—or even my life—without him. He has an almost mystical power over the dogs and wields a pair of grooming scissors like a magic wand. His efficiency and work ethic are a constant source of amazement to me, and even Miles jokes that if I leave it to Corny, Dog Daze will be on the New York Stock Exchange in five years. Of course, Corny can be a tiny bit eccentric—he doesn't own a car, for example, and rides his bike everywhere he goes—and more than a little dramatic. But his devotion to his job—and to me, and everything and everyone that's important to me—is almost fanatical. In short, there are maybe three people in the whole world I'd trust with my dogs, and Corny is one of them. That's the highest praise I can give.

Melanie giggled from the grooming table where she was perched, swinging her feet. "That was funny. He almost made it, too."

I kept my expression stern as I glared down at Cisco. "It was not," I replied. "He could have broken the door." But it *was* funny. I glanced over my shoulder to see Mischief and Magic help themselves to a chew bone each from the basket on the floor of the office, and then curl up on their beds behind my desk. My lips turned down dryly. "Why can't you be more like that?" I muttered to Cisco. "Back up."

He took two backwards steps, grinning up at me as though nothing whatsoever of consequence had happened, and then two more. That made me smile. Backing in a straight line is hard for dogs to do, but Cisco had mastered it beautifully. I dug a treat out of my pocket, tossing it to him as I opened the door. "Go lie down."

He snatched the treat out of the air, licked his lips, and looked at me as though hoping I'd change my mind. When I didn't, he walked a few steps away, turned in a circle and plopped down on the floor with a big sigh. I latched the door firmly behind me.

"We're getting Pepper ready for her big trip to Grandma's tomorrow," Melanie said, glancing at the soapy golden retriever in the tub. "I'm thinking of painting her nails pumpkin colored for Thanksgiving. What do you think?"

Melanie was at the age where she was starting to develop a sense of style—for both herself and her dog. That style was unique, to say the least. Today she had pulled up her curly black hair into a bushy top ponytail that was tied with a hot pink ribbon painted with glittery silver dog bones. Her red cat-eye glasses were decorated with rhinestones all around the frame, and so was her pumpkin-colored sweatshirt, which actually had rhinestone pumpkins on it.

I said, "I think all the other dogs at the beach will be jealous." What I *really* thought was that all the other dogs at the beach would be laughing, but I'm learning not to say everything I think.

The subject of the upcoming Thanksgiving holiday had been the source of tension around here for the past several weeks. Miles had wanted me to come with Melanie and him to Myrtle Beach and have Thanksgiving with his mother. I had wanted his mother to come here so that everyone could have Thanksgiving with Aunt Mart and Uncle Ro and me. It wasn't that I didn't like his mother—I liked her a lot, and who wouldn't love spending time at her luxury beach house with ocean views from every room? But I always spent Thanksgiving with my family, and besides, I had the kennel to think about. Miles pointed out, accurately, that his mother had invited me for Thanksgiving way back in the summer, and I pointed out that I hadn't accepted. Thanksgiving was a family holiday, and I should be able to spend it with my family, just like he should spend it with his.

It wasn't like we were married or anything.

So in the end, Miles pretended to be okay with my decision and I pretended to be okay with his, and of course neither one of us was okay at all. Every time we were together the subject lay between us like a mess someone had forgotten to clean up, both of us going out of our way to ignore it in order to avoid a fight. That was okay, I guess, because it kept us from talking about the real thing that lay between us, and the much bigger fight we refused to have.

"Dad said I could go with you to scout the trail for the tracking test," Melanie went on in a slightly accusatory tone, "but when I got here Corny said you had already gone and we should wash Pepper instead. You should have waited for me."

"Sorry," I said. In fact, what her father had probably said was that he would check with me, and if the terrain wasn't too strenuous she could go. I was familiar with Melanie's creative interpretation of her father's rules by now, and had learned to anticipate it. The terrain *had* been too strenuous, so I didn't feel bad about having missed her. It had just saved me an argument. "But it's just as well. I didn't get to scout the trail after all. You won't believe what happened."

Corny's eyes grew round as saucers while I told my story; Melanie was considerably less impressed— or at least she tried hard to be. This was probably because she had spent the past month throwing broad hints to her father about what an incredible educational opportunity it would be for her to spend her Thanksgiving break on the set of an actual movie watching actual Hollywood professionals at work, and how it probably wouldn't be any problem at all for someone like her dad to get a set pass for her because, after all, he knew *everyone*, didn't he?—only to learn that Miles had already made arrangements for them to spend the break at the beach with her grandmother. Since there was nothing she could do to change her father's mind—and I knew her too well to believe she hadn't tried—she had done what any self-respecting ten-year-old would do: pretended it didn't matter, and that the entire movie and everything associated with it was, in her words, "lame."

"It was really bizarre," I said, "to walk right into the middle of a movie scene. And that big camera crane thing sitting there in the middle of the woods…I wonder how they even got it up there. Helicopter? They were filming the master shot, whatever that is. At least that's what that fellow Lonzo, Mr. Rosenburg's assistant, said."

"Stein," corrected Corny, never taking his enraptured gaze off of me even as he did a thorough and professional job of buffing the excess moisture out of Pepper's rinsed and conditioned coat with a chamois. "Rosen*stein*."

"Right," I agreed. "I guess he's the producer. He was bossing everyone around like he was, anyway."

Melanie corrected, "Director. He's the writer and director, everyone knows that."

Corny paused with the drying chamois in mid-air. "Wait. You actually *met* Seth Rosenstein? *The* Seth Rosenstein?"

I shrugged. "I guess. I mean, we didn't shake hands or anything." I didn't have to pretend to be unimpressed. I hadn't even known Rosenstein's first name until now. "It was more like he yelled at me and I went away." I didn't see any reason to elaborate on exactly how I had blundered onto the set and ruined his shot, nor on how I had so foolishly mistaken a stunt for a real life-threatening incident. Whenever possible, I like to be the hero of my own stories—or at least to avoid looking stupid in them.

Melanie said, disgruntled, "Who cares? It's not like it was Beyoncé or anything."

Pepper, having been patient as long as could reasonably be expected, shook out her coat, spraying a mist of jasmine-scented water everywhere. Melanie wrinkled up her nose and made a show of wiping off her glasses with the hem of her sweatshirt. Corny opened the door of a drying cage and said, "All right, young lady, off you go." Pepper obediently trotted into the cage and lay down.

"Maybe not as exciting as Beyoncé," agreed Corny, adjusting the blowers, "but still." His fuzzy orange hair bounced with the decisiveness of his nod, eyes shining behind the giant white-framed glasses. "I mean, *still!* Seth Rosenstein is a legend! Every film he's ever made has been a smash! An absolute *smash!* Well," he corrected himself, "maybe not *every* film. There was that really awful *Bloodbath*, right at the beginning of his career. A real stinker-roo vampire/ slasher kind of thing. Glad he got over *that*."

"Oh sure," Melanie put in, "I saw that. It was totally lame."

I lifted an eyebrow. "Your dad lets you watch slasher movies?"

She shrugged. "As long as he watches them with me. But this one wasn't even scary. These stupid kids saved their own blood to make a vampire trap when *everybody* knows vampires only drink fresh blood."

I wrinkled my nose. "Yuck. Why didn't they just go to a blood bank?"

"Oh well," supplied Corny with the ease of someone who is intimately familiar with the storyline of every vampire movie ever made, "the whole plot hinged on this century-old vendetta the vampire had against this family, so it was important that the DNA be authentic."

Melanie rolled her eyes. "Like I said, stupid."

"Anyway," I added, discovering the morning's mail on Corny's desk, "Rosenstein seemed like kind of a jerk." I began to sort through the mail, tossing aside a brochure offering a free evaluation of my life insurance needs. "I felt sorry for his poor assistant. The woman, Dallas, was nice though."

Corny passed a questioning look to Melanie, and Melanie said with authority, "She probably wasn't anybody famous. They always send in the B team first."

Corny added, in possible defense of Mr. Rosenstein, "Geniuses are always jerks."

I shrugged and borrowed an expression from Melanie's vocabulary as I tossed the last of the junk mail into the trash. "Whatever. They thought I was the dog wrangler. What is a dog wrangler, anyway?"

They both seemed to be experts on that subject. "It's like a dog handler," offered Corny, "only he works for the production company."

"She's in charge of all the canine actors," Melanie clarified. "Like a trainer. Makes sure they hit their marks and know their tricks."

I grunted. "I didn't know there were dogs in this movie. What's it about, anyway?"

"Well," said Corny with enthusiasm, "it's actually based on a true story about this millionaire playboy back in the seventies who did away with every woman he ever dated—or married. Twenty women altogether, and he made every single murder look like an accident! Until the very end, that is. It was his last wife who caught on to him, and the whole story is from her point of view, going back to her childhood and everything. At least that's what the article I read in *People* magazine said," he explained. "It was really interesting. But I don't remember them mentioning anything about dogs."

"They're probably just extras," offered Melanie confidently. "But even extras have to be cleared by the production company, especially if they're dogs. *And* they have to have a Humane Society rep on the set at all times."

"Huh," I said, impressed as always by Melanie's vast repertoire of knowledge. "That's good, I guess."

Melanie said, "Too bad you didn't go into dog wrangling, Raine. There's a lot of money in it."

"Oh yeah?" I put the electric bill in the stack with the other unopened mail—gas bill, two credit card bills, homeowner's insurance bill, and a very intimidating looking notice from the county reminding me that my property taxes were due in three weeks.

"Sure," she replied confidently. "That's why the movie has a forty-million-dollar budget."

"Fifty-seven," corrected Corny. "I read it just this morning."

She gave him an annoyed look. "Forty million. I'll bet you twenty dollars."

The unfortunate thing about that bet was that Melanie probably had twenty dollars in her pocket. I wasn't so sure about Corny. I said sternly, "No gambling on the premises."

"No problem, Miss Stockton." Corny assured me earnestly, but he turned surreptitiously to the laptop where he kept the grooming records and clicked the mouse to access the Internet.

I changed the subject. "What time are you leaving for the beach, Mel?"

Her expression fell visibly. "I dunno. After breakfast, I guess. Don't worry, though." She cheered marginally. "I'm all packed so I can help you set up for the class this afternoon."

"Good," I said. "You didn't forget to pack Pepper's bag, did you? With her own dishes? Because no dog likes to eat out of someone else's dish." And no grandmother liked to have her good china turned into dog bowls, either, but I didn't mention that part.

She rolled her eyes at me. "Of course I didn't forget. That was the first thing."

I said, "I've got a bag of pecans from Aunt Mart's tree in my office that she wants you to take to your grandma." My aunt had become friends with Miles's mother, Rita, when she'd visited here over the summer, and they still Facebooked and e-mailed back and forth. Another reason why Rita should have come here for Thanksgiving. "I guess you all are having pecan pie for Thanksgiving. Don't let me forget to give them to your dad when he comes to pick you up."

"Yeah, okay." She sighed. "I wish you and Cisco were coming."

"That would hurt Mischief's and Magic's feelings."

"They could come too!" Her eyes lit up as though this were a real possibility.

"I'm sure your grandma would have something to say about that," I returned, trying not to grin at the thought. Rita was a lovely person and liked dogs as much as anyone else, but four full-sized canine houseguests would push even the most gracious hostess over the edge. "Besides, when you own a business you can't just take off whenever you want. Ask your dad about that. You have to be responsible."

One thing Miles and I did agree on was the importance of teaching Melanie a strong work ethic. She'd worked for me over the summer at the kennel—although for her it was more like play—and had even had a few solid ideas for how to improve business. She might have been born with a silver spoon in her mouth, but I could tell already that was a handicap she'd have no difficulty overcoming.

She pointed out, deliberately being difficult now, "You just took off this morning."

"Yeah, well, that was dog business. Besides, I have to get some perks for being the boss."

I turned to Corny, who was busily scrolling down pages on the laptop. "Corny, I promised to meet someone for lunch in town at 1:00, so if you want to go ahead and get something to eat, Melanie and I will finish up with Pepper."

"Aha!" he exclaimed. Triumphantly, he turned the screen around to us. "Told you!"

The headline read, **Fifty-Seven Million Dollar** *Deadfall* **Film Projected to be a Windfall for Hanover County.**

Melanie shrugged and rolled her eyes, and I tried not to chuckle. Until then, I hadn't even known the title of the film, but given the scene I'd witnessed that morning, it seemed appropriate.

But I don't think any of us could have guessed then just how appropriate the title would eventually turn out to be.

CHAPTER FOUR

In Hanover County we have a pizza place, a Chinese restaurant with take-out, some really good barbecue joints, and a steak house out on the highway where kids like to go on prom night. But for good home cooking at an affordable price, it's Miss Meg's Diner all the way. It's located in the middle of the block right downtown, which means it gets all the lunchtime business from the surrounding merchants, and at noon on a weekday it's hard to find a seat. Usually by 1:00 or 1:30, though, the working crowd starts to clear out, and when I arrived a little after 1:00, Sonny was holding a booth for us. Her service dog, a yellow Lab named Hero, was lying quietly under the table with his head on his paws, as he had been trained to do.

Sonny is probably in her fifties, and one of the most accomplished people I know, but unless she's in a courtroom or trying to intimidate an opponent, she looks a lot like a refugee from a hippie commune. She wears her prematurely gray hair in a long braid down her back, and dresses in flowered prairie skirts and chunky rock jewelry. She suffers from a debilitating joint disease that sometimes keeps her confined to a wheelchair or a scooter for days at a time. On those days Hero is trained to open and close cabinets and the refrigerator door in order to fetch things that she needs, to turn light switches on and off, to open and close doors, and even to dial 911 on a specially designed telephone with an oversized emergency dial button. On good days, like today, when Sonny is able to get around with a cane, he still goes everywhere with her, mostly to keep his skills sharp, but also because it's often too painful for her to bend to pick up a dropped object or even lift something as heavy as her purse. I had seen Hero take a credit card to the cashier and return with a receipt. He's amazing.

I didn't train Hero, but I'm a huge fan of the people who did. In fact, I have nothing but admiration for all those dedicated men and women who train service dogs for the physically and mentally challenged—the legitimate ones, that is. Unfortunately, there are far too many people out there, whether through greed, lack of scruples, or simple ignorance, who are selling dogs as service dogs that haven't been through anything resembling a training program, and who possess nothing more than average obedience skills. Presumably, that was what Sonny and I were here to talk about today.

The place was bustling when I sat down, and I wasted no time deciding on the daily special: Miss Meg's chicken and dumplings with a side of field peas and mashed potatoes. Sonny sensibly ordered a green salad and unsweetened tea. Good for her. But this would probably be my only meal today, and when I can get someone else to cook for me, I take advantage of it.

I entertained Sonny with the story of my brush with Hollywood while we waited for our food, and she told me that someone from the production had contacted her about sending a crew out to film some of her farm animals, but when they found out how far she lived from town they'd decided to use stock footage instead. I'll admit, Sonny's place isn't easy to reach—at the top of a mountain accessible only by a dirt road that's steeper and rockier than a lot of hiking trails I've been on—but it seemed to me that if they had been willing to helicopter a mini-fridge and a coffee bar to the top of a waterfall, they could have found a way to use local animals for their production.

"They pay for that, don't they?" I asked.

"I'm sure," she replied. "I heard the director is staying in the Hamilton place on the lake, and they're paying four thousand a week in rent."

The Hamilton lake house was something of a landmark around here, built by a railroad tycoon at the turn of the century as a family retreat. It was still used by the family as a summer place, and had been the most luxurious home in the county until Miles built his.

"Langston Blake got ten thousand for the use of his 1957 Ford truck in the film," Sonny added, "plus they insured it for the full value."

My eyes went big. "Holy cow."

"Of course, it's a restored classic." She made a wry face. "I doubt they'd pay as much for my goats. But it's good PR to spend as much money locally as they can. It makes the fact that most of us couldn't turn left on Highway 83 for two hours yesterday a little easier to swallow."

"I guess." I was still trying to get my head around that figure. "But you can almost buy a whole new car for that."

"Which Mr. Blake will probably do."

The waitress brought our food, and I dug in while Sonny took a more ladylike approach to her salad. But I was starving, and really, chicken and dumplings are no good unless they're piping hot. When my plate was half-empty, I slowed down enough to say, "So tell me about your case."

She reminded me of the particulars: A military veteran by the name of Kate Greene, who suffered from balance issues as a result of head injuries sustained in combat, had taken her service dog to a local softball game at which her nephew was playing. A family with a four-year-old boy was sitting in the bleachers next to her and, according to Greene, the child had been teasing the dog. The parents of the child denied that, of course. At any rate, the little boy had been bitten in the face, resulting in a $25,000 medical bill, a permanent scar, and "emotional trauma." The family of the child was suing for $1.5 million.

Sonny speared a piece of lettuce and looked at it thoughtfully before replying, "I don't know,

Raine. Maybe I'm not the right person for this case. It's never a good idea to make decisions based on emotions, and when I heard about this case it made me so angry...I *know* how valuable service dogs are and how important it is for them to be allowed to do their work." As she spoke, she dropped her gaze in the direction of Hero, beneath the table, and at the same moment, sensing her attention, he lifted his head toward her. That was the kind of bond a really good service dog team shared. "This kind of thing diminishes everyone with a service dog and might even eventually threaten public access. It is absolutely beyond me how anyone can have the audacity to take an untrained animal into a public place and try to pass it off as a service dog without any regard at all for the consequences. Personally, I'd like to see them do jail time."

As she spoke, her color rose and her voice grew crisp with anger. She paused to draw breath, looking a little embarrassed for the passion she'd displayed—she was usually much more laid back than that—and I said, "It sounds to me like you've already got your opening statement nailed. Anyway, you're preaching to the choir here."

So here's the problem. There is no law in the United States requiring that a service dog be certified, registered, trained, or even evaluated by a qualified agency. There's no universal standard for testing. There are a couple of legitimate agencies that oversee the standards and practices of service dog training programs—Assistance Dogs International and the International Guide Dog Federation are probably the most well known—but unless you're in the business, you probably wouldn't know to check a service dog provider for affiliation with one of those organizations. In fact, Google "service dogs" and you'll come up with five pages of places you can go to purchase a service dog vest and fake certification online, and there are thousands of people more than willing to take advantage of the opportunity. I can't tell you how many people have walked out of my therapy dog training class when they discovered that a therapy dog does *not* get to fly free in the airplane cabin with you, and it isn't guaranteed access to restaurants and movie theaters. And don't even get me started on so-called "emotional support" dogs. Every dog I've ever met is an emotional support dog, who are you kidding? That doesn't mean they should have the same privilege to public access as a fully trained service dog who actually saves lives.

I said, "So let me guess, you're representing the family of the little boy who was bitten, not the owner of the dog who did the biting, right?"

She said, "Actually, we're suing the trainer. Kate Greene, the dog owner, claims the trainer misrepresented the dog's temperament and will actually be a witness on our side. In a case like this you follow the money. The trainer—or I should say, the service dog provider—carries over a million dollars insurance on each dog she places. "

As a dog trainer myself, I can't say I approve of that kind of jaded approach to justice, but I suppose

I shouldn't expect anything else from a lawyer. I took another bite of dumplings and swallowed. "So what kind of dog is it?"

"Some kind of shepherd mix. This trainer rescues dogs from the pound and trains them as service dogs. Sounds like a win-win for everyone, right?"

Right. It always *sounds* like a win-win. Don't get me wrong: I love mixed breeds, and I tell everyone who's looking for a pet to go to the local shelter. But there is such a thing as genetic temperament, and the problem with mixed breeds is that you very often don't know what they're mixed *with*. Not to mention the fact that sometimes—and I hate to say this, I really do—dogs are in the shelter for a reason. Had this shepherd-mix bitten before? We might never find out.

I put down my fork. "I don't know what to tell you, Sonny. It sounds open and shut to me. Of course, I'm no expert on the law…"

She seized on that. "But you *are* an expert on dogs."

"Well," I said modestly.

"And that's why I came to you," she went on. "The former counsel hired an investigator, of course, and I'll put him on the stand. But the trial is going to be held here, in Hanover County, and you're local. Everyone knows you, and they'll believe what you say. I want to call you as an expert witness."

"Oh." You'd think that the daughter of a judge would be perfectly at home in a courtroom, but I had given one too many witness statements in my lifetime to think that going to court was a fun way to spend the afternoon. Suddenly I wasn't quite as interested in seeing justice served as I had been before. I couldn't keep the reluctance out of my voice as I said, "I don't know, Sonny…"

"You'd be paid the standard rate, of course."

I was surprised. "People get paid for this kind of thing?"

She gave a decisive nod. "A hundred dollars an hour for any research involved, and a thousand dollars for the courtroom appearance."

Wow. That would certainly make those car payments a little less painful. Still…"I'll have to think about it," I said.

Sonny was about to reply when someone called from across the room, "Hey! Hey, it's you!"

Over the past half hour, the bell over the door had become an almost constant background noise as people finished up their lunches and went back to work. When I looked up the diner was almost empty, except for the woman called Dallas, who was waving at me from the door. I waved back, and she started toward me, tugging a not-quite-as-enthusiastic Lonzo behind her.

Without the blond wig and suede jacket, she looked like anyone else on the street, and I might not have noticed her if she hadn't called out. Her brown hair, loosened from its braid, swung in a simple bob around her jawline, and the only makeup she wore on her fresh-scrubbed face was a little lip gloss. She was dressed in jeans and a faded navy sweatshirt with a picture of a cartoon mouse on the front. I noticed for the first time that she wasn't particularly pretty—not unattractive, but just ordinary looking. I remembered her being a lot more glamorous on the set.

"This is the woman I was telling you about," I said to Sonny as she reached our table. "The one from the movie set."

"Dallas McKenzie," she introduced herself, and gave Sonny's hand a firm shake. "And this strange-looking fellow here is Alonzo." She tossed him a questioning look over her shoulder. "What's your last name again, sweetie?"

As comfortable and at-home as Dallas looked here, that was how out-of-place Lonzo looked. It wasn't just his blue-plaid wool jacket and pink scarf looped oh-so-fashionably around his neck, or the spiked white hair or narrow-toed cowboy boots. It was the way he hunched his shoulders and kept his hands in his pockets, his eyes darting uneasily around as though he expected to be robbed at gun-point at any moment. And when Dallas spoke to him he replied with a scowl, "Bartinelli. How many times do I have to say it, already?"

Dallas grinned and elbowed him in the arm. "Just messing with you, kiddo. We always give the new guys a hard time," she explained to us.

Sonny introduced herself, and I added, "And I'm Raine Stockton. I don't think we actually met before."

Dallas started to pull out a chair and make herself at home, and then she noticed Hero under the table. "Good heavens, how many dogs do you have? Hey there, big fella."

She reached down to pet Hero, and Sonny said, "Hero is my service dog."

Dallas withdrew her hand. "Sorry. I didn't see the vest."

I appreciated the fact that she knew enough not to pet a working dog. You'd be surprised how many people don't. I've actually been out with Sonny and Hero, while she was in her wheelchair and his vest was perfectly visible, and watched people send their children over to offer Hero a dog biscuit. Not cool.

"I should've known he wasn't an ordinary dog," Dallas went on easily. "Way too well behaved. I had a Lab as a little girl and there wasn't enough rope in the county to keep him tied under the table when there was food around."

Sonny and I laughed, and I added, "It took a lot of training to get him to this point."

"Did you train him?" Dallas asked. "Because your two little ones—what were they?"

"Australian shepherds," I supplied.

"Yeah, they were amazing."

"Thanks," I said, trying not to show my pride. Actually, all three of my dogs were pretty amazing, but Mischief and Magic knew how to work a crowd. "Australian Shepherds are known for being quick studies. But I didn't train Hero," I added. "That's a little outside my skill set."

"Raine's one of the best trainers in this part of the country, though," Sonny put in, and I suspected the flattery was her way of furthering her case. "People come to her with their dogs from all around."

"Actually," I pointed out just to let Sonny know I wasn't swayed, "I'm the *only* certified dog trainer in this part of the country—or the county, anyway. So is filming finished for the day?"

"My part is," Dallas returned cheerfully. "So I'm in search of lunch. Lonzo here is still working. He's in search of tomorrow's breakfast. You wouldn't believe the donuts we had this morning. They tasted like they'd come from a World War Two vending machine."

"They didn't have vending machines in World War Two," Lonzo muttered.

"Exactly," Dallas tossed back.

Sonny said, "So you're an actress?"

Dallas shook her head. "Not quite. I do all of Bethany Parker's stunts, plus the stunts of the four wives who were killed before her. I get set on fire, pushed off a cliff, drowned in a river, thrown out of an airplane…it's great." The spark of enthusiasm in her eyes looked genuine.

"How long are you going to be here?" I asked, although I was sure everyone in town except me knew the answer to that.

"We're set to wrap the location shots by Christmas," she replied. "The rest of it will be shot on a set in Hollywood."

I could see Lonzo shifting his feet restlessly, but Corny and Melanie would never forgive me if I didn't get as many details as I could while I had the chance. "Where are you all staying?" I asked.

Dallas replied, "The director and the actors have all rented houses between here and Asheville somewhere. The rest of us peons are staying on site, at this compound out in the country not far from here. Actually," she admitted, "it's not that bad. I think I heard they used to have some kind of rehab program for rich kids there. The main building is really luxurious, with a gourmet kitchen and an indoor pool…"

I said, "You must mean the New Day Wilderness Outreach center." The center had closed down after the death of its operator last year, not to mention the scandal that had followed. I guess the lawyers involved in defending the multiple lawsuits that were being filed had decided to lease out the real assets to try to make up the deficit.

She said, "Could be. Anyway, they brought in some cute little trailers that look like log cabins for the overflow and there's good Internet and cable TV, so it's okay. Better than a lot of places I've holed up in, that's for sure." She elbowed Lonzo and grinned. "Remember that swamp we were in this summer? Mosquitoes the size of bald eagles."

Lonzo said impatiently, "Come on, Dallas, I'm supposed to be back in an hour. Let's just get a chopped salad to go."

Dallas rolled her eyes in his direction. "He's vegan," she explained.

I thought, but did not say, *Good luck with that around here.*

So Dallas said it for me. "I told him to bring his own carrot sticks. You don't come to a place like this to *not* eat." She drew a deep, appreciative breath. "Man, it smells like home in here."

Sonny inquired, "Where're you from, Dallas?"

"Texas." She grinned. "And no, my parents didn't name me that. No one in this business goes by their real name." She elbowed Lonzo again. "Except maybe this one. I mean, who'd make up a name like Lonzo?"

He ignored her, glancing at his watch. "Dallas…"

"Okay, okay. Nice seeing you all. Say," she added, just before she turned, "what's good?"

"The chicken and dumplings were amazing," I told her, "if there's any left. And Meg makes a great hamburger. Also," I added on an inspiration, "her sausage biscuits are the best. Maybe that'll help with your breakfast problem."

Dallas grinned her thanks at me, and she and Lonzo made their way to the far end of the counter. A waitress scurried to present them with menus.

"She seems nice," Sonny observed.

"Not what I expected," I agreed. "You know, for a movie person."

Sonny looked amused. I knew she thought I was a little unsophisticated at times. She was right.

Sonny reached into the oversized purse that was on the seat beside her and took out a manila envelope, passing it across the table to me. "Here's the investigator's report, the original police report, and some other information about the case. All I need you to do is talk to the trainer, check out her facility, look at her dogs, and give me an opinion."

I looked at the envelope, wrinkling my nose a little in a subconscious expression of how distasteful I found the prospect of spying on one of my own kind. On the other hand, if this person was turning out untrained service dogs, she certainly didn't deserve my protection, or that of anyone else.

I said, "So what if I decide she's on the up-and-up?"

"Then you'll tell me," she replied simply, "and your job will be finished. It won't stop the lawsuit, but it may persuade the client to settle out of court. If they do decide to go forward with a jury trial, I obviously won't put you on the stand."

I scowled, feeling slightly less valuable than I had a moment ago. "So where is this person, anyway?"

"Just outside of Greenville," she said.

"That's a two-and-a-half-hour drive."

"You get paid travel expenses," she assured me. "The hourly rate plus mileage."

One five-hour round trip could make a huge difference in my Christmas budget. I pulled the envelope toward me. "How soon do you need to know?"

"You can take a couple of days to think about it," she said. "But I'll need your report by the end of the month. The court date is December 13."

The tracking club event was the tenth, so that wasn't a conflict. And it wasn't as though I had much else to do this time of year, and definitely nothing that paid a hundred dollars an hour. I said, "I'll have to look at my schedule."

She smiled confidently. "Let me know by the weekend."

Miss Meg herself swooped down to place a dish of banana pudding before me. "You won't believe what just happened," she said in a hushed tone. She picked up our plates and nodded her head toward the counter where Lonzo and Dallas were sitting. "That fellow over there? The one with the funny-looking hair? He just ordered *two hundred* sausage biscuits for the morning! Two hundred! Paid for it with one of those platinum credit cards with the name of some fancy studio on it. I waited for the charge to clear," she added, just to make sure we knew she wasn't a fool. "But two *hundred*!"

I grinned and glanced in the direction of Dallas and Lonzo. Dallas was stirring sugar into her iced tea and Lonzo was still frowning skeptically over the laminated menu. The bell over the door rang again and I waved as Marshall Becker, our newly elected sheriff, came in. Miles says that Miss Meg's is the small-town equivalent of an outdoor cafe in Paris: if you sit there long enough, you're bound to see everyone you know. He was right.

Marshall waved back and started toward us, and I turned my attention back to Meg.

"Good for you, Meg," I said. "They're going to be here another month, maybe they'll make that a standing order."

She looked horrified. "Good Lord, I hope not! You know I only keep one cook on in the winter, and he goes home after lunch." With a flash of panic in her eyes, she added, "Raine, honey, you need to finish on up and get out of here. I've got to start making biscuits!"

She turned just as Marshall reached our table. "I've got your order just about ready, hon," she told him in passing. "Putting the fries in now."

Sonny waved her credit card at her and Meg snatched it up before hurrying back to the kitchen.

Marshall said, "Afternoon, ladies." He pulled out a chair from a table across the aisle and brought it to the end of our booth, straddling it backwards. "Mind if I join you for a minute?"

I had only gotten to know Marshall this summer, when he had run against the incumbent—my ex-husband, Buck Lawson—for sheriff. We'd become friends, more or less, when he adopted a rescue golden from me. He'd probably make a good sheriff, but he was a bit too by-the-book for my taste. To be perfectly honest, I still wasn't sure how much I liked him...except for the golden retriever part, of course. It was hard not to like anyone who loved a dog as much as Marshall loved Cameo.

I scooped up a spoonful of banana pudding. "We're about ready to leave. You didn't forget about class this afternoon, did you?"

"Cameo is in the car," he told me. This was no surprise, since he took her everywhere. "We'll be heading out to class from the sheriff's office. I just stopped by to pick up some sandwiches for Buck and me."

Marshall wouldn't take office until January, but my uncle, who'd been sheriff of Hanover County until Buck took over, had told me that a successful transition of office could take every bit of the two months between the election and the swearing in, especially when the incoming sheriff planned to implement as many new programs as Marshall did. Buck had been more than accommodating in working with Marshall, which didn't surprise me. For one thing, Buck was basically a nice guy and would have been gracious in defeat to anyone. But more importantly, he was glad to be out of the job and anxious to see someone else take over. The only reason Marshall had won at all was because Buck had dropped out at the last minute to take care of his new wife, a deputy who'd been injured in the line of duty. Still, I'd heard the write-in votes—mostly for Buck—had been the highest ever recorded in a local election.

Sonny said, "How're things going, Marshall?"

Like a typical lawyer—or politician—Sonny was friendly to everyone, probably because she never knew when she'd need them on her side. I had no idea who she'd voted for.

"Good," he replied. "It's a lot of work, trying to get caught up with where we are and what needs to be done before I take over, especially since Buck's leaving next week."

"What?" I looked up from my banana pudding, surprised. It wasn't that I expected to be kept informed of my ex-husband's every move, but it was a small town and I knew most things that concerned him. We still talked sometimes, after all, although not as much as we used to before he'd remarried. But come to think of it, we hadn't talked much at all since the election. Of course, I'd wondered what Buck would do after he left office; everyone had. Personally, I figured Marshall would find a place for him on the force, probably as chief deputy, since no one in Hanover County had more law enforcement experience than Buck, and Marshall would be foolish not to take advantage of that. But I think everyone assumed Buck would at least serve out his term.

Marshall said, "He's got about six weeks vacation on the books. I guess he decided to spend Thanksgiving with his wife and in-laws up in Asheville."

I'd heard that Buck's wife, Wyn, had gone to stay with her folks in Asheville after she got out of the hospital, and that Buck drove back and forth to see her on his days off. I guess her recovery was taking longer than expected, and there was a good rehab center in Asheville that her doctor had recommended. However, that was all I'd heard, and I did make it a point not to ask too many questions about Buck's personal life.

"So what's going to happen to the sheriff's office while he's gone?" I wanted to know.

Marshall smiled and shrugged. "Not my problem for another ten weeks. But usually the chief deputy takes over the rank-and-file when the sheriff is unavailable."

I wasn't even sure who Buck's chief deputy was.

I said, "Marshall…do you know what Buck's plans are? After, you know, January?"

Although he was too polite to say so, I got the feeling Marshall was one of those people who thought everyone would be better off if I learned to mind my own business. Whatever he thought, he'd become pretty adept at dodging my questions, and all he replied this time was, "We never talked about it."

I found that hard to believe, and I probably would have pressed him further if I'd had the chance. But just then Meg returned in a bustle with Sonny's credit card and receipt, and she swept my bowl off the table while my spoon was still in the air. I quickly took the last bite of my pudding before she took my spoon too.

"Your order's ready at the counter," Meg told Marshall and called over her shoulder. "Y'all have a good day now!" as she hurried off again.

"Boy, talk about the bum's rush," I muttered.

Sonny said, "That's what you get for trying to help a person out." She explained to Marshall about the movie people and the big breakfast order while Hero went to work. He braced himself beside the table while Sonny grasped his harness to pull herself across the bench seat, carefully swinging her legs into the aisle. She steadied herself by placing both hands on Hero's shoulders while she stood, at which point Hero swung himself around to press against her knees while she found her balance. All the while Sonny kept talking and joking, and we were all chuckling about Miss Meg and her sausage biscuits as we made our way to the front—or the humans among us were chuckling, at least. Hero walked quietly and attentively by Sonny's side, matching his pace to hers. Had he not been there, Sonny would have had to rely on Marshall or me for assistance getting up, which would have made her feel like an invalid. But with Hero at her side she was as independent as anyone else in the restaurant, a professional woman out for lunch with friends. You can't overestimate the importance of something like that.

Marshall's order was waiting when we reached the front, and he walked us out. "I guess I'll see you both Thanksgiving," he said, holding the door for us.

I knew my Aunt Mart had invited Sonny for Thanksgiving, but I hadn't heard Marshall was coming too. I wasn't surprised, however. He was friends with Uncle Ro, and Aunt Mart made it her mission in life never to let a bachelor, widow, or orphan eat a holiday meal alone.

I said, "And I'll see you at class this afternoon."

He crossed the street toward the sheriff's office, and Sonny and I went toward our cars, which were parked next to each other a few doors down. "I'll try to read the file tonight," I promised her, "or at least look at it. Maybe I'll see what I can find out about this service dog trainer and let you know... Oh, crap," I said, looking down unnecessarily at my empty hands. "I left the file in the booth."

She gave me a tolerant look and pointed the remote at her car. It beeped to unlock. "Just don't take too long to decide, Raine," she said. "If I'm going to take this case I need to present my clients with a strategy before Thanksgiving."

"Before the weekend, I promise," I assured her, and trotted back toward the diner to retrieve the file. Before I reached the door, my phone buzzed with a text. It was from Miles, and it said, *I'm bringing dinner tonight. Hope you're hungry.*

I grinned and typed back a reply. Like I said, I never turn down the opportunity to have someone else cook for me, and today it looked as though I'd hit the jackpot. I had just hit send when the door of the diner opened so abruptly it almost hit me in the face. I jumped back, startled, as Dallas burst through, screaming at someone over her shoulder, "Let go of me, you crazy bitch! Is this how you treat your customers? What kind of two-bit joint is this, anyway?"

Meg had Dallas by the elbow and one shoulder, and she gave her a final forceful push out the door just as Dallas jerked away, her eyes blazing. Meg's expression was equally fiery as she retorted, "The kind that don't tolerate your kind of BS, young lady, I'll tell you that much! And if you ever so much as darken my door again, I'll call the cops, I swear on my mother's grave!"

I watched, gaping, as Meg spun around and marched back inside. Lonzo barely managed to edge out the door before she slammed it with such force that I could hear the angry jangle of the bell from the sidewalk.

I said, "Dallas, what happened?"

She whirled on me, her color high and her eyes wild. "You saw that, didn't you? Didn't you? She put her hands on me!"

Lonzo, clearly uncomfortable, said, "Dallas, let's just go."

She turned on him. "You're a witness! You saw it! You did!"

"Dallas, for God's sake…" He tried to take her arm, but she jerked away from him.

"I should have known," she spat, "you worthless little wimp. Where's the damn car?"

Without waiting for a reply, she pushed past me and off the sidewalk, striding past the parked cars and into the street just as a pickup truck made a left turn from the intersection in front of her. I yelled, "Hey! Watch out!"

She stopped her forward momentum just in time, but the truck didn't slow down. In fact, there was a moment—I could have been wrong of course, but there was just a moment—when it looked as though the driver actually swerved toward her, as though he meant to hit her. He pulled back at the last minute, which caused the truck to slow enough for Dallas to lunge at it, banging her open fist on the tinted window. "Try it again!" she shouted. "Just try it! I'll kill you! I swear to God I will!"

The truck took off, maneuvering the turn as fast as was safely possible. I would have done the same.

People were staring. Heads turned on the street and peeked from the shop windows. Lonzo ran into the street and grabbed Dallas's arm. This time she let him. He half pulled, half pushed her the rest of the way across the street and into a black SUV. I watched until they drove away, and then hurried into Miss Meg's.

"What was that about?" I demanded, hoisting myself onto a counter stool.

Meg, tight-jawed, was attacking the countertop with a polishing rag and the devil's own vengeance. The cashier and waitress were hovered at the other end of the counter, casting furtive glances toward their boss, and the few customers who remained forked down their pie and drank their coffee with a determined concentration.

Meg said, "I don't care who you are, you don't act like that and think you can get away with it, not in my place of business you don't. Ain't no amount of sausage biscuits worth that!"

I insisted, "What did she do?"

"She attacked one of my customers, that's what! Walked right up and started yelling at him to get out—out of *my* restaurant, mind you!—and cussing up a blue streak, to boot! I never heard the like!"

I twisted on the stool, looking around. "Who? Who did she attack?"

"Never seen him before. One of them movie people, I reckon. Anyway, it don't matter who, you don't act like that in my place of business, and I told her so. Told her to mind her manners or get out." She reached beneath the counter and brought out the manila envelope I'd left behind, slapping it down on the counter in front of me. "Here. You forgot this."

I took the envelope and looked around again. "Where is he?"

"Gone. I don't blame him. That woman's got a screw loose, if you ask me. And," she added with a nod of satisfaction, "I tore up the charge slip for them sausage biscuits, right there in front of them both. I'll be glad to see the last of every blame one of them movie folks. Nothing but a menace and a pestilence, if you ask me."

"I'm sorry, Meg," I said. I couldn't help feeling responsible for sending them here. "She seemed nice when I first met her."

"A pestilence," Meg repeated firmly. "You mark my words."

I don't like to judge, but at that moment I can't say I disagreed with her.

CHAPTER FIVE

Every now and then I like to teach a stand-alone, just for fun class to supplement the obedience, puppy kindergarten, and agility classes that are my bread and butter. Last month it was Beginner Tricks, the month before it was Canine Musical Freestyle, and this month it was An Introduction to Nose Work. I had five students, all of them golden retrievers, which made me—and Cisco—very happy. In addition to Pepper, with her freshly groomed coat and pumpkin-colored nails, there were a couple of young goldens from my obedience classes, one woman who'd been talking to me about joining our tracking club in the spring, and the aforementioned Marshall Becker with his gorgeous English Cream Golden, Cameo.

Cameo had come to Marshall beautifully mannered and fully trained, but he'd still taken the time to take her through therapy dog training last month, which raised him a notch in my esteem. Of course, he had been in the midst of an election campaign at the time, and there just so happened to be an article in the paper when he and Cameo passed their therapy dog test that showed him in a very favorable light, so his motives might not have been entirely altruistic. On the other hand, the article hadn't done me any harm either. I'd filled up two classes after the paper came out that week, so I guess in a way I owed him one.

I think Marshall might have had an idea about eventually using Cameo in the sheriff's office, but I'd explained to him—to everyone who signed up, in fact—that this class would in no way qualify a dog as a tracker. What it would do was demonstrate the remarkable ability dogs have to distinguish and define various odors—even ones we humans can't detect—and teach the handlers some basic techniques for developing their dogs' skills. When I returned from lunch, Melanie and Corny helped me fill a dozen small containers with cotton balls soaked in things like alcohol, orange oil, and ammonia. Some of them had perforated lids, and those we "hid" around the agility room. The others would be distributed among the students as training tools. By pairing a food treat with exposure to a specific scent, we would teach the dogs to locate and alert to that scent when exposed to it again. Or at least that was the plan.

With a little over an hour left before the sun dipped behind the mountain, I started class in the outdoor training yard, a fenced enclosure that I used for advanced obedience classes, rally, and puppy play when no classes were in session. The yard was filled with scents, which was the point, and

I encouraged everyone to walk their dogs around to become familiar with the area and with each other. Cisco was my demo dog, and of course he had to greet everyone who came through the gate. When Cameo arrived, Cisco's ears perked up and his tail wagged with special enthusiasm. He had had a wild crush on the gorgeous white dog over the summer, despite the fact that she showed only the mildest interest in him. He was over the infatuation now, but Cameo was still one of his favorite playmates, and he was always glad to see a dog he knew.

While Cameo and Cisco sniffed and wagged and play-bowed, I told Marshall, "You missed all the excitement at the diner this afternoon."

He watched, smiling, while Cisco and Cameo checked each other out. "Oh, yeah?"

Briefly, I told him about the drama with Meg and Dallas. "Dallas was so upset she almost walked out in front of a truck, right in front of the sheriff's office too. I can't believe you guys didn't see it."

He said, "If the deputies are hanging out at the office watching traffic, they've got too much time on their hands. Meg should've called when the disturbance broke out."

He had a lot to learn about the way people handled things around here. "Meg's a tough old bird," I assured him. "She's used to taking care of her own troubles."

"Still, somebody should file a report."

I tried not to roll my eyes. It was going to be a long four years if this was how he intended to keep the peace in Hanover County. I was tempted to say something to that effect, but just then Corny came trotting up with the supplies I needed for class, and I saw it was past 4:00. "Okay, everyone," I called. "Let's get started."

"Pepper would've won," Melanie remarked as we stacked the dinner dishes, "if Cisco hadn't cheated."

Meals at my house were always served at the kitchen table, with a fire crackling in the woodstove in the center of the room and at least one dog sleeping nearby. I had a dining room, but it was currently being used to store the extra bags of dog food, cleaning supplies, and kennel merchandise that I'd moved out of the kennel when Corny moved into the back room as the on-site kennel manager.

Miles, Melanie, and I had gotten into the habit of having dinner together three or four nights a week since Miles had built the big, glass-fronted mansion on the hill that was within walking distance of my house. Sometimes I'd go there, sometimes we ate here, but he always cooked. Tonight my kitchen was redolent of beef stew with wine—or, as Miles and Melanie informed me, boef bourguignon—along with a touch of cinnamon and sugar from the apple pie that was warming in the oven. Miles liked to cook; I did not. Also, he was good at it; I was not. He was a great boyfriend.

I'd spent most of the meal retelling my adventure at the waterfall this morning, and then rehashing the drama at the diner. Melanie couldn't wait to tell her father about the nose work class, since Miles had only arrived in time to observe the last part of it.

All of the dogs had been great students and had picked up the basics of identifying and locating the scent vials hidden in the agility room with little difficulty. But I'd expected nothing less from golden retrievers. Some had done better than others, of course, but none had completely mastered the art of the alert by the time class ended at 6:00. The end game had been a timed exercise to see how quickly each dog could find and sit in front of the particular scent he'd been training for throughout the previous two hours, and that was what Melanie was referring to. There had been no winners or losers, though. All the dogs went home with an oversized, cellophane-wrapped dog biscuit for their efforts.

Upon hearing his name, Cisco looked up hopefully from the mat in the corner of the kitchen to which he had been relegated while we ate. Pepper, who had actually done quite well in the nose work class, was sound asleep on my sofa in the other room, completely unconcerned about her reputation.

"It wasn't a competition," I informed Melanie, turning on the water to rinse the dishes, "and Cisco didn't cheat."

As it happened, Cisco had demoed that class several times before, and naturally he had the routine down. For purposes of the class, he had been trained to hit on the scent of rubbing alcohol, and, having been repeatedly rewarded with leftover roast chicken for the entire hour of class every time I took the lid off the jar that contained the alcohol-soaked cotton pad, he practically tore up the matting in his hurry to find the hidden container that held "his" scent when we took the dogs inside for their search game. He was, after all, a search and rescue dog.

Well, okay. Maybe he cheated a little.

"Dad says everything in life is a competition," replied Melanie.

"Dad also says nobody likes a bad sport," Miles said. He finished storing the last of the leftovers in my refrigerator and turned to us. "Just for that, you can finish loading the dishwasher while the adults have our coffee on the porch."

She started to screw up her face with an "Aw, Daaad…" But he stopped her with a wink.

"Besides," he added, dropping a quick kiss atop her curly hair as he passed, "you're better at it than I am. You never leave spots on the glasses."

She tried to hide her pleasure as she shrugged away his affection. "I told you," she informed him archly, "you've got to rinse off the dishes with hot water before you put them in the dishwasher, or the grease will leave spots. We learned that in cooking class," she added for my benefit. "Of course…" She made a big show of turning the hot water on full blast before putting the first dish beneath the stream. "We have a commercial dishwasher that can rinse, clean, and sanitize a load in ninety seconds at school. Hand-rinsing is really just for amateur cooks."

Melanie went to an elite private school a half hour away that had classes in things like organic gardening and gourmet cooking. We'd called it Home Economics back in the day; apparently it was called Lifestyle and Sustainability when the tuition ran into the thousands of dollars per year.

"Anyway," she added smugly, "I know you're just trying to get rid of me so you guys can have smoochy time together. You're not fooling anybody."

Miles and I shared a smile while he filled our coffee cups. "I'd mind my own business if I were you," he told Melanie mildly. "Dessert is not a guarantee."

"I'm totally minding my own business," she assured him.

"Good for you." He handed a mug to me. "Then you can take the pie out of the oven when the timer sounds. It needs to rest fifteen minutes."

"Yes, sir, on it, sir!" She gave him a military-type salute with one sudsy hand, and we chuckled as we left her.

Cisco, who had fallen off his diet today too, nonetheless paused to check out the open door of the dishwasher, then followed Miles and me outside.

"Thanks for dinner," I said. "It was great."

"You didn't eat much," he observed.

"I had lunch at Miss Meg's," I reminded him.

"Oh, right." He gestured toward the swing at the end of the porch and we headed in that direction. "I had a load of firewood delivered this afternoon. The guys were talking already about the big fight there."

"Wow." We sat in the swing and Miles shook out a quilt that was folded over the back, draping it over both of us. "News really does travel fast."

"About something like this it does," he agreed. "When the movies come to town, everybody starts watching…and that's before the film is even made."

He stretched an arm around my shoulders and I leaned against him, sipping my coffee, relaxing into the night. The air was crisp and the only light came from the muted glow of the lamps behind the curtained living room windows. In the distance a couple of dogs barked back and forth, but there was no other sound. Cisco walked to the edge of the porch, sniffed the air, and seemed to debate whether or not to join the conversation across the ridge, then decided against it. He found a chew toy underneath the porch railing and carried it beneath the swing, where he lay down and went to work.

Miles said, "I left some coq au vin and a lobster au gratin in your freezer. All you have to do is microwave. Also, some soup bones for the dogs."

Seriously, who could ask for a better guy? I should have gone with him to the beach for Thanksgiving. I should have done whatever he wanted to do. What was the matter with me?

I stretched up to kiss him. "Thank you."

"You're welcome." I felt his smile against my lips, and he rested his forehead for a moment on mine. Then he straightened up and sipped his coffee, adding casually, "Can't have you starving while we're gone."

To that I said nothing.

We sat quietly for a moment, sipping our coffee, the chain creaking with the slow, slight rhythm of the swing. There was no other sound except Cisco gnawing on his rubber chew toy. The dogs in the distance had stopped barking, probably busy with their own suppers.

I said, "So why do I get the feeling you have something besides smooching on your mind?"

"What gives you that idea?"

"You didn't bring me out in the cold to look at the stars. If you have something to say, say it."

Miles said, "Do you want to go to Peru for Christmas?"

Some people might have found that an odd question, but Miles was always coming up with things like that. Before settling down in the mountains to become a full-time father—more or less—Miles was always flying here, there, or the other place to build a hotel or supervise a high-rise office complex or do who-knew-what. I thought he missed it, although he would never admit as much.

Still…"Peru?" I parroted. "For Christmas?" That was totally out of left field.

"I've got a luxury hotel going up there, beach on one side, jungle on the other. I need to go down and check it out, and I thought it would be a fun way to spend the holidays."

Fun? Maybe. Holidays, never. And I hated it when Miles tried to combine business with pleasure and convince everyone else that it would be "fun." Maybe it would be fun for him, but I couldn't think of anything I would rather do less than spend Christmas in a foreign country while he was busy building a hotel and Melanie and I were busy doing…what?

He sipped his coffee. "I thought it would be educational for Melanie."

Okay, so I just thought of something I'd rather do less than go to Peru for Christmas: spend Christmas without Melanie. We always had a party at Dog Daze for all our clients, and I was looking forward to decorating the place with her and baking bone-shaped cookies together, and I'd already ordered the custom cell phone case with a photograph of Pepper that I was going to give her for Christmas. Thanksgiving was bad enough, but Christmas…

I said, "Gee, Miles, I don't know. Aunt Mart and Uncle Ro aren't getting any younger, you know. Who knows how many more Christmases I'll have with them? And you know how busy it is around here during the holidays. I just don't see how I can." Then I added, trying to muster enthusiasm, "But that doesn't mean you shouldn't go. I'm sure Melanie would have a blast. I mean, how many kids get a chance like that? You should do it."

"No," he said. "We'll stay here." He took another sip of coffee. "It's just, first Christmas without her mom and all. I thought a break in the routine might make it easier."

Now I felt bad. Even though Miles had been divorced from Melanie's mother for seven years, and Melanie had lived with him for the past year, her mother had died violently only a few months ago. Of course it would be hard. I said earnestly, "Really, Miles, you should go."

He gave a brief firm shake of his head. "We're staying." He tried to soften the next words with a smile. "Wouldn't be the same without you, sweetheart. Besides, Mel wouldn't want to leave Pepper. It's fine."

Then why did I feel like such a cad?

We drank our coffee for a while without saying anything else, but the prickly silence between us was palpable. I hated being awkward with him, both of us tiptoeing around in our Sunday School manners. If there was one thing I'd always been able to count on with Miles, it was that I could be myself. Until recently, that was.

I said stiffly, after a moment, "Maybe you should spend Christmas at the beach with your mother."

"Oh for crying out loud." His tone was abruptly exasperated. "I thought we were done with that."

"I'm just saying, we don't have to spend every holiday together. Or any holidays. It's not like we're…" I broke off.

"Not like we're what, Raine?" I could feel his glare, hard on my temple, though I refused to look at him.

I sipped from my cup. "Just drop it, Miles."

"No, I don't think I will. Not this time. I'm tired of walking on eggshells around you, Raine, and don't pretend you don't know why. I'm starting to wish I'd never asked you to marry me. Do you want me to take it back?"

And there it was. The thing between us that we refused to talk about.

I retorted, "You didn't exactly ask."

"Is that it?" There was impatience in his voice, and he turned in his seat to look at me. "You didn't like my proposal? What, do you want rose petals and champagne? A ring?" And then he sat back in the swing, adding, "That certainly makes my Christmas shopping easier."

"No!" I exclaimed. "No ring! I don't want a ring." I was aware there was a note of panic in my voice, and I made an effort to take it down a fraction. "What I mean is, I can't wear a ring, with the dogs and all, I'd be sure to lose it and…just promise me you will *not* buy me a ring for Christmas."

He replied, "Does that mean I have my answer?" If he was disappointed at the thought, I couldn't tell.

I said, "It means I don't want a ring. I'm serious."

He waited.

I added in a moment, reluctantly, almost mumbling, "Not yet, anyway."

And he replied simply, "Okay."

I sighed, leaning my head back against his arm. "Maybe you *should* take it back."

"No, I don't think I will. I like seeing you squirm."

I punched him on the arm, not particularly gently either. After a minute I said, "It's just that I'm so bad at it. Marriage, that is."

"Fortunately, I'm an expert."

I made a wry face that he couldn't see. He was even worse than I was. Perhaps the one thing we had in common was our inability to sustain a healthy relationship.

I said, "I don't want you to think I'm not thinking about it. Because I am."

"Take your time," he said. "I'm not going anywhere. But while you're thinking, stop trying to be so damn nice. It makes me nervous."

I smothered a smile in my coffee cup. "Okay."

"Good," he said. "Now tell me the truth. What do you really think about the Peru idea?"

"It sucks," I told him flatly and with conviction. "I can't believe you'd even consider it. It's a third-world country, for Pete's sake, not some place you take a little girl for Christmas. That's the craziest thing I ever heard of. Don't do it. Period."

"That's more like it," he said, and I could hear the amusement in his voice. "I hate it when you try to try to be pleasant. Not a good look on you."

I made a face and moved my head away from his caress in pretend annoyance, but the tension was gone now. We sipped our coffee and moved our feet in unison now, enjoying the night.

My coffee mug was half-empty when I said, "Sonny wants me to be an expert witness in this case she has about a service dog biting a little boy."

"Who better?" He sipped his coffee. "Which side are you testifying for?"

I gave him a dry look in the dark. "What do you think?"

"I don't know, sugar. You can be a hard woman to figure out."

I decided to let that slide. "It sounds like a lot of work," I admitted. "And I'm not that wild about getting involved in a court case. But winter's coming up and I've got taxes due. I'll probably do it."

He nodded sagely. "You're lucky to have the offer."

"Right."

A lot of people might have looked for the irony in complaining to my mega-rich boyfriend about having to take on extra work to pay my taxes. But Miles and I had one strict rule: he could give me advice—which I might or might not take—but nothing else. The occasional tasteful birthday or Christmas gift was, of course, the exception—as long as the gift was not a ring.

Just then the front door opened and Pepper came out, wagging and sniffing her way over to us, followed closely by Melanie. She had my portable phone in her hand. "Some man is on the phone for you, Raine," she said, holding up the receiver. "He didn't say who he was. Do you want me to find out? Maybe it's a dog client. Pretty late to be calling somebody at home, though," she added suspiciously. Her part-time summer job at the kennel had turned her into a pretty good receptionist, and she took her duties seriously.

Cisco came out from under the swing and offered the chew toy to Pepper. A playful tug of war ensued.

I smothered a smile as I reached for the phone. "Thanks, Mel, I'll take it."

Miles looked amused as he told her, "It's none of your business who's on the phone, Mel, and it's only seven thirty. What time is that in Japan?"

She said skeptically, "He didn't sound Japanese."

Miles chuckled and stood up. "Come on, let's serve the pie."

Melanie handed over the phone and Pepper abandoned the tug game to follow the two of them inside. I heard Melanie call, "Hey, Siri, what time is it in Japan?" and then burst into giggles as her father chased her to the kitchen. Cisco looked momentarily hurt that people were having fun without him, then he happily placed his front paws on the swing, setting it to rocking, and offered his toy to me. I held one end, engaging a pretend game of tug while I said into the phone, "This is Raine."

"Miss Stockton." The male voice on the other end sounded tense, urgent, and vaguely familiar. "This in Lonzo Bartinelli from Phase Two Productions. We met this afternoon—"

"Oh," I said, sitting up a little straighter in surprise. Cisco pulled the toy from my unexpectedly loosened fingers, which was not at all what he wanted, then banged it down on my knee again to get my attention. I resumed the tug game. "Sure,

I know who you are." And I frowned a little in the dark. "How'd you get my number?"

"Facebook," he replied briefly, which led me to understand he'd checked my profile, which pointed to my website, which had my business phone number on it, which had a message on it after hours directing callers to my landline if the call was about a lost or missing dog. A normal person would have just looked up my number in the local telephone book.

Lonzo went on in the tense, rapid speech pattern I remembered from our encounter at the waterfall, "I hope you don't mind me calling you at home, but we're in a bit of a bind here and I remember you mentioned that you trained dogs, and Dallas suggested I call you. So if you can't help us out, maybe you know someone who can?"

I was interested. "I'll try. What do you need?"

"The script calls for a dog, not a big part but an important one. The dog we hired bailed at the last minute, tore an ACL on another job, of all the inconsiderate things, never mind that they're in breach of contract. But here we are on location and it's my head that's going to roll if I can't find a substitute by the day after tomorrow. Of *course* I've tried all the animal talent agencies, but no one can get a dog here in time, so that's when Dallas came up with the idea of using local talent. It pays the standard rate and all we need is two days on set. Can you help?"

"What kind of dog do you need?" I asked, holding the toy steady while Cisco jerked his end of it from side to side.

"It doesn't matter." He sounded desperate. "What about one of the ones you had with you this morning?"

"I don't know." I had to be cautious, of course, but I'm no more immune to the call of fame than anyone else, especially where my dogs are concerned. Why else would I spend hundreds of hours training and drive thousands of miles for nothing more than a blue ribbon and a chance to get my dog's photo in a show magazine? My skin was already tingling with excitement. "What would he have to do?"

"I could messenger a script over to you tonight," he said eagerly, "and a copy of the shooting schedule. It's only five or six scenes, and they'll all be shot here, no traveling."

Since I'd just turned down a trip to Peru—not to mention a chance to spend Thanksgiving at the beach with Miles and Melanie—I should have been relieved to hear that. But in fact I was a tiny bit disappointed. It would have been kind of cool to fly to Hollywood with my dog, and of course I would have taken Melanie with me.

I said carefully, "I'll have to make sure there's nothing dangerous involved. And that the movie doesn't show anything I wouldn't want to be a part of. Like, you know, animal torture or anything."

"Nothing like that," he assured me, "nothing at all, not even close. So can we count on you? Are you onboard?"

I let go of the toy and Cisco whirled away with it, then spun around to sit in front of me, grinning proudly around his prize. Sometimes it's good to let your dog win—just not too often.

"I'll look at the script," I agreed, stroking Cisco's silky ear, "and let you know."

He said quickly, "What's your address?"

I told him, and added, "But it's way out in the country. You don't have to send the script over tonight. Tomorrow will be soon enough."

"We have people for that," he replied briskly. "It'll be there within the hour." And he disconnected.

"Well, well, well," I told Cisco, barely holding back a grin myself as I pushed the "off" button on the phone. "What do you know about that? We're going to be in the movies!"

CHAPTER SIX

Miles was right: when the movies were involved, everyone paid attention. Everyone also, it appeared, had something to say, even Miles himself. Especially Miles.

"Don't sign anything," he advised me sternly, "without having my lawyer look at it first. I'm texting you the address."

"Sonny's a lawyer," I reminded him, already feeling a little over my head. "She can look at anything that needs looking at."

"And she'll tell you to send it to my lawyer. Entertainment law is a specialty, and this firm handles some of the biggest names on the east coast."

"I got the feeling this was kind of a rush job," I said. "I doubt that there'll be time for…"

"And don't let them take advantage of you," he went on. "There are rules about how many hours a child or an animal can be on set."

"I'm not an idiot, Miles. I'm not going to let anyone take advantage of my dogs. Besides, I think they have to have a Humane Society rep there while the animals are working."

"Who's being paid by the production company," he pointed out. "You just be careful."

Melanie chimed in, "Maybe we should stay here, Dad, in case Raine gets in trouble. You know how she is."

Well, of *course* Melanie had an opinion. Her reaction to the news that I had been approached about having one of my dogs appear in a major motion picture had ranged from excitement to jealousy to pouting to scheming to advance her own agenda, in which she—and no doubt Pepper as well—went to the set every day with me. And all of this was before we even finished our pie.

Her latest attempt at manipulation caused me to roll my eyes and her father to fight with a grin. "I do know how she is," he agreed, "and experience has taught me that she can get into enough trouble without your help, so I think the best thing for us to do is stick to our plan."

Before she could do more than sputter another "But Dad…" he added firmly, "And we're leaving at six in the morning so let's go home and get some sleep. I'll call you from the road, Raine. Let me know if you need anything."

He left me to do my own dessert dishes, which was a fair trade, I suppose, since I left him with a very unhappy daughter and a long road trip to look forward to.

Somehow a skinny young man in a movie poster sweatshirt and a shock of blue hair managed to find my driveway in the dark and deliver the script, which, frankly, didn't make for very compelling reading, given the fact that the only pages that were included were the ones in which a dog appeared. Before I even finished looking through the script, three different assistant producers called, none of which was Lonzo. The first one said I had a six o'clock call on Friday morning. I wasn't entirely sure what that meant but thought someone would probably call me at six o'clock on Friday to tell me where to be. The second said I should disregard the first call and be ready to shoot my first scene with the dog at two o'clock on Friday. When I asked where, exactly, I was supposed to show up for this shoot, he seemed at a loss and said he would call me back. But when the call came ten minutes later it was from an entirely different assistant producer who said that the director wanted to choose the dog himself, so I should report to the film company compound at noon tomorrow morning with a "selection" of canine actors for his perusal.

Show business.

By this time it was ten o'clock, pretty late for a country girl, and after another quick glance through the script I decided to call it a day. The good news was that none of the highlighted parts seemed to be beyond any of my dogs' skill level: bark three times (speak), run through a grassy field (go out), comfort a weeping little girl (visit), curl up on a rug and go to sleep (all of my dogs' best thing).

"It's not like anybody has to jump through a broken window or anything," I told Corny the next morning. "I mean, there's this one scene where he has to walk across a log over a stream, but that's no harder than the dog walk at an agility trial, right? No wonder they weren't worried about replacing their dog at the last minute. Any dog could do it."

"Oh no," he assured me fervently, "not *any* dog. I mean, just think of the kind of focus it takes to even concentrate in the middle of all the noise and lights and reflective screens, and people running here and there shouting and banging things and shooting guns...I assume there're guns, right? There are *always* guns. Plus, they have to work away from you and listen to you but focus on the actor...oh my, no, not just any dog!" He beamed at me as he spritzed extra shine on Cisco's coat. "Only a star!"

The "star" of the moment shook out his golden coat, which fell back into place so beautifully he could have been auditioning for a part in a dog shampoo commercial instead of a suspense thriller. The moment he'd heard the news, Corny had snatched up my dogs and begun grooming them within an inch of their lives. I always like my dogs to look their best, but they'd all had baths only this weekend, and they weren't actually filming today, just parading in front of a director. Besides, this was about skill, not appearance. When I said as much, Corny looked at me as though I'd just uttered a blasphemy and declared breathlessly, "Everything is about appearance, Miss Stockton, *everything*! Especially in Hollywood."

I didn't bother pointing out that we were not in Hollywood, as I'm sure that protest, too, would have fallen on deaf ears. I made my escape with three shining, fluffy, glamorous-smelling dogs before Corny could translate the critical glance he gave my own attire into words. I wasn't sure what a dog wrangler was supposed to look like, but I was pretty sure the jeans and scuffed running shoes that I wore to train dogs were perfectly appropriate attire. If I gave Corny even half a chance, he'd have me looking as tricked-out as a show dog, and I had enough of those on my hands today.

According to the directions that had been e-mailed to me at 2:00 a.m.—and which I had read shortly after 8:00—the production staff compound, as they called it, was exactly where I speculated it was when Dallas first told me about it, about ten miles outside of town in what once had been the location of the New Day Wilderness Outreach program for troubled youth. It was a perfect location for both enterprises: virtually in the middle of nowhere, at the end of a dead-end road on twelve acres surrounded by chain-link fencing and electronic gates. Today a security guard was manning the main gate at the front of the compound. He checked my name off a list and handed me a laminated security pass on a chain that was to be worn around my neck before he buzzed me in.

My chest tightened a little as I made the turn that brought the big, A-frame glass-fronted building into view. My memories of this place were not all that great. Cisco and I had taken a job as "excursion specialists" on a winter hike for the New Day group and had ended up trapped in a blizzard. Two people had died. The fact that they were bad people did not mitigate the horror. I had not been out this way since.

The surprise was that except for the building itself, which I'd actually only been in once, nothing else looked familiar to me. A portion of the parking lot had been commandeered for equipment storage, and there were large metal containers with the name of a rental company painted on the side lined up against the curb. A couple of sleek black vans with tinted windows and several jeeps, along with what looked like half a fleet of limos, took up most of the rest of the parking lot. There were two big box car-type containers parked at the side of the building which I guessed held more equipment. The rest of the grounds had been completely taken over by a collection of cute little modular cabins, the kind that can be moved in and out with a trailer and a pickup truck. There must've been two dozen of them. The paper had said filming here would last two weeks; the production company had definitely spared no expense in making sure their stay here was comfortable.

All of that was interesting, but none of it was what captured my attention. There were two Hanover County Sheriff's Office units pulled up in front of the A-frame building, flasher bars going, blocking the entrance. One of the deputies leaned up against her vehicle, making notes in her field book. Another deputy was talking to someone at the top of the stairs. A small crowd of people in jeans and sweatshirts, some of them holding paper cups of coffee, had gathered a short distance away, watching.

I pulled into what might or might not have been a parking spot at the edge of the lot, rolled the windows halfway down so that the dogs could have fresh air, and dropped the chain with my security pass on it over my head before I left the car. I don't like to leave my dogs in the car in a strange place, but until I found out where I was supposed to be and who I was supposed to see, it seemed like the smartest thing to do. And I didn't want to do anything until I found out what the police were doing here—particularly since the officer I'd recognized standing by her unit was not precisely a huge fan of mine.

I walked past a big open tent with long tables laden with food and urns of hot coffee. The people who weren't milling around outside watching the police activity seemed to be gathered in the food service tent, but since I didn't see anything that indicated canine auditions were being held there, I proceeded toward the building. I thought I might be able to get past Deputy Smith without her noticing me, so I made a point of walking on the opposite side of the car from where she was standing. I had barely reached the passenger door when she said, without looking up, "That's far enough, Stockton. This is a crime scene."

I looked from her to the building, where another deputy was standing in front of the door, interviewing a man with long hair and glasses wearing another one of the ubiquitous film-poster sweatshirts. "Hey, Jolene," I said. Ignoring her previous admonishment, I came around the car to stand beside her. "I think I'm supposed to be in there." I nodded toward the building. "What's going on?"

She looked up from her notes to gaze at me, expressionless. Her eyes rested briefly on my security badge and she turned back to her notebook. "Why am I not surprised?" she observed flatly. "Every time I turn around, you're somewhere you're not supposed to be."

We had a history, Jolene and I. For one thing, she was the sheriff office's only K-9 officer, and I was the county's primary canine search and rescue volunteer, so our paths crossed a lot during the course of our work—*cross* being the operative word. For another, I had been married to her boss, Sheriff Buck Lawson, and she not only suspected me of exercising undue influence over him but resented me for receiving special treatment from the sheriff's office, whether that treatment was real or imagined. She and Buck were not on the best of terms, and I think sometimes she took out her frustration with him on me. I can't think of any other reason she would actively dislike me. I'm the easiest person in the world to get along with. Most of the time.

"Seriously," I said. "I'm supposed to see someone inside."

She murmured, "Of course you are."

"So if this is a real crime…"

"Of course it's a real crime. We hardly ever bother with fake ones." Once again she did not bother to look up from her notebook or to raise her voice to me. Either she was in a particularly mellow mood today, or she was actually starting to warm to me. Somehow I found it difficult to get onboard with either of those explanations.

"There's no crime scene tape," I pointed out.

"We finished our investigation." She snapped the notebook closed and tucked it into her uniform shirt pocket.

"Investigation of what?" I asked. "What happened?"

She said, "What are you doing here, Stockton?"

"They needed a dog for the movie," I said. "I'm supposed to see Lonzo Bartinelli at…" I glanced at my watch. "Five minutes ago."

"Well then," she replied pleasantly, "you'd better get on with it, hadn't you?"

I regarded her suspiciously. "You told me not to move."

She turned to open the car door. "I'll tell you what, Stockton. Since this is probably the last time I'm going to have to overlook you interfering with a crime scene, I'm going to cut you some slack. Go on and do what you have to do."

I wasn't so easily sidetracked. "What do you mean, the last time?"

She looked over her shoulder with a smile. "Haven't you heard? There's a new sheriff in town."

For some reason I felt compelled to leap to Buck's defense, and my scowl was automatic. "Not until January."

She quirked an eyebrow. "Are you sure about that?" And her self-satisfied smile only deepened as she got into her unit and closed the door, leaving me, for one of the few times in my life, speechless.

CHAPTER SEVEN

To tell the truth, I probably would have knocked on Jolene's tinted window to demand what she meant, but just then I spotted Lonzo, looking harried and stressed as he consulted a clipboard in his hand, coming out of the building. He was dressed today as nattily as he had been yesterday, in a navy wool peacoat and a Burberry scarf, with a pair of sunglasses pushed up atop his bleached hair. He paused at the top of the stairs to speak with the officer waiting there, and I raised my arm in greeting as I started up the stairs.

"Lonzo," I called. "I'm here!"

He turned, looking at me blankly. "Raine Stockton," I reminded him as I reached him. "With the dogs." I turned to the deputy, whom I recognized, and said, "Hi, Tim. What's going on?"

"Hi, Raine," he said, and answered my question with a shrug. "Just a little vandalism, nothing serious. Probably just some kids on a prank." He winked at me. "You gonna be in the movies?"

With the exception of Jolene, most people in the sheriff's office like me.

I was about to reply when Lonzo, still staring at me, said, "Oh! Right. The dogs. Hold on just a minute." He turned back to the deputy. "Officer, do you have everything you need? Can I send the painters in now? Because we have *got* to get that scene filmed today, and we're already three hours behind."

While he spoke, I had the opportunity to see through the open door behind him into the vast room beyond. The only thing that was familiar from the last time I'd visited it was the massive stone fireplace on one wall. Behind that fireplace someone had placed a spiral staircase that ended at the ceiling, and opposite it a heavy paneled door that went nowhere. On the far wall was an extremely realistic-looking mural of the view of a summer garden through arched windows. Mounted high on all four walls were giant industrial lights that had absolutely nothing to do with the elegantly furnished room below, and I gradually understood that this room had been transformed into a movie set. There were cream-colored, silk-looking sofas and subtly patterned rugs and glass tables and elaborate flower arrangements. Completely out of place on the long, east-facing wall, centered between two gold-framed paintings, was a single word in giant, red spray-painted letters: BITCH.

I would have had no way of guessing whether this apparent vandalism was part of the set or part of the crime if I hadn't seen Dallas inside, half-turned away from the ugly spray-painted word with her arms folded tightly across her chest and her head bowed.

I thought she might be crying, but I couldn't tell for sure because a man stood close to her, partially blocking my view, trying to urge a glass of water into her hand. It was the director, Seth Rosenstein. He said something to her I couldn't hear, and she said, shaking her head, "I'm fine." He said something else, and she said, more violently. "I said I'm fine, damn it!" She shoved his arm so hard that water splashed on the floor, then strode away, down the hall that I recalled led to the dorms. Rosenstein, tight-jawed, thrust the almost empty glass into the hand of a nearby assistant, and spun on his heel toward the opposite hallway.

That was no way to treat your boss, if you ask me. But I guess they did things differently in Hollywood.

I turned back to Tim. "Any idea who it was?"

He replied, "One or two." Which was more than I would have gotten from Jolene. He said to Lonzo, "We'll be in touch, Mr. Bartinelli." And to me, "See you around, Raine." He touched the brim of his hat to us and went down the steps.

Lonzo, blowing out a breath of relief, impatience, or simple dispelled tension, returned his attention to me. "So, Miss, uh…"

"Stockton," I supplied.

"Right. Sorry, it's a little hectic around here this morning."

"Not a problem." I didn't bother pointing out that it wasn't morning any more. "So wow, somebody broke in and destroyed the set, huh?"

"Not exactly destroyed," he corrected absently, shooting a glance back over his shoulder toward the open door. Then he looked at me. "You know that police officer?"

I shrugged. "Small town." I gestured toward the open door. "Looks like somebody is pretty mad at somebody else."

He frowned. "It's a nuisance, that's all. But it did put us behind. This shouldn't affect you, though. I'll introduce you to the production assistant who'll be in charge of the dog's role, and we can get started. Where are they, anyway? The dogs."

"In the car." I followed him down the stairs. "When did it happen, last night? Wasn't the building locked?"

"It's a hot set," he replied impatiently, "of course it was locked. They broke a window in back. We didn't discover it until a couple of hours ago, when it was time to set up for the indoor scene."

"What's a hot set?" I asked.

The look he shot me this time was the one you might give a demented four-year-old—surprise mixed with pity mixed with amusement. "We shoot multiple takes of each scene," he explained in an overly patient, almost professorial tone. "Usually these takes are edited together to compose the final scene, so everything in the background has to look exactly the same for each take. If a lampshade is crooked or a flower petal drops, it can ruin the whole scene. So a hot set is one that's still being filmed. We take photos at the end of every take, and the set is sealed between takes so that nothing will be disturbed."

"Wow," I said. If a dropped flower petal could ruin a scene, I couldn't imagine how much damage something like this would do. "So I guess this scene is pretty much trashed, huh?"

"It could have been worse," he admitted. "Aside from the spray paint, not much was touched. The crew will have it restored in half an hour."

I remembered Dallas's quick-change artistry from the day before. The magic of Hollywood.

"Do you think this might have something to do with what happened yesterday at the diner?" I suggested. We were on the lawn now, and I had to increase my stride to keep up with him. These movie people always seemed to be in a hurry.

He shot me a quick, dark look, not slowing his stride.

"You know," I reminded him, "that guy Dallas got into an argument with? Or maybe the one whose truck she banged on when she almost stepped in front of it? People are pretty particular about their trucks around here."

He scowled, not looking at me. "Probably just some local yokels trying to get their kicks. Who knows why?"

"Oh," I said, trying not to take offense at the "local yokel" part. I was fairly sure the police theory on the crime was more in line with my thinking than with his, but I had a feeling I was approaching that point where I'd be told to mind my own business, and I didn't see what good it would do to make an enemy of Lonzo. So I just smiled and said, "By the way, how'd those sausage biscuits work out for you this morning?"

He slanted me a glance, his expression like stone. Then he lifted his clipboard in a gesture to someone over my shoulder and called out, "Adrian."

A young man in jeans and a ponytail came trotting up, and Lonzo said, "This is Adrian Phillips, he'll take over from here. Adrian, the woman with the dogs. Bring them up to the office in what? Fifteen minutes? I'll tell Mr. Rosenstein."

Adrian turned out to be a lot more easygoing than Lonzo, and he actually liked dogs. He walked with me to the car and spent some time rubbing ears and clucking chins when I let my three shiny-coated, fluffed out beauties out of the car. He heaped the appropriate amount of compliments on them and they all practically wiggled out of their skins with pleasure. I took all three leashes in my hand, mostly because I wanted to show off how well behaved they were, as we walked back toward the building. Mischief and Magic, on my right, were perfect little ladies. Cisco, on my left, seemed to understand what was at stake and put on his best manners, prancing like a racehorse and swishing his tail with such enthusiasm that I could feel the breeze. I would have hired him on the spot for the size of his smile alone.

"They've never really done any acting," I confessed to Adrian as we walked, "but the scenes that were marked in the script pages I got were pretty straightforward. I don't think any of them will have any trouble with the behaviors."

"Awesome," he said. "We'll need health records and waivers, and there's like a mountain of paperwork for you to sign after we finish with Mr. Rosenstein. Do you have an act or something ready for him to see?"

I stared at him. "Um, no. I mean, no one told me I had to do anything." Frantically I started going over the possibilities in my head. All three of the dogs were therapy dogs, and they sometimes entertained at schools and nursing homes with the standard repertoire of counting tricks, say your prayers, play dead, and find the toy, but I wasn't sure how impressive any of those would be to a Hollywood director. "I thought were just going to practice the things they have to do for the movie. But I guess they could do some tricks. Is that what you mean?" Shake, roll over, spin…I hadn't brought any props with me, not even a ball, and Cisco had only recently mastered putting a faux basketball through a hoop. If only I'd known.

"Oh yeah, sure, whatever," Adrian said with a wave of his hand. "No biggie."

Easy for him to say. His dogs weren't about to be humiliated in front of a big shot director and a couple of dozen Hollywood types, not to mention half the county when the word got out.

"How about a cup of coffee?" Adrian directed me toward the big food tent. "Craft Services is set up all day. Help yourself to whatever. The food hasn't been half-bad so far. Except for breakfast." He wrinkled his nose. "But what can you expect at 5:00 in the morning, right?"

I was surprised, "People start to work around here at 5:00 a.m.?" And yet nobody had noticed the vandalism until close to 10:00, according to Lonzo.

"Oh sure, some of the makeup people and stuff. And pretty much everybody is sleeping onsite, either in the cabins or the building. So Craft Services starts early and stays late."

Cisco's head swung right and left as we walked through the tent, taking in the buffet which, from his point of view, must look like doggie heaven. There was a salad bar on one side, a hot bar on the other, and an entire table devoted to pastries and desserts, not to mention the dozens of people sitting at tables throughout the building with steaming plates of noodles and beef medallions and eggplant parmesan and chicken cordon bleu before them. Diners nudged each other and grinned when the dogs passed, and I have to admit I was rather proud of my canine crew as we got in line for coffee.

"So," I asked Adrian, "what part does the dog play in the movie? I mean, how does it fit into the story line?"

He grinned at me. "What, does he need to know his motivation?"

I shrugged. "Just curious."

We moved forward in line, and Adrian said, "Mostly the dog is just for color, you know. The scenes he's in are supposed to be from the heroine's childhood. It makes her seem like a regular person, more relatable, you know."

I nodded as though I did, in fact, understand.

Adrian took a paper cup from the stack beside the coffee urn and began to fill it with coffee. I noticed there was a cappuccino machine next to it with a variety of flavored syrups and I thought I might give it a try. I was about to reach for my own paper cup when there was a commotion behind me, laughter and shouting and—to my everlasting horror—the sound of gobbling. I whirled around to see Cisco at the end of his leash, his front paws on the buffet table and his face in a platter of cold cuts.

I cried, "Cisco, off!" and jerked the leash hard. He landed on all fours and began to scarf up the scraps of meat that had landed on the floor.

Adrian stared at me, shocked, and a woman in a white chef's coat hurried toward us. "I'm so sorry!" I gasped. "I should have been watching. I'll pay for the damage, of course..."

Adrian said, "Umm, maybe you'd better just wait outside."

I scurried off, cheeks blazing, three dogs in tow. Of course, I knew the futility of scolding a dog for something he's already forgotten about doing—not to mention the fact that there was no punishment I could devise that would in any way diminish the joy Cisco had taken from devouring a platter of cold cuts—but if ever there was a time when I came close to forgetting everything I knew about positive reinforcement, that was it. And it was a pretty sure bet Cisco had just blown his chance to be a movie star.

"I'm so sorry," I said again, miserably, when Adrian came out. By this time I had all three dogs in a sit, and Cisco, who knew enough not to push his luck, gazed at me with the kind of innocence that suggested he had never even heard the phrase "cold cuts." "I guess you'll want to look for another dog handler, huh?"

"Hey, no probs." He handed me a paper cup of coffee and added, "Maybe leave the dogs outside next time, though."

"Oh," I said quickly, both relieved and surprised. "Right, absolutely."

I shifted all three leashes to one hand and accepted the cup of coffee he offered. Cisco walked in absolute lock-step with me, almost outdoing the Aussies in the perfection of his heelwork. Like I said, he's a smart dog—when he needs to be.

"So," Adrian said, gesturing with his coffee up to the sprawling building in front of us, "this is where the magic happens. You probably won't be working here, since most of your scenes are outside, but the front part of the building has been converted to a silent stage, so when that red light is on…" He indicated a caged light above the front door. "Absolutely no admittance."

I asked, "What's a silent stage?"

"It means we don't film any dialogue here, and all the sound will be added post-production. That's pretty much standard for location shooting."

"Are they using the whole building for a stage?" I asked, thinking about the break-in last night.

He shook his head. "Offices, an editing room, props, wardrobe, electrical…it's all right here."

"Wow. Sounds like a lot of expensive equipment. And nothing was stolen last night with the break-in?"

He shrugged. "Not that I heard about. Anyway, it's all insured. Hold on," he added as we reached the bottom of the steps. "I'll see if they're ready for you."

Adrian bounded up the steps, around the porch to the left, and through an entrance I had never used before. I sipped my coffee—not cappuccino, but good nonetheless—and put the dogs in a sit in front of me. I'd waited less than five minutes when Adrian reappeared, beckoning from the doorway for me to join him.

I took the dogs up the steps and through a set of French doors, where Seth Rosenstein sat at a long table scattered with papers and lined with computer screens. There was a much-used whiteboard on one wall and a giant television screen on the other. A couple of people were leaning over Rosenstein's shoulder, pointing at something on the computer screen at which he was working. Others were moving around purposefully, tacking notes up on a wall, flipping through binders, making marks on papers. I looked around for Dallas; I don't know why. She wasn't there.

Adrian gave me a reassuring wink and I felt an unexpected surge of butterflies in my stomach. I still had no idea what we were going to do to impress the director and I was beginning to wonder if all this anxiety was worth it. I edged the dogs away from the open door and told them to sit. Seth Rosenstein made a note on a paper in front of him and glanced briefly up at us.

"The black and white one," he said, and turned his attention back to the computer screen. "Okay," he said to one of the men leaning over his shoulder. "Set up Camera Three here, just south of that boulder, and tell Jonas I want the shot filtered through the trees. Get Dave in here, tell him we're cutting three and a half minutes out of the fireplace scene."

"Yes, sir, Mr. Rosenstein."

The man hurried out of the room through the exit into the hall, and I looked at my dogs, surprised. The black and white one? But golden retrievers were the most popular dogs in the world. *Every* movie had a golden retriever in it. Clearly, word of Cisco's disgrace had reached the production office before we had. He really had blown his big chance.

I looked from the dogs to Adrian, still a little confused. "They're both black and white," I whispered.

Rosenstein twisted around in his chair and said, "Speaking of fireplaces, how're they coming on that set? I need to get my cameras in there."

Somebody muttered something into a cell phone and then said, "Five minutes, Mr. Rosenstein."

Adrian said, "Excuse me, Mr. Rosenstein? Which one of the black and white ones?"

Rosenstein turned back to his computer. "Both," he said, not glancing at us. "We'll cut the shoot time in half and still keep the Humane Society off our backs."

"Yes, sir, Mr. Rosenstein." Adrian turned to me with a smile, gesturing toward the door. "All righty then," he said. "Let's go sign some papers."

So just like that, I guess we were hired.

CHAPTER EIGHT

It was midafternoon by the time Adrian finished shuffling the paperwork, giving me the tour of the facility, and answering all my questions. We had lunch at the commissary—with the dogs safely crated in my SUV—and it was pretty good. Lots of vegetarian dishes and salads, but also a pretty decent hamburger. Most importantly, no one seemed to recognize me from the incident with Cisco earlier. I kept in touch with Miles and Melanie via text—yes, of course I was getting paid for both dogs, not just one, and yes, the contract had already been e-mailed to that lawyer Miles was so wild about, and as a matter of fact, Adrian had brought it up before I even had to. No, I hadn't seen any stars, and no, I hadn't gotten to see any more scenes being filmed, and no, I didn't think Mischief and Magic were going to get their own trailer. It turned out I was wrong about that, kind of, which I learned when Adrian walked me down to the edge of the compound, behind the row of little cabins, and showed me a portable chain-link kennel with a tarp roof that he said the former dog wrangler had ordered. He assured me running water and electricity were available if I wanted to set up a temporary grooming station to keep the dogs looking fresh between takes. I hadn't even thought about lugging grooming equipment and crates all the way out here. I was beginning to understand why dog wranglers got paid so much.

I was cautioned to keep my cell phone on and with me at all times—pretty much the same instructions Miles gave me every time he left town—since the schedule often wasn't confirmed until 1:00 or 2:00 in the morning on the day of the shoot. Someone would call me at least twelve hours before I was supposed to report with the dogs. I would check in with Adrian here at the compound each morning I was called in, where I would receive the shooting schedule for the day. Of course, I had a general idea of the order in which the scenes would be shot, but things could change at the last minute, and often did. Oh, and good news: not only was I being paid for two dogs instead of one, I also got paid if I showed up and didn't get to work, for whatever reason. I was beginning to think Melanie was right. I should have gone into the dog wrangling business.

By the time we headed toward the parking lot it was almost 4:00, my head was practically bursting with everything I'd learned, and the dogs were exhausted. That was more or less my plan—to allow Mischief and Magic to explore every inch of the compound, to become so familiar with the sights and sounds and ins and outs of the place that by the time they returned tomorrow they would be completely at home and ready to give their full attention to the tasks at hand. Even Cisco, who hadn't yet realized he'd been passed over for the job, was dragging a little. I felt confident in dropping his leash while I got the Aussies settled in their crates in the back of the SUV. I had just pressed the button on the remote that closed the back hatch when I heard a cheerful voice behind me.

"Hey, girl!"

Dallas was coming toward us in a pink cowboy hat and embroidered cowboy boots, hands tucked jauntily into the pockets of her sequined denim jacket. By the time I turned around, Cisco was halfway to her, and I had a flash of horror about dirty paw prints on designer jeans and, worse, dog toenails on sequins. I lunged for Cisco's leash, but he astonished me by screeching to a halt in front of Dallas, dropping to a sit, and giving a single sharp bark.

Dallas laughed, "How cute is that?" She bent down to greet him. "Hello to you, too, young fella!"

She certainly was being friendly for someone who'd been acting like a raving lunatic the last time I'd seen her. I picked up Cisco's leash and approached her somewhat cautiously. I said, "He must really like you." Of course, Cisco liked everyone from toddlers to serial killers. The only thing that puzzled me was that his normal behavior when he liked someone was to fling himself upon them in an abundance of uncontrolled affection. Dallas didn't know how lucky she was.

Dallas patted her pockets. "I should give him something, but all I have are gummy bears." She pulled out a crumpled cellophane package from her jacket. "I don't suppose…?"

Cisco looked at me expectantly, just as though he really did deserve a treat for not jumping on her. Unfortunately for him, I still had visions of flying cold cuts dancing in my head. "That's okay," I said quickly, before she could actually offer him the candy, and pulled him close to me. He had the audacity to look insulted, the scoundrel.

Dallas grinned at me. "So! You got the gig, huh? Good deal."

I said, "Thanks for the recommendation. Lonzo said it was your idea."

She shrugged. "De nada. It seemed a shame to cut the whole dog character just because of one snafu, and script rewrites are a pain. They throw everything off schedule, and Seth *hates* being off schedule."

"He must be pretty upset about the vandalism this morning then," I said.

She replied easily, "It could have been worse."

I waited a beat for her to elaborate, but she just reached down and stroked Cisco's ear, smiling and cooing at him. I said, "Any idea who would do such a thing?"

"Nah."

I thought, *Seriously?* and was about to question further, but just then she straightened up.

"All I know is it didn't affect any of my scenes so I've got the rest of the day off," she said. "Say, wanna go hit the dives? I bet you know some killer honky-tonks around here."

I hate to admit it, but my days of honky-tonking, beer-chugging, and line-dancing had ended with my twenties...or maybe with my divorce from my number one honky-tonking partner, Buck Lawson. Listening to country-western songs isn't nearly as much fun when your life actually starts to sound like one.

"Not really," I said, a little apologetically. "There's this place out on the highway that has kara-oke Thursday and Friday nights though."

She said wistfully, "I bet they serve Cuervo with lime and the greasiest nachos this side of El Paso. Man, I miss home." Then, "So what do you say? Let's go blow the place down."

I was tempted. Who wouldn't be? Miles was out of town and I hadn't had a girl's night out in...well, forever. It'd be fun to kick up my heels for a change, and with a Hollywood stunt woman, no less. Besides, there was a lot more I wanted to know about Dallas McKenzie, who'd been as happy as cherry pie one minute and thrown a temper tantrum at the diner the next; who'd been so upset over the vandalism this morning that she was not only crying, but had yelled at her director when he tried to comfort her, but now pretended it was no big deal, and who, for whatever reason, seemed to want to be my best friend. But every now and then—not often—I listen to my better instincts, and I had a 6:00 a.m. call.

"I can't be out late," I said. "I'm supposed to be back here with the dogs at the crack of dawn." She looked disappointed, which surprised me. I added uncertainly, because I *still* had a few things I wanted to talk to her about, "But we could go get a pizza if you want. I have to stop by the house and feed the dogs first."

She grinned broadly and started toward my car. "Cool," she said. "You're driving."

Dallas was enchanted by my house, my dogs, my kennel, and my training business. She kept saying, "You're so lucky! What a great life!" and, frankly, I didn't argue with her. I *did* have a great life.

Corny was completely starstruck, and must have taken a dozen selfies with Dallas. I kept thinking how much Melanie would have enjoyed meeting her, and I couldn't resist texting a picture of the two of us to her with the message, *Having pizza with my new friend from the movie. Call you later.* I got back an emoji with a tongue stuck out. I wasn't entirely sure whether that was good or bad, but figured she couldn't be too mad at me because in the next minute she sent a picture of Pepper on the beach wearing sunglasses. I showed it to Dallas, who laughed as much as I did. She really did seem just like a regular person. Now, anyway.

I got the dogs fed and settled for the evening and left Corny to close up the kennel. When Dallas and I were seated in our red vinyl booth with a couple of beers before us, she said, "When I was a little girl I wanted to grow up to train horses. I was going to have a ranch with two or three nice paddocks, a stable with a concrete floor like the rich folks have, and a big house just like yours." She smiled and saluted me with her beer. "I actually worked my way through nursing school on a dude ranch."

That surprised me. "You were a nurse?"

She grinned. "For about two minutes. That's how long it took me to find out I liked horses way more than hospitals. But hey, at least I've got something to fall back on when my luck runs out, right?"

I sat back against the sticky vinyl seat and picked up my beer mug. "So," I said, looking at her frankly. "What happened at the diner yesterday?"

She shifted her gaze in a brief gesture of impatience. "Oh, that."

I tried to quash my annoyance, but I'll admit my tone was a little sharper than normal when I said, "Meg is a friend of mine. She was pretty upset."

Dallas had the grace to look embarrassed. I had no way of knowing how sincere it was. "Look, I acted like an idiot, okay? I shouldn't have made a scene. This dude…" There was the briefest of hesitations, as though she was debating how much to tell me. "He said something rude to me and I totally went off on him. Completely overreacted. It's a bad habit of mine. I should go apologize to the woman." She sipped her beer and added with a decisive nod, "That's what I'll do. I'll apologize."

I didn't think it would serve any purpose to point out that Meg would be unlikely to let Dallas back in her restaurant for any reason. I said instead, "Don't you think there might be a connection between the vandalism on the set and the disturbance at the diner?"

She sighed. "Probably. I told the police about it. I guess they're looking into it."

"This guy who was bothering you," I pressed. "Any idea who he was?"

She took another quick drink from her mug. "Do we have to talk about this? Really, I just wish it had never happened."

I had to bite my tongue, but I let it drop.

I cast around for something neutral to say. "So how did you get into stunt work?"

She shrugged. "I wasn't pretty enough to be an actress."

I started to protest, because really, what do you say to something like that? But she stopped me with a chuckle that was only a little self-deprecating.

"I actually started out in the rodeo," she said, "as a stunt rider. Then Seth gave me the job doing stunts for *The Horsewoman*, and I got completely sucked in by the whole Hollywood thing. I thought for sure acting was the life for me. I had an agent and every-thing, did a couple of commercials, some walk-on TV roles…but it didn't take me long to figure out I wasn't cut out for the big time. I just don't have the kind of face people remember. If I heard it once, I heard it a million times. Forgettable. Blend-in-able. I was never going to be a star." She grinned. "Besides, stars are few and far between, but you know who's always in demand? Someone who can be anybody. Someone who can do the things stars can't, or won't, or aren't allowed to. That's me. I've always been an athlete, but once I started to learn the stunts…" She gave an appreciative shake of her head and took another sip of her beer. "Man, it's a rush. Seriously, nothing like it in the world. I mean, how many people can say they get to jump out of twelve-story buildings for a living?"

I don't exactly consider myself a shrinking violet: I like rock climbing, spelunking, wilderness camping, and was looking forward to being SCUBA certified next summer so that I could go cave diving with Miles. I'd never been sky diving, but that's only because I'd never had the chance. Still, I wasn't sure I could ever embrace being pushed off cliffs and set on fire the way Dallas did.

I said, "Don't you ever worry about getting hurt?"

She laughed. "See this?" She pointed to her collar bone. "Broken in three places." She held up her right hand, and I noticed her pinkie finger was a little crooked, zigzagging at the knuckle. "Got it caught in a safety rope, of all things, almost amputated it. But I finished the scene." She pushed up her sleeve, and I must have winced a little at the nasty black bruise on her forearm. "Oh, that's nothing," she said. "Broken ulna, once, radius twice. The second time the bone didn't knit just right, you can see the bump. Dislocated my shoulder four times, I can practically pop it in and out at will. And look." She swung her leg up on the seat and pushed her jeans up above her boot. I leaned over the table to see. There was a deep scar on her shin, and just above it a nasty looking red wound that looked fairly recent. "Compound fracture of the tibia. That one kept me out of work for almost eight months. I thought I'd go crazy."

She started rolling down her pants leg, and I said. "What about the other one?"

"No clue. Mosquito bite probably." She swung her leg back to the floor. "I don't even notice the small stuff anymore."

I sat back. "None of my business, but…"

She read my thoughts. "Oh, yeah. I get hazard pay. And believe you me, I'm making a lot more now than I ever would have done if I'd stayed with acting. Besides…" She lifted her mug again, and though I couldn't be sure, I thought I saw a slight hardening of her features. "Fame is highly overrated."

I said, "Wait a minute. *The Horsewoman*. I saw that. You were in that?"

She grinned. "Not so that you'd notice. Like I said, a good stunt woman never lets you see her face."

"Wow." I was impressed…and I now understood why Melanie and Corny had been so impressed by the name Seth Rosenstein. I wasn't one to read the credits or follow entertainment news, but I did remember *The Horsewoman* had been all over the red carpet scene when it first came out. I just hadn't realized until now that it had been a Seth Rosenstein film. "So you and Mr. Rosenstein go back a while, huh?"

She nodded and sipped her beer. "All the way back to Houndstooth, Texas." Again she flashed me that infectious grin. "Yeah, there really is such a place, not too far from Lubbock. Population 2100. Seth and I went to school together, and we've been best friends since then. Our graduating class had seventy-six people in it."

"Sounds a lot like my high school." I thought about my best friend, the one I'd married. My relationship with Buck went back to elementary school, and you can't know a person that long without going through some stuff, good and bad. But were we still friends? I wasn't sure.

Our pizza arrived, piping hot and filling the air between us with the smell of pepperoni and garlic. My mouth watered, and neither of us lost any time transferring a slice to our plates.

"It was hard for Seth, growing up, you know," Dallas went on. "Hard for me too. My dad was a mean drunk, and my mom was too scared of him to leave or even call the cops…" A shadow of bitterness flickered over her face. "So anyway, Seth and I, we ended up kind of taking care of each other. The difference between us was that Seth was smart, I mean really smart, and ambitious too. His very first screenplay won a Golden Globe. And after *The Horsewoman*, well, he could just about write his own ticket. Two Oscars for best director by the time he was thirty." The pride that swelled in her eyes was as genuine as if the accomplishments had been her own. "We've been together ever since, more or less."

I said, "Oh." That explained the solicitation I had sensed in the director's manner when I'd seen them together this morning, not to mention the flippant way Dallas had reacted to his threat against her job yesterday at the waterfall. "That must be interesting. I don't think I could get used to working for someone I was, you know, dating."

Dallas looked surprised, and then amused. "Dating? Seth?" She shook her head, watching me as she bit into her pizza. "He's married. Everyone knows that."

I took another bite of pizza and tried to indicate by my sophisticated silence that I wasn't so naive that I didn't know how things like that worked in Hollywood. She leaned forward with twinkling eyes and added, "To a man."

I blinked. "Oh." I guess everyone knew that, too...except me. I really should start paying more attention to Corny and Melanie.

Dallas lifted her hand to the waitress and ordered another beer. I shook my head when she turned an inquiring look on me. "I want to be fresh for my first day on the set," I told her.

"Bring a book," she advised me sagely. "It's mostly hurry-up-and-wait."

The waitress brought her beer, and Dallas asked, probably just to be polite, how I'd gotten into dog training, so I told the story, which wasn't all that interesting compared to hers. Still, she seemed impressed by my search and rescue work, and said, "Say, I'll bet you know all the good hiking trails and camping spots around here."

"Sure," I agreed. "The one I was on the other day, by the waterfall where you were filming, it branches off a few hundred feet farther and goes up into some beautiful country. It meets up with the Appalachian trail eventually, but before you get there it's just miles and miles of you and Mother Nature. Fern grottos, hidden falls, pine forests, and if you go high enough you're actually walking through clouds. It's one of my favorite trails."

She sighed. "Sounds like heaven. Gosh, I'd love to do some camping while I'm up here. You know, the real kind, with nothing but a campfire and a sleeping bag."

"Sure," I said. "There are a couple of good spots for wilderness camping off that trail, if you don't mind the cold."

Her eyes lit up. "I *love* winter camping. Last year I spent my whole Christmas vacation camping in Montana. I had to snowshoe in. Gosh, it was the best time I'd had in years."

We fell into an easy conversation about camping and horses and dogs, and once again, she seemed like just another girlfriend; easy to talk to, fun to be around. We had each plated our third slice, and were each pretending we were only going to eat one bite of it, when I got a text from Miles: *Don't forget us*

common folk when you're a star. Call when you get home.
Mom sends her love.

Dallas must have read my smile because she said, "Boyfriend?"

I texted back a smiley face and put the phone away. "He's out of town for the holiday."

Because she seemed interested, I told her about Miles and Melanie, and added a few funny stories about Pepper that made her laugh. We were getting chummy enough that I was just about to ask her what she was planning to do for Thanksgiving when her attention seemed to be caught by something over my shoulder. I felt a shadow fall over me as a male voice said, "Well, if it ain't the high and mighty Miss Hollywood."

I twisted around to see Mitch Dobbs glaring down at us from his six-foot height, muscles bulging against the material of a USMC tee shirt that was much too tight and a little lightweight for the weather, if you ask me. Mitch had finished a stint in the Marines six months ago and taken a job as a trainer in a gym in Boverton, a little crossroads town about forty-five minutes away. He liked to look the part with tight jeans, crew cut, and perpetual sneer, but he really wasn't such a tough guy when you got to know him. His mother was Meg of Miss Meg's Diner. Still, it took me a moment to get the reference to Hollywood.

He leaned in, glaring at Dallas. "You're her, ain't you? You're the one that called the law on my momma?"

Dallas swallowed hard and pulled her purse in beside her on the bench. She looked really scared. Scared enough to open her purse and slip her hand inside.

I scowled at Mitch, who was leaning way too close to me for comfort, and said, "What's the matter with you, Mitch? What are you talking about?"

He didn't move. "She knows what I'm talking about. You fancy-ass movie types come prancing in here, thinking you can push people around who've been living here and working here and paying taxes here all our lives. Well, let me tell you, this is one redneck who ain't going to stand for it, you hear me? You start messing with my momma and you're going to have to answer to me!"

With this last, his voice rose and he leaned in so forcefully that I shrank from the feel of his hot breath on my neck. "For Pete's sake, Mitch!" I planted a hand in the center of his chest and gave him a push. "Back off, will you?"

He took a step back, but turned his churning glare on me. "Yeah, I might've known. Raine Stockton, always poking your nose in where it don't belong. Well, you just better watch your back, because—"

"Evening, ladies." The voice was male, pleasant, and familiar, and it came up behind me, just like Mitch's had. "Everything okay here?"

I turned my head to see the face of my ex-husband, Sheriff Buck Lawson.

My back was to the door, which was why I hadn't seen either Mitch or Buck enter. Buck was not in uniform, but Mitch knew who he was. Even in jeans and a fleece-lined denim jacket, even with his sandy-blond hair rumpled by the wind and his eyes tired and his smile forced, everyone knew who he was.

Mitch muttered, still glaring at me, "Yeah, Sheriff. Everything's fine. Just fine." He turned and strode away, pushing his way out the door with such force that the bell continued to clatter a good three seconds after he was gone.

I cast an uncertain glance first to Dallas, then to Buck. I said, "Umm, Dallas, this is Buck Lawson. He's the sheriff around here. Buck, Dallas McKenzie. She's with that movie they're making."

Buck smiled that smile that made every woman he met want to sleep with him. I guess it wasn't his fault that so many of them had no impulse control. He said, "Miss McKenzie, glad to meet you. I hope you're not getting a bad impression of us, based on the last twenty-four hours."

Dallas drew a breath, released it shakily, and removed her hand from her purse. "Thanks Sheriff." She managed a smile. "I'm from Texas. I'm used to dealing with rowdies."

Given her behavior at the diner, I thought that was an understatement. I could see by the slight flicker in Buck's eyes that he, too, had heard about the incident and was of the same opinion.

Dallas looked back at me, her smile becoming slightly more genuine. "If you're about done, Raine, I'll get the check. I've got an early call, too."

While I stumbled over my thanks, Buck said, glancing at the door, "I'll stick around and walk you ladies to your car."

Dallas turned a full-voltage smile on him as she slid out of her seat, "Chivalry!" she exclaimed. "I'd almost forgotten about it. It's great to be back in the South!"

I hadn't realized how much attention our little contretemps had attracted until I saw the sideways glances of the other diners when the three of us walked to the front. Dallas went to the cashier's counter to pay, and Buck and I waited by the door. I said to Buck, "So. Any idea what that was about?"

He shrugged. "We were called in about the vandalism on the set. After the incident at the diner yesterday, we had to question Meg. I guess Mitch took that the same as us accusing her of something. He'd be a prime suspect in the vandalism, but he spent the night with his girlfriend over in Boverton, no time to drive back and do the damage. Still, he's a hothead. I'd steer clear if I were you...or your friend." He looked at me, his expression no more than mildly interested. "So how do you know her, anyway?"

"They needed a dog for the movie," I explained briefly. "But you don't seriously think Meg had anything to do with what happened on the set, do you?"

"No," he admitted. "But we have to question everybody. People like Mitch don't get that."

"I guess." I frowned a little. "But that set was secure. I just don't see how anybody could have gotten on it after dark. And what about the guy that

Dallas said was harassing her in the diner? Seems like he'd be the first one you want to talk to."

"Right." His tone was a little dry. "We've got this, Raine. But listen." Now he was the one who frowned; just a tiny crease between the eyes that the average person might not even notice, but which I knew meant he was uncomfortable about something. The frown deepened, just a fraction. "Your friend's got a temper. That kind of acting out can bring her more trouble than she can handle if she's not careful. And another thing. Last night we pulled over a car for speeding. My guy swore it was a woman driving, but by the time he got them stopped, it was a man behind the wheel. He suspected they switched drivers but couldn't prove it, gave them a warning mostly because the car was a rental registered to Phase Two Productions. The woman—the one he suspected was driving but who was a passenger by the time he stopped them—was drunk as a skunk. He got her name: Dallas McKenzie." When I remained stone faced he added, "Just thought you should know."

There was another uncomfortable beat, to the background of conversation and laughter and good natured jostling at the hostess stand. He didn't take his eyes off me. I refused to look away from him. He said, "And if you get a chance, you might want to remind Miss McKenzie of the North Carolina concealed carry laws. I'm not going to call her on it, but she's been drinking, and she had her hand on a .38 inside that purse."

Crap, I thought. I'd suspected as much, but still…crap.

I said, after a moment, "How is Wyn?"

"Good." He seemed almost relieved to talk about something neutral, or almost neutral, even if it was the woman he had left me for, and married. "Better," he qualified. "She finishes physical therapy next week. They think she'll be fit for duty by the first of the year."

"That's good," I said, and meant it. The woman had practically died trying to save my life, after all. "So you're spending Thanksgiving in Asheville?"

He nodded, and once again that frown appeared between his brows, making him look uncomfortable. "The fact is…"

But just then one of the girls from behind the counter called, "Sheriff Lawson?" She held up a pizza box. Buck excused himself to pay for his purchase, and he didn't finish his thought. Too bad, because I'd wanted to ask him who was taking over while he was gone, and, more importantly, what he planned to do come January, when he was no longer sheriff.

While he was gone, Dallas returned, and, with the cheerful exuberance I'd come to associate with her, said, "Okay, all set!" She linked her arm through mine companionably. "Great idea, Raine, hit the spot. Ready to hit our marks in the morning, right?"

I smiled a little uncertainly. "Right."

Buck pushed open the door for us and, pizza box in hand, walked with us out into the cold night air. There were less than a dozen cars in the lot, and I didn't see Mitch anywhere.

Buck said, "You driving, Raine?"

I slid a dark glance at him. "I only had half a beer."

He smiled at me. "Just wondering which car we're heading to."

I gestured toward my red SUV, a few dozen steps away, and then stopped dead, a horror washing over me that was icier than the November night. "What the…?" But my breath left my lungs and I couldn't even finish the exclamation.

I had parked under a street light, and it was plain to see. Someone had gouged a scratch all the way from the headlight to the tail light into the glossy finish of my brand new car.

CHAPTER NINE

It seemed to me that 6:00 a.m. came earlier than usual the next morning. After driving an unusually tense and silent Dallas back to the compound, stopping by the sheriff's office to sign a complaint, waiting for deputies to track down and interview Mitch, and then spending an hour or so on the phone with Miles, I was drained. The problem with Miles—with most men, actually—was that he wanted to fix things. Call the insurance company, pick up the key to one of his cars to drive while mine was in the shop, take it to the body shop on the highway, not the one at the dealership. I didn't want to be told how to fix things. I *knew* how to fix things. I just wanted someone to let me be mad for awhile. The SOB had keyed my car. My *new* car. I had a right to be upset, and I didn't want to think about fixing things until I was finished being upset.

Miles did have a point about one thing, though. "That woman, Dallas," he observed, "seems like a trouble magnet to me. I'd watch my back if I were you, sugar."

I'd come to something of the same conclusion myself, even though Dallas did have the grace to say, just before she got out of the car in front of the cabin, "I'm sorry, Raine. I feel like this is my fault."

I wasn't going to argue with her there.

She added, "I didn't mean to cause such a mess. And I'm really sorry you got caught up in it."

I said, "Yeah. Me too." I wanted to ask her about that drunk driving incident Buck had told me about, but she was already out of the car. She said, "Thanks for the lift." She slammed the door and hurried into her cabin, the whole thing apparently settled for her. But it wasn't for me.

So I wasn't quite as enthusiastic as I might once have been as I packed up the dogs the next morning for their first day of work. Corny, of course, was horrified over the previous night's adventure, and clucked and cooed over the damage to my car the whole time he helped me fit everything I needed for the day's excursion into the cargo hatch. He brushed out Mischief and Magic and spritzed down their coats again with a glossy conditioner, but I drew the line at letting him tie matching bandannas around their necks. After all, I told him, when he looked hurt, that was what the wardrobe department was for.

Cisco, who wasn't accustomed to being left behind on any trip, followed me inquisitively from house to car as I packed crates, an exercise pen, jugs of water, treats and toys, a shade canopy, and a portable grooming table. More than once I had to tell him to get out of the car, and once he raced into the house, brought out his stuffed duck, and dropped it into the back of the SUV next to the canvas bag containing my grooming kit. I removed the duck and knelt on the ground next to him, ruffling his ears. "Not today, buddy," I told him. "You stay with Corny. It's your own fault, you know. Next time maybe you'll think twice when you see a buffet."

But Cisco did not seem mollified, even when Corny lured him back to the office with crispy chicken-flavored treats. I felt bad when I saw Cisco standing with his paws on the windowsill, watching me get into the car, and even worse when I could hear him barking as I drove away, begging to come with me.

Maybe I should have listened to him. I probably would have found out the truth a lot sooner if I had.

Okay, I admit it: I'm an adventure junkie. Maybe that's one thing Dallas and I had in common. I like doing new things, learning new things, going new places, challenging myself in new ways. I like competing…and winning, of course. Most of all, I like showing off my dogs. So despite the bad mood in which I'd gone to bed, and despite my disillusionment with certain cast members, I was psyched to show up on the movie set for my first day of shooting.

I pulled up at the gate and showed the guard my ID badge. He checked it against his list and made a note. "Dog wrangler, huh?" He glanced at the backseat, where Mischief and Magic were strapped in and looking around with interest, then grinned. "Cute mutts."

"Thanks." I accepted the ID he returned to me. "They're Australian Shepherds. This is their first movie."

He winked at me. "Break a paw, then."

I said, "Thanks…I guess."

He glanced back at his clipboard. "You're supposed to meet Adrian Langley at the production office, main building. You go straight up the drive here…"

I smiled and waved at him. "Got it." I started to put the car in gear, then looked back. The name embroidered on the pocket of his white uniform shirt was Gary, so I said, "Say, Gary."

He looked at me inquiringly.

"Do you guys man this gate all night?" I asked. "Because when I came through last night after dinner there was a guard here, and I was just wondering."

He shook his head. "Nah. We go off duty at midnight. But no worries—this place locks down tighter than San Quentin when we leave. Has to, you know, because part of it's a sound stage."

I nodded as though I knew what that meant.

"I think that's why they picked this place to set up in," he confided, "because of the security. I mean, there's razor wire and crap on top of the fence at the back, for Chrissakes, and security cameras every hundred feet or so…I think it used to be a detention center for juvies."

Again I nodded, not bothering to correct his misimpression. "It didn't do much good yesterday," I observed. "You know, with the set being vandalized and all."

He gave a small derisive snort. "If you could call it that."

"What do you mean?"

He shrugged and shifted his gaze away, seeming uncertain for a moment whether to say more. But I've found that almost everyone considers himself an expert on something, and deep down everyone wants to share that expert opinion. All most people need is a little encouragement.

So I said, "I mean, I don't want to be a baby about it or anything, but if somebody can break through all that security…Well, they said we might be working late some nights and I've got my dogs to worry about, you know."

This time he gave a muffled guffaw of laughter. "Believe me, miss, you and your dogs can rest easy on that score."

I looked at him hopefully. "Oh?"

He nodded. "Our office checked the perimeter security footage and didn't find anything in terms of anybody breaking into the compound that night. Of course, there might be a few dead spots where the cameras didn't reach, but the fact is, it was a pretty considerate vandal, if you ask me. Broke into a hot set and didn't even wrinkle a rug or bump a chair out of place? Did his damage on a wall that could be painted over in ten minutes and put the whole schedule behind by less than two hours? He couldn't have done less damage, production-wise, if he'd planned it out that way. Your ordinary vandal doesn't go out of his way to keep the film on schedule." Again he shrugged. "At least that's the talk around the office."

I said, "Huh." Very interesting. Then I smiled and put the car in gear. "Thanks, Gary. I feel a lot better."

He touched a finger to his forehead in a small salute. "Hey, maybe one of your dogs will put his paw print on a movie poster for me."

I grinned and returned a wave. "You bet," I called as I drove off.

Adrian met me at the check-in station and told me that we would be shooting today's scenes with the dogs on the north side of Quail Hollow, and that a van was standing by to transport me, my dogs, and all my equipment to said location. When I told him I was familiar with the location and could drive myself, he wouldn't hear of it. Instead, five young men transferred the equipment from my SUV to a cargo van, and the dogs and I were directed to our own special van, all to drive less than a quarter mile away. No wonder movie tickets were so expensive.

Mischief and Magic were assigned their own producer, camera crew, and something called a "sequence director," because apparently Mr. Rosenstein did not do hands-on supervision for scenes in which human actors did not appear. This meant, according to Adrian, that we would spend the day shooting our scenes from every possible angle, in every possible light, with every possible detail emphasized and de-emphasized, so that Mr. Rosenstein could choose the best possible take for his final product. Again, think about that next time you pay $20.00 for a movie ticket.

Although, to be honest, by the time I got home that night, $20.00 a ticket seemed like a bargain.

The director, whose name was Jay and who looked to me as though he might have graduated film school last month, looked Mischief and Magic over critically as they lounged on their colorful rubber play mats inside the exercise pen. "They're twins?"

"Not really," I said. "Mischief has a patch over her left eye, and Magic has a patch over her right eye."

He gave a short approving nod. "So we shoot one from the right and one from the left. They look like the same dog."

So *that* was why the Aussies had gotten the job. Maybe that would make Cisco feel a little better. He'd never had a chance, buffet or no.

Jay explained the scene to me, in which Mischief and/or Magic was supposed to run from east to west through a flat winter meadow for approximately twenty yards. That wasn't even the size of a regulation agility course. Piece of cake. But when Jay looked at me uncertainly and finished with, "Your dog does action scenes, yes?" I felt obliged to tell the truth.

"Actually," I said, "We've never done a movie before. We were only called in because..."

He interrupted, "What do you do, commercials?"

"Not really," I began.

I could see panic rising in his eyes. "Television?"

I shook my head.

"*Photo shoots?*"

Yes, that was definitely the voice of panic.

"Dog shows," I explained simply.

Young Jay thrust his hands into his bushy hair and let out a muted cry of distress, gripping his skull. "I've got forty-eight hours to shoot six scenes, and they send me a dog who can't even hit its mark? A wrangler who's never even shot a *commercial?* What am I supposed to do with this? *What?*"

It was starting to look to me as though everyone in the movie business had a flare for drama, not just the actors. I turned to Jay. "Where do you want her to stand?"

He looked at me as though I had spoken a language other than English. "What?"

"Tell me where you want my dog," I repeated patiently, "and I'll send her there."

He gave me a long, skeptical, despairing look, then randomly pointed about ten feet to the north. "There," he said. "Over there. Make her go over there."

I took a clear plastic yogurt container top from my utility bag, walked to the area he had indicated, and placed it on the ground. I returned and released Mischief from the pen, pointing to the yogurt top. "Mischief, go place," I said.

Mischief noted the direction of my arm, trotted over until she found the marker, sniffed it, and then turned her attention to me, waiting for her next command. I looked at Jay. "So," I said, "did she find her mark or what?"

You know, I've taken some flak in my day for being the dog trainer whose golden retriever leads tracking officials on a four-hour wild goose chase through tick-infested woods, whose enthusiastic greetings have been known to knock full-grown deputy sheriffs to the ground, who leaps up on buffet tables and helps himself to other peoples' lunch… well, let's just say I've seen that skeptical you-do-*what*-for-a-living? look more times than I like to count. So it's nice to get the opposite look every now and then, the one that says "Okay, I'm impressed" or "How'd you get her to do that?" That was the look I saw on the director's face now, mixed with a good portion of grudging respect, and even though that particular behavior—"go place"—was one even Cisco had known since he was six months old, still, it was nice to see.

"Well, okay," he muttered. "This might work after all." He swung away abruptly and shouted, "All right, setting up the first shot! Setting up!"

I wish I could say everything went as easily as that, but for the most part Dallas was right: it was mostly a game of hurry up and wait. I'm not saying every agility or obedience trial I ever entered moved at lightning speed; I know how to be patient between events. But at least at a trial I knew when to rest my dogs and when to warm them up, and when their event was over, it was over and I went home. I spent most of the day sitting in a lawn chair beneath our pop-up canopy, checking e-mail, texting back and forth with Melanie and Corny, trying to stay warm. I played tug with Mischief and Magic to keep their muscles limber and took them through some basic tricks to keep their minds alert. Every once in a while we'd be called to action, and then it was nonstop. Stand here, run there, pause, repeat, do it all over with the other dog. I met the Humane Society rep, who greeted the dogs, made sure I had water and sun shelter for them, asked the director a few questions, and then stayed out of the way. In fact, he may have left, for all I know. By then I was too bored to care.

At noon we broke for lunch, and everybody trundled back to the compound for hot coffee and a hot meal. I was told that we'd be setting up in a new location after lunch; the same five guys were busy packing and loading all our equipment into the van while the crew, the dogs, and I stepped aboard our luxury shuttle—complete with CNN playing on the overhead screen—and were transported back to the compound.

Okay, so there were a few things about being on a movie set that were better than a dog show.

Mischief and Magic were happy to curl up in their crates in the back of the SUV and chew on bones while I went to the commissary tent for lunch. I got a bowl of thick mushroom soup that smelled like it was laced with white wine and a hot sandwich that they called grilled cheese, but which was really three kinds of exotic French cheeses melted onto a buttery brioche with caramelized onions and apples. It wasn't something I'd usually think to order for myself, but it reminded me of the kind of thing Miles might make me for lunch, so I decided to try it.

The place was pretty crowded, and I was about to sit with the crew from my shoot when I spotted Lonzo sitting at the end of one of the long tables with two empty chairs on either side of him. I took one of them. "Hi," I said, placing my tray on the table. "Anyone sitting here?"

He barely glanced up from his phone. "Dunno," he said, and, still thumbing the screen of his phone, took a bite of what looked to be a bunch of bean sprouts wrapped in pita bread.

He was dressed today in another fashionably tied wool scarf—yellow with a pale blue stripe—and a camel-colored suede coat, despite the fact that the temperature by now was in the mid-fifties and patio heaters throughout the tent kept the place cozy. I guess those California people must get cold easily.

"The dogs finished their first scene today," I said as I sat down. I unfolded my paper napkin and placed it on my knee. "It went great." A slight prevarication, but he wasn't listening to me anyway.

He grunted something that might have been, "Good."

I tasted my soup, and I was right about the white wine. It was amazing. I said, "I heard you and Dallas got to see some of our town the other night."

Now he glanced away from his phone, mildly interested. "Where did you hear that?"

"I have some friends in the sheriff's department," I explained innocently. "He mentioned he gave you a warning for speeding. It's kind of a big deal around here, you know, getting to meet movie people."

Lonzo frowned. "Well, it wasn't me they met." He turned back to his phone. "Who knows who that woman's been running around with?"

"We went out for pizza last night," I said. "Dallas and I."

"Good for you."

I put down my spoon. "We had a run-in with one of the locals over what happened the other day while you two were at the diner. It got kind of ugly. What *did* happen that day? What did that guy say to her that made her go ballistic? And who was he, do you know? Meg said she thought he was somebody from the movie. Was he?"

He put down his phone with a long-suffering sigh. "Look, Miss, uh…"

"Stockton," I supplied.

"Look," he repeated, "you seem like a nice person. But I wouldn't get too involved with people you meet on the set, if I were you. I don't know Dallas personally, not really, but you hear things, you know what I mean?"

I said, naturally, "What kind of things?"

He shrugged uncomfortably, then released a long breath. "Okay, so before we left to come out here I guess there was some kind of incident with some guy she was dating, he filed a complaint against her or something, I don't know, but the police were nosing around, talking to people she'd worked with, that kind of thing. I don't know how it turned out, but I do know Mr. Rosenstein did have me call the production company's lawyers, and I think it was about whether or not we could get out of our contract with her."

That did surprise me. "I thought they were friends."

He said, "They are. But the film always comes first. Always."

He picked up his phone again. "It's just that she's got a reputation, you know, around the business. Walking off the set, showing up too messed up to work or not showing up at all…I guess Mr. Rosenstein felt sorry her. I don't think anyone else would give her a job."

That didn't sound at all like what Dallas had told me last night, and I was about to open my mouth to question. But just then I heard a sound that made my heart hit my ribs, one that I unfortunately knew too well: the sharp report of a pistol.

I snapped my head around toward the sound, half rising from my chair. I gasped, "What was that?" Even though I knew perfectly well what it was.

Lonzo had glanced up at the sound, but seemed unconcerned as he scrolled down a page on his phone. "Right," he said, checking whatever was written there. "They're rehearsing one of the murder scenes on the set. Dallas has to fall down the stairs. Bethany will do the rest of the scene when we get back to the lot."

But as I watched, the door to the main building across the compound was flung open and someone ran out, followed by several others. One was waving his arms and shouting something, one was on his phone, another had a hand pressed to her face and seemed to stagger a little. They all looked terrified. I said uncertainly, "That doesn't look like a rehearsal."

Lonzo turned curiously to look, and I got to my feet, starting toward the exit. More people streamed from the building, and I had only gone a few steps before I heard one of them cry, "Medic! We need a medic! Somebody help! Dallas has been shot!"

CHAPTER TEN

B uck always used to say that my biggest problem was that when someone yells "Fire!" I run
toward it, not away from it. He was right, of course,
but in this particular case it wasn't just my instinct
for being in the thick of the action that propelled
me. As a search and rescue volunteer, I'm trained in
advanced first aid, blood loss suppression, and CPR.
When someone calls for help, I go.

I pushed through the chaos at the front door
and tried not to trip over the wires and cables that
snaked all over the floor as I made my way through
the front room. Dallas was at the bottom of the
fake spiral staircase in a half-sitting position with a
bloody towel pressed to the side of her face. Among
the people surrounding her were Seth Rosenstein,
who knelt beside her with his hand on her shoulder,
his narrow face drawn with tension and fear. The
man on the other side of her was pulling on a pair
of medical gloves from the canvas bag filled with
emergency supplies at his feet. My heartbeat slowed
a fraction with relief to see a qualified medic was on
the scene, but I continued forward.

"What happened?" I asked of no one in particular.

"I don't know," someone said.

Someone else said, "We rehearsed that scene half a dozen times…"

And someone else, "It was a blank! I just don't see how a blank bullet could have done that kind of damage!"

I looked around until I saw what everyone was talking about. The big gilded mirror adjacent to the staircase was shattered, and big chunks of glossy glass were scattered on the floor and embedded into the carpeted treads. I didn't see how a blank bullet could have done that kind of damage either.

The medic carefully removed the towel from Dallas's face and replaced it with gauze, dabbing gently at the blood. Dallas said weakly, "My face. Is it bad? Will it scar?"

He replied reassuringly, "A few stitches by a good plastics man and it'll be like it never happened. The ambulance is on its way. You were lucky, though. Looks like a piece of flying glass caught you, but it was pretty close to the eye."

Dallas flashed Seth Rosenstein a terrified look and I saw Seth's mouth tighten grimly. He gave Dallas's shoulder a reassuring squeeze and murmured, "You're okay, baby. You're fine."

Dallas shoved him away angrily. "My *face*!" she cried and burst into tears.

A big bald man was standing next to me, wearing a sweat-stained tee shirt that had "Props" stenciled on the back. He was breathing hard and drops of perspiration glistened on face. He had a gun in his hand. "My God, Mr. Rosenstein, I don't know what happened. I've never seen anything like this before. You should be able to fire one of these blanks at a teacup and not even knock it off the saucer." As he spoke he fumbled open the chamber and shook one of the rounds into his hand. He stared at it for a long moment. So did I.

Slowly, he lifted his gaze back to Seth Rosenstein. He looked slack-jawed, stunned. "Except," he said, "these aren't blanks. And this isn't the prop gun."

It was, in fact, a .38 Special. The same kind of gun, according to Buck, that Dallas had had in her purse last night.

Dallas was taken away in an ambulance for stitches and X-rays of her various bumps and contusions, but I heard the EMTs giving her the same reassurance the first medic had—a couple of stitches, no scarring, she'd be fine.

Three sheriff's office cars arrived within moments of the ambulance, which was probably two more than were needed. Among them was the K-9 unit. Jolene Smith locked her eyes with mine as she got out. I returned her gaze innocently.

Jolene and her police dog, Nike, were a gift to Hanover County from the Department of Homeland Security. Although Nike had already proven her worth in lives saved—including mine—on more than one occasion, the need for a bomb-detection dog in our small community was somewhat less than full time, as was the need for her other skills, such as take-down and drug-detection. So when she wasn't working as a K-9 handler in her area of expertise, Jolene performed the role of any other deputy: patrolling the roads, taking reports, investigating cases. The bonus was that she got to take her dog to work with her, just like I did.

Apparently one of the cases she'd been assigned was the disruption on the movie set. It didn't take much imagination to determine, from the look on her face, that she wasn't particularly happy about that.

She stood for a moment, eyes scanning and assessing her surroundings, while the other deputies positioned their cars and awaited their orders. Because of her rank, if she was on the scene she was almost always in charge, even though she had been a member of the sheriff's office for less than six months. This didn't sit well with anyone, although the deputies were too well trained to complain about it. She walked over to where I was standing near the front door of the building, hands resting lightly on her utility belt, eyes squinted at the sun over my shoulder. She said, "I swear to God, Stockton, if I respond to a crime scene one more time and find you hanging around, I'm going to slap cuffs on you whether you did anything or not."

I returned coolly, "I'm a witness."

Her gaze raked me up and down. "Is that a fact? What are you a witness to?"

I briefly told her what had happened, up to and including the part where the prop man had opened the cylinder of the pistol and found it loaded with real bullets instead of blanks. She listened without any discernible change of expression, jotted down the names of a few people I happened to mention, and then said, "Stay here."

"I can't stay here," I told her, mostly to be contrary. "I'm working."

She repeated sternly, "Stay here." And turned to deploy the other deputies to take interviews and gather evidence.

I didn't stay there, of course. I had left Mischief and Magic crated by themselves too long, so I went to check on them. They were both sound asleep, and I didn't blame them. They'd had a hard morning, and there was more to come that afternoon, or at least as far as I knew there was. I gave them fresh water and another smear of peanut butter on each bone, and opened the back hatch window for air circulation even though the temperature gauge on my dashboard told me it was 52 degrees outside and I was parked in the shade. I didn't like leaving my dogs in the car unsupervised, and I went to find Adrian to ask him how much longer it would be. Instead, I found Lonzo standing outside the open door of the main building with his phone pressed to his ear, looking frantic. He waved me over with a harried gesture and covered the microphone of the phone with his hand when I arrived.

"OMG!" he exclaimed, eyes big. "Can you believe this? The police are actually questioning Mr. Rosenstein! As if he didn't have enough to worry about!"

I had noticed that about people in a crisis. Half an hour ago Lonzo could barely be bothered to look up from his phone to talk to me; now, apparently, we were besties.

"All he wants to do is go to the hospital to be with poor Dallas," he went on, "and they won't let him leave! I'm on hold with the hospital now," he added with a roll of his eyes. "Honestly, don't they know who I *am*?"

I said, "Why are the police holding Mr. Rosenstein?"

His eyebrows shot up. "My dear, didn't you hear? He's the one who fired the gun!"

I started to say something, but he spoke suddenly into the phone. "Yes! Yes, I'm holding for a Dr. Breverton, he's treating Dallas McKenzie..."

He plugged his other ear with his finger and hurried down the steps and away from all the activity at the doorway. I didn't bother trying to follow him, and when I looked around, Jolene was just coming out of the building. She caught my eye and jerked her head to the side, indicating we should step out of the stream of traffic around the door. I followed her to the side of the building, where we had a view of the lawn below, the Craft Services tent, and the path that led to the private cabins.

She said, "How well do you know this Dallas McKenzie?"

I shrugged. "Not well. I know she's from Texas, and that's not her real name."

"Sarah Jane Littleton," Jolene supplied, glancing at her notebook. "That's her real name. You had dinner with her last night?"

I was surprised, and then realized it must have been in the report about the vandalism to my car. "Just pizza. Mitch Dobbs came up and started making trouble." I looked at her intently. "You don't think this whole thing could have something to do with what happened at the diner, do you? I mean, that somebody came on the set and deliberately switched guns, do you?"

She did not appear to be inclined to answer, not that I expected her to. "Do you know if she carried a handgun?"

I hate it when cops ask questions they already know the answer to, I really do. "Buck was at the restaurant last night," I replied impatiently. "He said he saw a .38 in her purse. I didn't see anything."

She nodded, as though approving of my reply. "What do you know about her relationship with Mr. Rosenstein?"

"They're old friends, grew up together I guess. She said he gave her a start in the business." I felt no responsibility to share what Lonzo had told me at lunch. She was the detective, let her do some detecting.

She asked, "Have you ever witnessed them arguing?"

My eyebrows shot up. "Are you serious? You can't really think that Seth Rosenstein deliberately tried to shoot his own stunt woman with fifteen people standing around watching!"

She waited without expression for me to answer her question. "No," I replied perfunctorily. "I never saw them argue. The director yells at everybody. That's his job. If you ask me, what you should be looking at is…"

"Didn't ask you, Stockton," she replied, flipping closed her notebook. "You can go."

I spun on my heel to do so, and then turned back. I painted a pleasant expression on my face and said, "Hey, Jolene."

She glanced at me and I smiled. "What're you doing for Thanksgiving?"

As I had learned all too well over the past six months, the easiest way to annoy Jolene was to be nice to her. But this time it didn't work.

She said easily, "I'm spending it with my family. You?"

I blinked. "Umm, yeah." Then, "You're going back to New Jersey?"

"Raleigh," she said. "That's where my mother is. Why else do you think I'd request a posting to North Carolina?"

I hadn't known that. Not the fact that she had family in North Carolina, nor that she had requested to be assigned here. "Oh," I said, somewhat deflated. "Well, have a good one."

She actually smiled. "You too."

I started down the steps, and halfway down darted a look back. She watched me go, still looking amused.

Jolene and I have a strange relationship.

"The police weren't actually holding Seth Rosenstein," I told Miles on the phone that night, "just questioning him like they were everyone else. And it turns out it actually *was* Dallas's gun, stolen from her purse apparently. The prop gun was on the shelf in the prop room where it was supposed to be, except for the fact that the prop manager swore he put it on the set that morning. It was a Smith and Wesson revolver, too, only a slightly different model, but not so much that the average person would notice right away, I guess. They use real guns in the movies, did you know that? Just with blank bullets. Or at least they're supposed to be blank."

Miles made a sound that might have been noncommittal or it might have been skeptical—or it might have expressed a complete lack of interest altogether. I went to the refrigerator, with Cisco, who had finished his own dinner half an hour ago and was clearly famished, trotting along beside me with an expression of avid expectation on his face. He watched intently as I opened the freezer door and peered around until I found one of the containers Miles had left for me. I didn't check the label; whatever it was would be fabulous, and I hadn't had more than a couple of spoonfuls of soup for lunch.

"So," I went on, closing the freezer door, "I guess when they rehearsed the scene, they fired the gun to give Dallas the cue to fall down the stairs. Or maybe it has something to do with the sound guy, I don't know." I crossed to the microwave, Cisco's toenails clicking on the floor beside me, his tail waving a happy breeze behind me. "They'd done it four or five times already that morning, but when they came back from lunch, Mr. Rosenstein fired the gun and a real bullet hit the mirror. It broke and it was the glass shrapnel that hit Dallas. Good thing he didn't aim for her, huh?"

Again, nothing but a neutral grunt.

I put the container in the microwave and slammed the door. Cisco licked his lips. "How many minutes on this frozen thing?"

"Which one?"

I opened the microwave door and checked the label. "The coq au vin."

"Take it out of the plastic container," he replied, "put it in a casserole dish, cover it, and microwave for five minutes. Be sure to stir it halfway through."

I sighed and retrieved the container. That sounded like a lot of trouble to me. I didn't even know where my casserole dish was, and I was sure I didn't have a cover for it.

I said, "The props room is just down the hall in the same building, so it looks like someone switched the guns during lunch."

Miles said, "You'd think that fellow Rosenstein would have noticed he was handling a different gun."

I found the casserole dish beneath a mound of orphaned plastic bowls without tops and dragged it out, dislodging a couple of aluminum pie plates in the process. "Not really," I said over the clatter. "Like I said, they didn't look that different, and besides, Mr. Rosenstein wasn't the one who usually fired the gun. That was some other dude's job—they have *way* too many people working on this movie—but he wasn't back from lunch or something."

I upended the container of coq au vin over the casserole dish and shook it, trying to dislodge the contents. Cisco watched alertly, hoping for an accident.

"Dallas was okay," I added. "I didn't get to talk to her, but she was back from the hospital before I left for the day. I heard they're going to go ahead and shoot the scene tomorrow."

Again, Miles replied with nothing but an enigmatic grunt.

"What's that supposed to mean?" I demanded, exasperated. I got a spoon from the drawer and tried to dig the frozen stew out of the container.

"I don't know, sugar," he said. "This whole thing reminds me of an old *Rockford Files* plot." Miles watched a lot more late-night television reruns than

I did, and if it hadn't been for him I wouldn't even have known what a Rockford file was. "Real gun substituted for prop gun, real bullets instead of blanks… and you don't think it was a little convenient that it was the director who picked up the gun right after the switch? And that his aim was good enough for a near miss, but not good enough to do any real damage—or shut down the movie?"

I scowled, stabbing at the frozen block inside the plastic container. "Yeah," I said. "I do." In fact, all of that was exactly what I had been thinking, even though I had been called back to my own shoot before the deputies had finished their interviews and I hadn't had a chance to get any more details. Jolene, as usual, was no help. I had simply wanted to get Miles's unbiased opinion on the story because he sometimes—make that most of the time—saw things I didn't.

"I also thought it was pretty convenient that Dallas's gun was a .38 revolver, just like the one on the set." I gave up on freeing my dinner from the container, put the whole thing in the casserole dish, and popped it in the microwave. Cisco's ears dropped in disappointment.

"What do you want to bet this whole thing ends on up *ET* tomorrow?" Miles said.

"Seems like a pretty crazy stunt to pull just for publicity," I said doubtfully. "Dallas could have been seriously hurt. That was real blood, and the cut was pretty close to her eye."

"I'm not saying he meant to hurt her," Miles countered. "But you've got to admit, it would have been a lot more serious—not to mention expensive—if it had happened to his leading lady instead of a stunt woman."

"I guess," I admitted.

"And didn't you say she's going back to work tomorrow? He didn't even lose any shooting time."

"Just like yesterday," I agreed thoughtfully. "They had the set repainted as soon as the deputies finished taking pictures. And Miles, there's really no way anybody could have gotten in from the outside to vandalize the set. There's security everywhere, not to mention people up and about at all hours. Someone would have noticed a stranger lurking around. It had to be somebody who was already inside the compound, or who was at least supposed to be there."

Miles said, "Rosenstein's star doesn't exactly appear to be in the ascendency. His last film lost $25 million, and most of the money to make this one came out of his own pocket."

"Wow," I said. I couldn't help it. "Fifty-seven million. Who has that kind of pocket change?" Aside from Miles, of course.

"Apparently not Rosenstein," Miles said. "Not yet, at least. He just put his Bel-Air mansion on the market for $62 million. Of course, he's still got an estate in Belize, and another in Cannes. They seem to be unencumbered. Unfortunately, in order to get talent like Bethany Parker and Josiah Blackstone, he had to promise them a significant portion of the back end, so even if the movie is a hit, his margins are close. And he needs this movie to be a hit."

"Wait a minute." I frowned suddenly. "How do you know all this? You were researching on the computer the whole time we've been talking," I accused him. "I hate it when you do that."

"The point is," Miles replied, "this project needs all the publicity it can get, and it's never too early to start. Do you know how many people bought tickets to *Spiderman* on Broadway in hopes they'd see someone get hurt?" At my silence he explained, "The show had a reputation for being cursed because of all the accidents and mishaps that occurred before it opened. The ghouls turned out in droves to buy tickets, hoping they'd get to see somebody die for real onstage, I guess."

"That's sick."

"That's show business."

"Jeez, Miles. You're such a cynic." The microwave beeped and I opened the door. The kitchen was immediately suffused with the aroma of chicken in wine. Cisco, who had given up hope and plopped down with his chin on the floor, now scrambled to a sitting position, his tail sweeping back and forth across the linoleum.

Miles said, "Do me a favor, baby. Don't eat that out of the plastic container."

I took the phone away from my ear and stared at it suspiciously. There is such a thing as knowing somebody too well. I returned the phone to my ear, at the same time plucking at the hot plastic bowl with my fingers, and said. "Don't call me..." I stopped, remembering something.

"Baby, I know," Miles finished for me, as he always did. "But if you're going to microwave my coq au vin and then eat it out of a plastic bowl—standing up, no doubt—I reserve the right to call you anything I want."

Seth Rosenstein had called Dallas "baby" that afternoon when he was comforting her. Was that what Hollywood people did? Even gay men who were married to other men?

I said dryly, "I'll put it on a plate. And sit down at the table."

"Atta girl. Say, here's something interesting." There was a brief pause while he apparently scanned an article. I rummaged in a drawer for silverware. "It looks like Rosenstein was involved in some kind of intellectual property dispute four or five years back. A writer got an injunction against the production company, claiming that *Deadfall* was based on a book he'd written."

I dumped the contents of the plastic container onto a paper plate. "I thought the movie was based on real life."

"Exactly. But this author claimed he owned the rights to the story before Rosenstein did. Eventually the case was settled out of court, but it cost the company a lot of money and most of its backers, and delayed production by several years." He made another one of those enigmatic grunting noises and was silent for a moment. I rolled my eyes. "Another lawsuit was filed the following year, and the year after that. Looks like somebody didn't want this movie made."

"The real-life killer?" I suggested.

"Probably not," Miles replied. "He died in prison in 2006, before the book or the movie were even thought about. More likely it's just one of those projects that was snake-bit from the start. No wonder he had so much trouble getting investors."

"You'd think a director with his credentials would just find something else."

"I would," he agreed. "But who knows about these creative types? Hold on a minute, hon, Mel wants to talk to you."

"Say, Miles," I said before he could turn the phone over to Melanie, "as long as you've got whatever kind of file open that you have on Seth Rosenstein…what does it say about his marital status?"

He sounded amused. "Thinking of leaving me, baby?"

"Not yet," I replied. "But if you call me 'baby' one more time…"

He said, "Married twice, divorced twice, both times to actresses he met on the set. One of the perks, I guess. Currently unattached, in case you've got any ideas. But," he added, "if you're interested you'd better hurry, because it's already been eight months since the last divorce, and that appears to be a new record for him."

"Yeah, well, I'll keep that in mind," I replied absently, frowning. "Let me talk to Melanie, okay? And hey, Miles?" I added, because he really was the best boyfriend in the world, and I still didn't understand what I'd done to deserve him. "Thanks for dinner."

I could almost see his smile. "Love you, sweetheart. Enjoy. Here's Mel."

I ate my dinner—from a plate—under the watchful eyes of Cisco while I told Melanie all about Mischief and Magic's big day in the movies, and she told me all about the trip to Charleston she and her dad and grandmother were planning the next day. I'm sure I was properly enthusiastic and said all the right things, but in truth only part of my attention was on Melanie. Mostly I was wondering why Dallas had lied to me about Seth Rosenstein's marital status, not to mention his sexual orientation, and what else she had lied about.

One thing was for certain: I had every intention of finding out.

CHAPTER ELEVEN

Miles was right. "Terror on the Set" was the headline on two of the daily entertainment business television shows the next day, and, according to Corny, at least three websites devoted to celebrity gossip. Even a show business neophyte like I was knew that kind of thing didn't happen by accident.

Mischief and Magic finished their scenes by midafternoon. Adrian told me, beaming proudly, that it looked as though they'd be able to use almost a full minute of the footage it had taken the dogs and me ten solid hours of hard work to shoot. But, he cautioned, I shouldn't be too disappointed if a lot less than that made the final cut. The eventual decision would be made by the director when the whole film was shot, months from now.

You'd think that being on the set of a major motion picture—not to mention having my dogs actually featured in said motion picture—would be the highlight of my year, or at least my day. Not even close. The whole thing was a lot harder than I'd imagined. Mischief and Magic had fun doing their tricks for the cameras, even when the trick was something as simple as chasing a flying disc, but trying to keep them interested and entertained during the long down periods between takes was exhausting. The only thing that made me smile all day was the series of texts and photos from Melanie in Charleston. I sent back my own photo chronicle of Mischief and Magic doing their collective thing, with funny captions when I could think of them: Mischief with her head tilted inquisitively toward the camera saying *You want me to do what?* and Magic sound asleep saying *Nice work if you can get it.* That kind of thing.

We worked through lunch—which meant somebody ran back to the Craft Services tent and brought back a bunch of sandwiches that we ate when we could—so I didn't have any idea how things were going with the rest of the filming after all the drama yesterday. At 3:00 somebody called, "Okay, that's a wrap on the dogs." And we all shuffled back to the van that would deposit us back at the compound. A couple of hefty guys loaded my equipment into my car while the dogs and I said good-bye to the crew. One thing about working with dogs: hardly anyone is ever in a bad mood. Adrian reminded me to stand by for a couple of weeks in case reshoots were needed, told me my check would be mailed from California within thirty days, and sent me on my way. I was looking forward to life getting back to my normal.

My pretty girls and I were walking back to the car when I saw Dallas walking down the path to her cabin. She had her phone to her ear and didn't see me wave, so after a moment's debate I veered away from the parking lot and took the shortcut across the dead winter lawn that led to the cabins.

I remembered which cabin was hers from the night I'd dropped her off after pizza, but if I'd had any doubt, the sound of her voice inside reassured me. The doors and windows of the modular cabin were cheap plywood and single-pane glass, and sound carried clearly. Before I even reached the door, I could hear the shouting. *Great*, I thought. *The many faces of Dallas.* I almost turned with my dogs and walked away, but curiosity got the better of me. I still hadn't gotten the full story about the shooting accident, and if anyone would know, Dallas would. So I kept going.

"I'm *done*, do you hear me?" I heard Dallas cry behind the door. "Not another day, not another minute, it stops *now*!" A pause, and once again I considered a cowardly exit. Then, "No! No, you listen to *me*! We have a deal, damn it. We're sticking with the plan!"

I was starting to feel a little creepy, standing on the doorstep eavesdropping, so I resolutely raised my fist and knocked loudly enough to be heard over her tirade.

I heard a crash and a loud, "*Damn it!*" This was followed by a sharp, "Who is it?"

I called back, "It's Raine Stockton. This is my last day and I just came to say good-bye." The silence from behind the door went on so long that I added, "If this is a bad time I can come back."

I heard her murmur something, probably ending her phone call, and then she opened the door. Her hair was slicked back in a ponytail so that the white bandage on her forehead was clearly visible. Her face was pinched and her lips compressed, and when she looked at me she said distractedly, "Oh," as though she had forgotten who I was.

She opened the door wider and gestured me inside. I noticed a slight shakiness to her hand as she did so. "Sorry. I was on the phone. Men can be such asses sometimes. I knocked over a lamp. I guess it broke. Watch the dogs' feet."

I put Mischief and Magic in a down stay on the dead grass by the door and stepped inside, glancing around. The room was about 12x12 with a narrow door that probably concealed a bathroom. The bed was unmade and piled with clothes and the floor was strewn with shoes, magazines, and used paper plates. No one has ever accused me of being a neatnik, but even I felt compelled to start cleaning up.

I said, "I didn't mean to eavesdrop." That was a patent lie, but the best I could do. "You sounded pretty mad."

She shrugged, still looking upset and distracted. "Just stupid work stuff. This is a hard business."

I murmured, "Yeah, I'm beginning to see that. So, are you okay?"

She looked at me blankly, and I gestured to the bandage on her head.

"Oh," she said. "Oh, yeah, fine. A couple of stitches, aspirin for pain. Stupid freak accident. They're part of the job."

I observed, "I don't know. That one seems a little more freaky than normal."

She just shrugged.

There were two nightstands flanking the bed, both of them scattered with food wrappers and crumpled paper cups. One of them had a glass-shaded lamp sitting on it; the twin to that lamp lay in pieces at the foot of the opposite wall, where Dallas had apparently "knocked it over." She knelt to begin picking up the pieces, speaking rapidly now. "Sorry about the mess. We're supposed to have maid service. Listen, I'm glad you stopped by. All finished, huh? Lucky you. I don't suppose you see a broom around here anywhere, do you? They should at least give us a broom."

I agreed a broom would be a good idea, but the room was clearly too small to conceal one. I knelt to help her pick up the broken glass. "Anyway, I'm glad you're feeling better," I said. I found a paper plate that wasn't too dirty and dumped a handful of broken lampshade onto it. "That was a close call."

"You're telling me." She dropped more glass onto the plate. "So listen. I've got the whole Thanksgiving weekend off, Wednesday through Sunday, how about that? I was thinking about actually making that camping trip happen. Is there a good outfitter in town?"

"You can find most everything you'll need at Patterson's Hardware and Sporting Goods," I said. "But if you want the fancy stuff, like MREs and solar-powered camp stoves, you'll have to go to Asheville."

"Great," she said, plucking up more glass with her fingers. "I'll go into town as soon as I finish my scene tomorrow. So I just stay on that trail that goes up past the waterfall, right? What did you call it? Overlook Falls?"

"Right," I said. "It's a pretty easy hike. About an hour past the waterfall there's a beautiful overlook, and not far past that a foul-weather shelter. No real campgrounds, and it's not patrolled, but this time of year there aren't a lot of campers so you should be able to set up camp right at the shelter if you want to."

"Sounds perfect."

I dropped another piece of glass onto the paper plate and sat back on my heels, looking at her. "So let me ask you something," I said. "Why'd you tell me Seth Rosenstein was gay?"

I thought I saw a flicker of uneasiness cross her face, and then she slanted a half smile at me. "Who knew you'd take me seriously? I mean, don't you have Internet or anything?"

I was annoyed, but tried not to show it. I probably didn't do a very good job. "Was it to hide the fact that you're having an affair with him?" I persisted. "Because that's pretty stupid. Why would I care?"

With a jerky movement, she dropped another sliver of glass onto the paper plate. This time a drop of blood appeared on the white paper beside it. She sucked in a hissing breath and clutched her injured finger. "Damn!"

She stood up and headed toward the small bathroom. "Be right back."

All right, so maybe I'm not the most tactful person in the world. But it had been a long day, my two dogs were in a down stay outside, and I was tired of whatever game Dallas was playing. Scowling, I picked up the paper plate filled with broken glass and glanced around for a trashcan. I found one next to the bed and dumped the glass inside. When I did, the contents that were already inside the trashcan were dislodged. I stared at what I saw.

It was a hypodermic needle. And next to it, half-hidden by tissues and torn packets of alcohol swabs, was another. And another.

"Crap," I muttered.

I looked for a moment at the closed bathroom door, where I could hear the faucet running. And suddenly I just didn't want to be there anymore. I turned and left the cabin without saying good-bye.

"It explains a lot," I told Miles wearily over the car's speakerphone as I drove home. "Everything, really. The crazy mood swings, the lies, the DUI—even though she didn't get caught for that one. She's probably been high half the time we were together. I'm such an idiot."

"But a well-meaning one," Miles said.

I probably should have taken issue with the fact that he didn't disagree about the "idiot" part, but that only goes to show how dispirited I was. I hate it when I misjudge people. "I'm just so disappointed," I said. "Not in her, in me. I mean, I knew she had issues, but I never suspected drugs. She seemed like such a regular person when we had dinner that night."

"I think that's why most people turn to drugs," Miles reminded me. "To feel like regular people. My guess is half the people in Hollywood are dealing with that problem, to one extent or another."

"This is more than a 'problem,'" I replied bitterly. "There were at least three needles in that trashcan, probably more that I couldn't see under the trash. How bad off do you have to be to shoot up that often? What do people even use hypodermics for these days anyway? Meth? Crack?"

"Someone in her income bracket can probably afford the good stuff," Miles answered. "Are you going to narc on her?'

I pulled a sour face, even though he couldn't see. "To whom? Her boss? He's probably her dealer. She practically admitted they're sleeping together." She had done no such thing, but at this point that hardly seemed to matter. "And Jolene would tell me to mind my own business because it has nothing to do with the case. She'd be right about that," I admitted. I pounded my hand on the steering wheel in frustration. "Why do I keep *doing* this? Taking everybody I meet at face value, thinking every one is a nice guy."

"You're a lot like Cisco that way," Miles pointed out, which took the edge off my foul mood and even came close to making me smile. There were certainly worse things to be compared to than a golden retriever.

"Well," I admitted grudgingly, "you turned out okay, I guess."

"Although if I recall you didn't care for me in the least when we first met, so I guess your point is well taken. You're a terrible judge of character."

"Thanks, Miles. I can always count on you to tell me the truth."

"My pleasure, sweetheart. Any little thing I can do to help." Then he said seriously, "Raine, you are not an idiot and you're not gullible. You made a couple of bad calls, and now you're questioning your judgment about everything. Don't do that. Everybody makes mistakes."

"Even you?" I said, because I couldn't actually remember Miles ever admitting he was wrong about anything.

He replied dryly, "Three marriages, remember?"

"Oh." I stopped at the crossroads and signaled the turn that led to my house. "Right." I made the turn and added, somewhat morosely, "Dallas probably switched the gun herself yesterday."

"That doesn't make a lot of sense," Miles pointed out. "Why would she want to make sure someone fired real bullets at her?"

I scowled a little, knowing he was right. "Drug addicts aren't supposed to make sense."

He said thoughtfully, "What I don't understand is how she got past the insurance physical. I mean, I guess you can fake your way through a drug test with enough help, but if she's shooting heroin, or something similar, it wouldn't be easy."

"Lonzo said no one would give her a job except Rosenstein," I said. "This is probably why." Then, "What insurance?"

"It protects the investors in case the film shuts down," Miles explained. "Having a cast member go into rehab in the middle of a shoot can cost tens of millions. The insurance company wants to avoid that kind of payout if it can."

I said, "You know this because…?"

"I've invested in a couple of films," he replied easily.

Of course he had.

I sighed. "Anyway, I'm just glad to be out of it. I feel like I need a shower, and not just because I worked all day, either. So what are you doing tonight?"

He replied without hesitation, "Missing you."

I had to smile. He was smooth. But mostly sincere. "And?" I prompted.

"Dinner reservations at six, early bed and back to the beach tomorrow. It's supposed to be sunny this weekend and Mel wants to get in a little more beach time, but we should be home Sunday night."

I said softly, "It'll be good to see you."

"You too, sweetheart. Enjoy your afternoon off, and take care of yourself, will you?"

"Don't you worry," I assured him. "That's exactly what I intend to do."

I have a sign in my mud room, right above the leash hooks, that says "A Day Without a Golden Retriever is Like a Day Without Sunshine." Truer words were never spoken. I saw Cisco leap up with his forepaws on the glass door of the Dog Daze office as soon as I pulled in outside the gate, his beautiful white belly exposed, his tail swishing madly, his happy bark of greeting clearly visible, if not audible. I gave Mischief and Magic a big hug each, told them how proud I was of them, and released them to the play yard. There they wasted no time starting an exuberant high-speed game of sister-tag, completely unimpressed with themselves.

Corny had Cisco in a nice sit by the time I reached the door, which my darling dog completely forgot the minute I opened it. Cisco barreled toward me with such force that I almost slapped myself in the face with the door, then he hit my knees so hard they buckled and I went down, holding on to my golden for dear life—literally. Was his behavior acceptable? Of course not. Was I going to correct him? Not a chance in this world.

Corny exclaimed, "Oh, Miss Stockton, I'm so sorry! Are you all right? Cisco, what were you thinking?" While I laughed and rubbed my face against sweet-smelling golden fur and tried to dodge the doggie tongue that wanted to swipe my eyes and nose. It took only moments for that pure sweet golden goodness to wash away all the ugliness of the outside world. I was a lucky woman.

"So," Corny said, bright-eyed, after I'd finally disentangled myself from Cisco and the three of us went back inside the building. "How was it? Amazing? Did you meet any stars? Are you invited to the premier?"

I looked at him wearily and said, "Let me put it this way. It's good to be home."

Corny helped me unload all the dog equipment from the car and put it away, and I volunteered to take over kennel duty so he could have an early night, but with only four boarders remaining until the weekend, there was hardly any need for my help. That suited me fine. I set up a circular jump course in the agility yard and let Cisco run it until we both were dizzy, then I played some hide-and-seek games with him to sharpen his search skills, but mostly just because they were fun. I knew I was acting like a working mom who was trying to make up for her neglect with "quality time," and also that Cisco would have been happy with a belly rub and a few liver treats. I didn't care. I'd missed my guy, and I was glad to be home again.

As twilight fell and Corny closed up the office, I gathered up the paperwork I'd neglected the past couple of days and took it, along with my three amazing dogs, to the house. I found some cooked chicken breast in the freezer and as a reward for everyone warmed it in chicken broth and poured it over the dogs' kibble. While they scarfed it up, I sat at the kitchen table and checked my messages. Miles had sent a video of Melanie and Rita sending greetings and throwing kisses from a horse-drawn carriage, ending with a view of their magnificent historic hotel on Meeting Street and the words, "Wish you were here, sugar." Suddenly I did too.

I smiled through a couple of texts from Melanie complaining about the school report she was tasked with writing about her trip. I smiled because I knew perfectly well that the only thing Melanie liked more than writing reports that allowed her to pose as an expert on a subject was complaining about how hard she had to work to get the inevitable top marks for that report. Then I sat up straight at an unexpected text from a number I didn't recognize, although I knew before finishing the first line who it was from.

Hey girlfriend! What happened to you? Mad at me?

I wrinkled up my face and muttered, "Seriously?" I deleted the text, and the two more after that. I moved on to the next message, which was from Sonny, who was wondering if I'd made a decision on helping with her case or, as she added wryly, whether Hollywood had gone to my head. I was about to send a reply when my phone chimed. It was Dallas again.

Hey, it said. *I'd really like to talk to you. Dinner?*

I actually hesitated, wondering what it was she had to say, and then I gave myself a firm shake and typed back, *Sorry. Busy.*

And with that I mentally dusted my hands and went to the refrigerator in search of nutrition.

I thought about video-chatting with Melanie while I warmed up last night's leftovers, but decided to check in with her father first. I texted Miles, *Are you at dinner?*

He sent back a selfie of Melanie, his mother, and himself seated at an elegant white cloth-covered table in a restaurant patio surrounded by palm trees and decorated with thousands of tiny fairy lights. All of them had their glasses raised to me and the caption read, *72 degrees, filet mignon, cherries jubilee. The only thing missing in this picture is you.*

No kidding. Sometimes I really wonder about my judgment.

I ate the rest of last night's coq au vin while reading through the file Sonny had given me on her case. Cisco settled down under the table, resting his chin on my foot, just in case I needed a dog to share the leftovers with and couldn't find one. I thumbed through all the legal stuff until I came to the report the previous attorney's investigator had made on the Heroes of Hope Dog Training Facility. The owner, Jenny Toliver, was accused of providing an untrained service dog to military veteran Kate Greene, who suffered from PTSD and minor balance issues related to a traumatic head injury. The dog, Rambo, had only been with his new owner six weeks when he bit the face of an eight-year-old boy, Billy Kiddleson. The Kiddlesons were now suing the Heroes of Hope and its owner, Jenny Toliver, for negligence and fraud. To the untrained eye—that would be me—the case would seem open and shut. There were affidavits from a dozen witnesses who had been at the baseball game where young Billy had been bitten in an apparently unprovoked attack, and the investigator had provided a page-long list of names of other people who were willing to testify in court to having seen the same thing. But I guess the argument wasn't whether or not Rambo had bitten the kid, but whether or not Toliver, the trainer, had knowingly provided a service dog who wasn't safe in public. And how was I supposed to determine that from somebody else's interview and surveillance photos?

I glanced at my watch and saw it was almost 6:30. If she ran her operation anything like I ran Dog Daze, the office would be closed and she'd be busy feeding and exercising dogs before tucking them in for the night. I was hoping to get the answering machine when I dialed, and so I did.

"Hi," I said when prompted to do so. "My name is Raine Stockton. I own Dog Daze Boarding and Training in Hansonville, North Carolina, and I'd like to talk to you about service dog training." All perfectly true. "I'm going to be down your way tomorrow and was wondering if I could stop by around 1:00. Could you call me back on my cell? I'd appreciate it." I left my number and hung up, then texted Sonny simply, *On the case.*

"All right," I congratulated myself, satisfied with a good day's work—and with the anticipation of the two substantial paychecks I'd be receiving before the end of the year. I smiled down at my canine dinner companion. "Cisco, my man, it's starting to look a lot like Christmas around here."

Cisco looked up at the sound of his name, his eyes brightening in anticipation of a treat. He might have gotten one, too, just because I was in a good mood, but before I could find something on my plate that wasn't covered in wine sauce, Cisco suddenly scrambled out from under the table so fast that he bumped his head on my chair and raced toward the front door. He was already there, tail swishing in excited greeting, before I saw the flash of headlights on the kitchen window. I took my plate to the sink and saw the glint of the sheriff's office emblem on the car door as the cruiser triggered the security lights. And I also saw the face of the driver.

I went to the front door and switched on the porch light, holding Cisco's collar until Buck got out of the car. He saw us standing at the door and smiled in acknowledgement, then dropped to one knee when I released Cisco's collar. Cisco exploded across the threshold in a cataclysm of golden fur, spinning tail, and ecstatic barks. Buck caught my wild dog against his chest, staggering back a little to maintain his balance, laughing and rubbing his ears and exclaiming the usual inanities that come from a human when he is completely and totally in love with a canine. I know because I've heard them coming from my own lips.

I knew better than to waste my breath trying to bring Cisco under control, so I grabbed a heavy sweater from the hall tree and pulled it on, waiting on the porch until Cisco and Buck had completed their greetings. Buck gave Cisco's ears a final vigorous rub and stood, meeting my eyes with a rather shy smile. Cisco scrabbled up the steps ahead of him, panting with happiness now that his two favorite people were together again.

"Hey," I said.

He replied, "Hey." He reached inside his jacket and brought out an envelope. "I just thought I'd drop by the police report on your car. You'll need it for the insurance. Mitch confessed to 'accidentally' scratching it." He made air quotes over the word "accidentally." "You can press charges if you want."

I took the envelope from him, shaking my head. "No. I just want my car fixed."

He said, "I figured."

It was an agreement, not a judgment. Nice to have someone who understood me.

I looked at him. His face, in the unkind glow of the porch light, look drawn and tired, his color weak. I said, "You could have e-mailed me this."

"Yeah, well." He glanced around the porch restlessly. "It was on my way home."

I made an uncertain gesture toward the door. "Do you want to come in?"

He shook his head. "That's okay. I can't stay."

But instead of turning to leave, he bent down and scratched Cisco's ears. Cisco's tail thumped ecstatically against the porch post, which drew a one-cornered smile from Buck.

I said, "So who's going to be in charge while you're on vacation?"

"Deke's got seniority," Buck replied. "He'll be running the desk."

I couldn't help wrinkling my nose. Deke was a thirty-five-year-old man going on thirteen who, despite having spent his entire adult life in law enforcement, was still at his most competent writing speeding tickets and directing parade traffic. No wonder Buck needed a vacation, if Deke was the best he could do for a second-in-command.

Buck saw my expression and agreed wryly, "Yeah, I know. But the guys like him, and somebody's got to sign the paychecks and file the reports."

I said, "I hope you're not going to be gone long then."

He hesitated. "It depends."

"On what?"

He met my gaze. "Wyn and I have been talking about making a move. We'll be looking for a house while I'm up there. I'm hoping we can find something in the next couple of weeks so I can get everything wrapped up down here by the first of the year."

"Oh," I said. I sank down into the swing, clasping my cold hands between my knees. "Wow. You're leaving." My voice sounded a little hoarse. "I never thought…Wow."

After a moment, he sat down on the other end of the swing. Cisco, not to be left behind, scrambled up between us, sending the swing to rocking and causing Buck to chuckle as we both grabbed Cisco's collar to keep him from falling. Oblivious, Cisco turned in the swing to find a comfortable position and then flopped down on the cushion, his chin on Buck's knee, his tail in my lap.

To tell the truth, I barely even noticed Cisco, although I was vaguely aware of my fingers absently combing the silvery strands of his tail feathers across my thigh. There was only one reason Buck would leave town, and that reason was Marshall Becker. If he refused to let Buck stay on in the sheriff's office, what choice did he have but to seek work elsewhere? A quiet outrage simmered inside me on Buck's behalf, but I was careful not to let it show. I said, "Um, what about work? What'll you do up in Asheville?"

His reply didn't sound particularly enthusiastic. "There's a job coming open on the police department in January, but I don't know. Maybe it's time to get out of law enforcement. I'm looking around." Again he smiled, though without humor. "If you ever have kids, don't let them get a degree in criminal justice. It really limits your options in the corporate world."

I didn't know what to say. I really didn't. I couldn't believe Marshall would be so stupid as to let Buck go. What could he possibly be thinking?

Buck said after a moment, "Things have been a little rough for Wyn, you know, since the shooting." He stroked Cisco's floppy ear, concentrating his attention on the motion. "For us," he corrected himself quietly. "It's been a strain on us both. On the marriage. This is going to work out for the best. A change of scenery, and Wyn's family is there…she needs to be near them now. She's talking about going back to school, getting a degree in early childhood education. She's got another month's medical leave coming, but Marshall knows she'll be turning in her resignation. It's all going to work out for the best."

I drew in a breath, and let it out. "Well," I said. The word fell flat. "Lots of changes."

"Yeah." The silence lingered a beat too long. I could feel his gaze on me, though I did not meet it. "Anyway, I just wanted to let you know. Sometimes we're not too good about communicating things."

Now I did look at him, and he corrected himself. "Sometimes I'm not. Most of the time," he admitted.

He rubbed Cisco's nose affectionately with his knuckles and stood. "I'd better get going."

I stood up too, and we spent a moment just looking at each other. Then he leaned forward and lightly brushed my cheek with a kiss. He smelled like gun oil and old leather. It occurred to me that this might be the last time I ever smelled that scent.

He said, "You have a good Thanksgiving, Raine."

"Yeah," I managed. "You too."

I watched him go down the steps, get into the cruiser, and drive away. I turned off the porch light, but I didn't go inside. I returned to the swing and sat there with Cisco in the dark and the cold until it was time to go to bed.

CHAPTER TWELVE

At 9:00 a.m. the next morning, Jenny Toliver called from Heroes of Hope Dog Training to say that she'd be glad to meet with me if I didn't mind waiting until 2:00 when she had staff coming in to take over puppy training. That suited me fine, since it gave me the rest of the morning to help Corny in the kennel and take care of my own dogs. According to my GPS, the drive would take just under two hours, so at noon I grabbed a granola bar for the road and set out. This time, Mischief and Magic stayed behind with Corny while Cisco, tail waving proudly, bounded into the back of the SUV.

I had been instructed to park in front of the house and take the path around back to the training building. When I pulled up in front of the modern cedar-sided one story with its neatly kept lawn, pumpkin-lined stone steps, and window boxes filled with colorful mums, I caught a glimpse of the building behind the house, and I have to admit, I was impressed. A stone path led to an almost exact replica of the main house, only smaller. It had the same cedar siding, the same window boxes, the same bright yellow door. An American flag hung from one corner of the building, and a set of chain-link kennels ran along the side. I have a nice setup at Dog Daze, thanks to an unexpected gift from a former client and Miles's building contractor, but I have to admit I felt a tiny pang of jealousy. Why hadn't I thought of window boxes?

I could hear dogs barking as I got out, always music to my ears.

I left Cisco in the car, both because it would have been impolite to bring a strange dog into someone else's territory without asking permission, and because I wanted to check for safety issues before exposing my dog to an unknown environment. After all, the woman was accused of selling a vicious canine as a service dog; who knew what her standards were? Although, to tell the truth, my initial impression of the place was that her standards were probably higher than mine.

I turned to start down the path toward the building when the front door of the house opened and a middle-aged woman in jeans and a logo sweatshirt came out. She had a pleasant, square face that was tan from working in the sun, and short salt-and-pepper hair. She came down the steps, her hand extended. "Raine Stockton?" She shook my hand with a firm grip. "I'm Jen Toliver." She glanced toward my car, where Cisco had his nose pressed to the crack in the window, and smiled. "You're welcome to let your dog out, as long as you keep him on leash. I keep new pups in quarantine until they've had all their shots, so we won't be going into that area, but I'll be glad to show you the rest of the operation."

Already I liked her, which both surprised and concerned me. After my experience with Dallas, I was more than a little skeptical about my ability to make character judgments.

"Thanks," I said. "It was a long drive and I'd like to give him a chance to stretch his legs, if you're sure it won't disturb your dogs."

"It'll be good distraction training for them," she assured me with a wave of her hand.

Cisco looked over my shoulder with eager sparkling eyes as I unfastened his seat belt, shifting his weight on his paws impatiently and swishing his tail at about 120 beats per minute. I gave him my sternest warning look before releasing him from the car. The last thing I wanted was to be humiliated in front of another dog trainer, especially one I was supposed to be investigating for incompetence.

To my everlasting relief, Cisco chose this opportunity to show off his manners, and approached the stranger with wagging tail and happy grin, at an eager pace but without trying to pull me off my feet. Jenny Toliver smiled her approval and waited until he sat before her to say, "What a good dog"—just like I would have done. She glanced at me. "May I give him a liver treat?" Again, that was exactly what I would have done.

She brought a treat from her jeans pocket and offered it to Cisco, palm up. He gobbled it up and looked at her for more, but she just laughed and ruffled his ears. "Beautiful dog," she said. "Championship stock?"

"Well, yes," I admitted, pleased that she'd noticed. "But I don't show him in conformation."

She nodded. "Right. He's your search and rescue dog."

And so my cover was blown.

She smiled. "I'm not an idiot, Miss Stockton. You're from Hansonville, where I go before a jury next month to prove my innocence in a negligence suit. I checked you out on social media. I know my lawyer didn't send you, so you're obviously from the opposition team." She gestured me toward the path. "Feel free to look around and ask any questions you want to."

All right. So I would. "You get your dogs from shelters?" I asked as we walked down the path, Cisco sniffing the trail curiously.

"Some," she said. "Some are donated from breeders with a reputation for turning out solid dogs with stable temperaments. We take goldens, Labs, and shepherds, mostly, along with any mix of those breeds. But we've recently found that border collies make excellent diabetic alert and seizure alert dogs."

"How do you evaluate the shelter dogs for service work?"

"We perform thirty different temperament tests over a period of three days on the dogs we pull from shelters before they ever go into program. Those who show a talent for the work begin an eight-month training program that focuses on basic obedience skills and public access. During this time most of the dogs live with volunteer foster parents, who bring them to training class twice a week. Would you like to observe a class? My assistant is in the middle of one now."

I readily agreed. She'd probably arranged the class just so I could see it, but that was okay. That was what I was here for.

I was impressed. I watched as six handlers left their dogs in a sit-stay and stood across the room from them while the instructor bounced a tennis ball in front of the dogs. Only two attempted to break their stays—both of them retrievers, naturally—and they were quickly and quietly corrected by their handlers. The real test came when Cisco was asked to move freely among the dogs, but even my butt-wagging, paw-scuffling, sniffing and bouncing golden retriever was no match for the discipline of those well-trained dogs.

"They're only a week from graduation," Jen told me. "After that they'll move in here and begin advanced training for whatever specialty they've been assigned to." She pointed to a black Lab. "Miraj will be assisting a quadriplegic with things like turning on lights, retrieving dropped objects, and acting as a general wheelchair assistance dog. He'll be in skills training for another six weeks, with his new owner coming in twice a week to work with him."

I said, "My friend Sonny uses a chair sometimes. Her service dog goes shopping with her and gets things off the shelves that she can't reach, then he gives her credit card to the cashier." I stopped abruptly, remembering that Sonny was the opposition counsel. I darted Jenny an embarrassed look and, to hide it, bent to pet Cisco's head.

But she either didn't know that Sonny was the lawyer who was suing her, or she was too polite to let on. "Wheelchair assistance dogs are amazing," she agreed. "They also require the most extensive training. Most of the dogs we place are more task-specific—balance dogs, for example, for victims of traumatic brain injury, general support dogs for autistic patients, medical alert dogs for various conditions. But the vast majority of our dogs go to victims of PTSD."

The class instructor called an end to the sit-stay exercise, and the six handlers called their happy dogs to them. Jen smiled. "We really couldn't do this without our foster parents. They are a bunch of incredibly dedicated folks."

She went on to explain that every foster parent had a list of places they were supposed to take their dogs each week to expose them to new situations—places like churches, movie theaters, schools, playgrounds, malls, bus stations, big box stores, and restaurants. Once a month the entire group went on a field trip to test the dogs' behavior and comfort level in public places. By the time they were placed with their new owner, the dogs had been on public transportation, had ridden in boats, and, in many cases, had flown in the passenger cabin of an airplane.

They were tested for steadiness around children of all ages, other dogs, and farm animals.

I tried to remain skeptical, I really did. But I didn't see how anyone could ask for a better public-access training program than that.

We watched as the class instructor, a pretty sharp dog handler himself, called to heel a light-colored German Shepherd who'd been quietly lying in a corner, watching the class. Head up, paws striding, taking every corner with a lyrical, almost telepathic synchronicity, the dog heeled in perfect rhythm with his handler as they wove through the line of student dogs and their people. It was like watching music.

A few of the student dogs turned their heads or had to be reminded to keep their focus, but for the most part they held their sits. I'd been to obedience trials with far less successful results. And my dog was usually one of those less successful ones.

"Wow," I said as the instructor sent the demo dog back to his rug in the corner with a single lift of his finger. The shepherd practically flowed back to his place. "That was impressive."

"That," she said, smiling, "was Rambo."

My brows flew up. "The demo dog?"

She nodded. "Would you like to meet him?"

I glanced down at Cisco. He had never met a dog—or a person for that matter—that he didn't like, so I was pretty sure that if there was anything fundamentally wrong with Rambo, he'd let me know. I said, "Sure. Is it okay if they greet each other?"

"Absolutely."

She called Rambo out of class, and the two dogs sniffed and circled each other until they were satisfied. Cisco's tail wagged his approval, and I asked Jen's permission to run through a few simple temperament tests with Rambo. I opened an umbrella in his face to test his startle reflex; I had him hold a sit while I pummeled him with liver treats and let Cisco chase a ball a few feet away from him to test his focus, and I made an abrupt, menacing gesture with a cane to judge his flight-or-fight response. He passed all my challenges with flying colors, as I'd known he would.

"So did the owner turn him in?" I asked when she'd returned Rambo to the class instructor.

"After the incident, we all agreed it was best," she said. "To tell the truth, the owner was so busy with her new life I don't think she would have missed him much, even without the bite issue. Of course, I won't place Rambo again, which really is the tragedy of this whole thing. He would make a great assistance dog. When he's not helping Scott teach classes, he lives with us, as a pet."

She gestured toward the door. "Would you like to see the kennels?"

"Sure." I called out a thank you to the instructor for letting me watch the class, and followed Jen out of the room.

Buck had once jokingly accused me of being a service dog groupie, and he was right. I'm fascinated by the things these amazing dogs can be taught to do, and by the training that goes into teaching them.

I could have watched classes and asked questions all day, but I reminded myself I had a job to do.

"So did you follow up with Rambo at home after he was placed?" I asked as we started down the lino-leum-floored corridor toward the kennel area.

"At two and four months," she replied. "The two of them seemed to be doing well, so I didn't think further follow-up was necessary."

"What does a PTSD service dog do?" I wanted to know.

"It depends on the specific need, of course, which is why we try to match dogs and owners before we complete the training. Some people need help with depression and stress relief, others need a dog who can remind them to take their medication or help them avoid stress triggers. We had one client who was on the verge of becoming agoraphobic, but with a dog to accompany her she felt safe leaving her house again. Quite a few of our clients suffer from flashbacks triggered by crowds or by people invad-ing their space. A trained service dog can help keep a safe distance between someone who feels threat-ened and the situation he finds threatening."

She pushed open a swinging door to the ken-nel area and we were greeted by some excited barks. Cisco looked as though he wanted to return the greeting, but I lifted a warning finger to him and he changed his mind.

"We only have three dogs in residence now," Jen explained. "Two of them are going home next week. "This is Whisper." She stopped before the kennel of what looked like a golden/collie cross, a pretty sable girl with white patches. "She's going to live with a little boy with Down Syndrome. She'll help him get dressed in the morning, carry his books in her backpack when they go to school, but mostly she'll help him integrate socially. Won't you, sweet girl?" She smiled and took a treat from her pocket when the dog sat at the gate. "That's really what these dogs do best, you know."

The kennels were as clean and roomy as mine, with appropriate chew toys and elevated cots. She went over their training, play, and exercise schedule, staff-to-dog ratio, and nutritional guidelines. As hard as I tried, I couldn't find fault with any of it. She introduced me to a sturdy Lab mix destined for life as a balance dog with a military veteran with a traumatic brain injury, and a goldendoodle who was being trained as a PTSD dog. Both were alert, friendly, and well trained, even when I forgot myself and let Cisco get too close to the gate.

I said, "Do a lot of your dogs go to military veterans?"

She gestured the way back down the corridor toward the office. "Unfortunately, modern warfare has resulted in a need for more service dogs than there are service dog providers. That's why my husband and I started Heroes for Hope."

"Also," I supplied, just to prove I'd done my homework, "the VA pays for it."

"In some cases," she agreed. "In others, a charitable organization will cover the difference between the cost of a dog and what disability insurance will pay."

"Disability insurance?"

"If a healthcare professional determines that a service dog is necessary for mobility or independence," she said, "insurance generally treats the service dog the same way it would a wheelchair or a prosthetic."

I asked, "How much does one of your dogs cost?"

"Obviously, it depends on the level of training involved," she replied. "On average, between fifteen and twenty thousand dollars."

I probably stumbled a little in my surprise, but she didn't notice. If she placed ten dogs a year… holy cow, no wonder her place was so nice.

"Of course," she added, pushing open the door to her office, "if an applicant comes to us in need and can't afford a dog, we pick up the cost whenever we can. We donate about twenty percent of our dogs. Come in and sit down. Can I get you a cup of coffee?"

"Thanks," I said. "That'd be nice."

I sat on a blue velour sofa—comfortably sagging and sprinkled with black and white dog hair, I noticed—and Cisco stretched out at my feet. I folded his leash over his shoulders, which was his signal to relax until I told him otherwise, and studied the photos on the wall while Jen poured two cups of coffee from the coffeemaker in the corner. The pictures were all of dogs and people, successful placements, I guessed. Jen confirmed my speculation when she brought me my coffee, telling me the story behind each of the photographs: the little girl with the golden mix was hearing impaired, the young woman with the yellow Lab had MS, the man with the leg brace was a former police officer who'd been wounded in the line of duty and relied on his German Shepherd mix for balance. By the time she finished going through the photos, I was beginning to feel as though I had done nothing with my life worth mentioning at all. But the kicker was when she turned around the photograph on her desk to show a handsome middle-aged man in a wheelchair with two prosthetic legs and a white German Shepherd by his side.

"This is my husband Jake," she told me. Her expression as she looked at the photo was filled with pride and affection. "He lost his legs in Iraq, and without Moses—that's the shepherd—I don't think either one of us would have gotten through the rehab. Moses was our inspiration for starting Heroes for Hope."

If I had been on the jury, nothing in this world would have convinced me to find Jennifer Toliver guilty of anything but sainthood. Sonny definitely had her work cut out for her.

I said, "So tell me about Rambo."

Jen sat in a scuffed black leather chair across from me and cupped her mug in her hands. "He was a shelter pick at four months old, scored high on temperament tests, a really quick study and eager to please. One of the mellowest dogs I've ever met, great with children. When Michelle came to me looking for a PTSD dog, it seemed like a perfect match. She'd had German Shepherds all her life and fell in love with Rambo on sight."

"What kind of PTSD did Michelle have?" I asked. "I mean, what was he trained to do?"

"She had panic attacks that were so bad she couldn't leave the house some days. She took medication for depression but often forgot to take it. Rambo was trained to ring a bell twice a day to remind her to take her meds, and to lean against her when her respirations started to increase at the beginning of a panic attack, which was often enough to signal her to go into her relaxation exercises and ward off an attack."

"Wow," I said, intrigued. "How did you teach him to do that?"

She smiled. "Ringing the bell was basic operant conditioning, and I worked with Rambo and Michelle, under the supervision of Michelle's therapist, for almost a year to help with the panic attacks. It must have worked," she added. "She went from someone who was virtually housebound to getting married last fall. I love the success stories." But even as she said it her smile faded. "Even if they don't exactly look successful at the moment."

"Have you talked with Michelle since the biting incident?"

"I've tried. Mostly our lawyers have talked."

"What do you think happened with Rambo?" I asked.

She looked at me frankly. "I have no idea. In fact, one of the reasons I wanted to go to court was to find out."

I was surprised. "You wanted to go to court?"

She nodded. "The lawyers wanted to settle, but my reputation—the reputation of my business—is at stake. And like I said…" She frowned. "I wanted to get to the truth. Something's just not right."

While we talked, Cisco had remained lying at my feet with his chin on his paws. His head lifted now and swiveled toward the door a moment before a teenage girl came inside. "Hey, Mom, I'm on my way…"

Cisco scrabbled to his feet before I could grab his leash, ran over to the girl, and sat in front of her with a single expectant bark.

I followed quickly and snatched up his leash. "Sorry," I said.

But no one seemed alarmed. Jen said, "Raine, this is my daughter Kendra. Kendra, this is Raine Stockton and her dog Cisco."

Kendra glanced at us. "Hi." She looked back at her mother. "I didn't know anyone was with you. I just wanted to tell you I'm going to Sandy's. I'll be back before dinner."

Cisco, holding his sit in front of the girl, looked up at me and barked again.

Jen gave me a look of puzzled amusement. "He wouldn't happen to be trained as a diabetic alert dog, would he?" To her daughter she said, "Did you check your blood sugar?"

She rolled her eyes. "It's fine."

"When did you check?"

"A minute ago." And as proof she held out her index finger, the tip of which showed evidence of a recent pinprick. She rolled her eyes again. "Honestly, Mom, like I've never done this before."

Jen fixed her daughter with a firm stare. "What was the reading?"

The teenager blew out an exasperated breath. "Oh, all right! One eighty-seven. But I just had a glass of juice and…"

"And you don't get behind the wheel of a car with a blood sugar over 180," her mother said. "Wait half an hour and test again."

Kendra said in the uniquely teenage-girl tone, "Mom!" But Jen ignored her.

Jen looked again at Cisco, thoughtfully. "Some dogs have a natural ability to sense a change in ketones," she said.

"I don't think Cisco is one of them," I replied. "At least, I've never known him to be." Still, I was puzzled. Sitting and barking was Cisco's signal that he had found what he was sent for. In fact, the last time he'd given that alert…"Rubbing alcohol," I said suddenly, understanding. To both women, I explained, "I've been rewarding Cisco for alerting to rubbing alcohol in a scent-training class. You must've swabbed your finger with alcohol before pricking it, right?"

Kendra, momentarily over her pique with her mother, grinned and rubbed Cisco's ears. "Right.

That was pretty good, though. Maybe you should think about training him." She looked at her mom. "Seriously? Half an hour? Sandy's waiting, and Cookie is already in the car."

"Cookie's her border collie," Jen explained to me. "And she's an official diabetic alert dog. If she hadn't already been in the car she would have let you know your glucose was too high," she added to her daughter. "Call Sandy, tell her you'll be late."

Kendra stuffed her hands in her pockets and slumped out of the room. Jen smiled wryly after her.

"Kendra was diagnosed with juvenile diabetes when she was thirteen," Jen told me when the door closed—somewhat forcefully—behind her daughter. "We got Cookie six months later—the second service dog to join our family. She had already started training as a diabetic alert dog, but the key to shaping a reliable dog is to continue the reinforcement at home every single day, and that's what we did. Kendra is seventeen now, and most days she only has to inject herself with insulin a couple of times a day. But I know Cookie has saved her life at least three times."

She came over to Cisco and scratched his ears, and Cisco grinned his appreciation back at her. "You're probably right," she said. "Most likely he was just alerting to the scent of the alcohol swab. But you shouldn't dismiss the possibility that he might also have sensed a change in Kendra's blood sugar. Some dogs are sensitive enough to alert to changes so minor that they don't even show up on a test strip."

I said, "Huh." Of course, I would have loved to learn more—everything, in fact—but something else was on my mind. I fixed my gaze thoughtfully on Cisco as I tried to remember where, besides the scent training class, I had seen my dog perform that particular alert behavior recently. But it completely eluded me.

I turned back to Jen, giving in to my professional curiosity. "So," I invited, "how do you go about training a medical alert dog, anyway?"

CHAPTER THIRTEEN

Thanksgiving at my Aunt Mart's is a community event, which means that no one in the county has any reason to eat alone on Thanksgiving as long as Aunt Mart is cooking. In past years she has had as many as thirty-two people sharing her table—or in that particular case, tables—which included cousins, in-laws, neighbors, widows, bachelors, and all the misplaced friends of the same. This year was what she called "a small table" with just my oldest cousin—who, with her two children and husband, had driven in from Alabama for the weekend—Corny, Sonny, Marshall Becker, and me. I was sure that my sweet aunt would have also invited Buck, oblivious to any awkwardness it might have caused, had he not planned to be out of town. In fact, even though we'd been apart for years now—off and on, anyway—it seemed odd to walk into my aunt's neat brick ranch and see Marshall, not Buck, watching the Thanksgiving Day Parade in the family room with cousin Dave and Uncle Ro.

The house was redolent of roasting turkey, sage and onion dressing, and apple pie spices; bright with autumn sunshine and the crackle of a wood fire in the fireplace. I was greeted by the sound of dog claws scrabbling on the hardwood floors, and, of course, before I greeted anyone else, I hugged my beautiful collie Majesty, who was dressed for the occasion today in a pumpkin bandanna that was all but concealed by her magnificent white mane, with a saucy orange ribbon clipped behind one ear. I had rescued Majesty as a year-old pup, and she had been part of my family for almost three years, until she abruptly decided that she much preferred life as Aunt Mart's dog. Aunt Mart adored her and fussed over her almost as much as Melanie fussed over Pepper, which constantly reminded me that Majesty had made the right choice, even though I missed her every day.

After politely allowing me to hug her neck and bury my face in her sweet-smelling fur, Majesty raced outside to join the children, who had discovered the tire swing and were doing their best to annihilate each other with it. I stopped in the family room to hug my uncle and introduce Corny to cousin Abby's husband, Dave, but I didn't linger. Marshall looked a little puzzled at my cool response to his hearty, "Happy Thanksgiving, Raine!" but I didn't care. What kind of sheriff lets his most experienced officer go before he even takes office? And after everything Buck had done for this county, after Wyn had almost *died* trying to keep it safe. I knew Uncle Ro was friends with Marshall, but I didn't see how he could overlook the kind of character flaw that would allow a man to treat someone like that. I knew I couldn't. So while Dave and Uncle Ro tried to pull me into the family room to watch the rest of the parade with them, I politely—or at least as politely as I could—excused myself to go find Aunt Mart and cousin Abby in the kitchen.

No one who knows me ever asks me to bring anything edible to Thanksgiving, so I always bring the centerpiece—usually a bunch of Shasta daisies from the grocery store wrapped in orange tissue paper. This year, Corny—who was spending Thanksgiving with us for the first time—had taken my daisies, arranged them in a hollowed-out pumpkin, spray-painted some twisty branches gold, and made a real centerpiece. Aunt Mart was enchanted, and my cousin Abby and I hugged and exclaimed over each other while my aunt added water to the vase inside the pumpkin that held the flowers. Corny, in his colorful cornucopia sweater, plaid pants, and orange high-tops, went outside with the kids to collect maple leaves for a table runner. Aunt Mart watched him go with a bemused expression on her face. "I really *must* find out where that boy does his shopping," she said.

Abby and I spent a few minutes catching up before Sonny arrived. Abby teased me about my millionaire boyfriend, and I'm not ashamed to say I enjoyed it. After ten years of being the only one at every family event who showed pictures of dogs, not children, and whose reply to the question "So what have you been up to?" was always met with looks of either pity or confusion, it felt pretty good to bring up pictures on my phone of Melanie in her school uniform and of Miles and me at his house in St. Bart's and of celebrities hanging out at Miles's pool with evidence of a recent over-the-top party in the background. Miles himself looked particularly hot in that one, if I do say so. Of course, to be perfectly fair, I couldn't resist sharing a few pictures of Cisco with his blue ribbon, and things really got fun when I got to the pictures of Mischief and Magic on the movie set.

And that was only one of the reasons I'd wanted to spend Thanksgiving with my family this year. The only thing that would have made it better was if Melanie and Miles and my award-winning, movie-star dogs could have been there in the flesh to show off. Don't judge. After ten years, it was my turn.

Sonny had made a sweet potato casserole, which Corny brought in from the car for her, but no dog. I was disappointed, because I love to watch Hero work, but Sonny joked that it was his day off. My dogs, too, had the day off, but their Thanksgiving would come later, when they feasted on the turkey giblets Aunt Mart always sent home for them. In fact, Aunt Mart informed me, she had bought extra packets of giblets from the butcher this year so that there would be plenty to go around for all the dogs in the family. She was a woman after my own heart.

Even though it probably wasn't polite to discuss business at Thanksgiving, not to mention the fact that my aunt had a strict rule against police talk at the dinner table, I knew Sonny wouldn't thank me for keeping the results of my visit with Jen Toliver to myself for another day. So while we helped Corny arrange maple leaves and candlesticks down the center of the long dining table, which was already covered with a white linen cloth and set with holiday china and sparkling silver, I laid out the facts for her.

"I couldn't find a single thing to criticize," I summarized apologetically. "In fact, you'd probably be better off paying *her* as the expert witness. Really, Sonny," I added sincerely, "I've never met a more professional dog trainer, or seen a cleaner operation. Totally aside from the fact that she has a husband in a wheelchair and a daughter with juvenile diabetes—both of whom use service dogs that *she* trained—by the time her lawyer trots in twenty or twenty-five witnesses whose lives have been changed by her service dogs, there won't be a dry eye in the house. And you *really* don't want to let Rambo in the courtroom. He's only the most mild-mannered, perfectly trained dog I've ever met."

Sonny said, "In other words, we're going to get slaughtered in court."

I was surprised she was taking it so well. "I still have to talk to Rambo's owner. Maybe there's something in his environment—former environment, I mean—that might have turned him into a biter. But if I were on the jury...well." I lifted one shoulder helplessly. "You might want to speak to your client again about settling out of court."

Sonny sighed. "I was afraid of that." She glanced at Corny, who was expertly tweaking the fat candlestick that I had—apparently erroneously—placed next to a tall, skinny one. She lowered her voice slightly and added, "I've already met Rambo. He says he's never bitten anyone."

I replied, "Oh." And tried not to wince. Little known fact about Sonny, an accomplished attorney and otherwise perfectly normal person: she talks to animals. Worse, they talk back. No, the worst part is that most of the time what the animals tell her—or at least what she claims they tell her—is right. Over time my skepticism has turned to reluctant resignation, although I still haven't quite been able to convince myself to completely rely on her information.

Corny had overheard and was completely unfazed. What else could I expect from someone who could quiet a kennel full of wild-eyed barking dogs with a single lift of his finger? He barely glanced up from fanning a spray of orange and red leaves around one of the water glasses as he commented, "My grandfather handled a Pyr once who was accused of killing a sheep on his neighbor's farm." Corny's grandfather had been a world-renowned dog handler who'd put more championship titles on more breeds than the average person was likely to meet in a lifetime. "Can you imagine anything more ridiculous? First of all, championship stock, *hello*, bred from six generations of working dogs whose only job was to *protect* the flock..." He took a napkin that I had slapped down willy-nilly beside the fork and deftly began to fold it into an envelope shape. "Secondly, as though the Pyr had the time or the energy to go hunting on the neighbor's farm after working all day and training to show on the weekends. I mean." He inserted the silverware into the envelope he had made of the napkin, arranged the napkin just so atop the plate, and decorated it with a tiny wildflower. "It turns out," he said, moving on to the next napkin, "that there was a lone wolf coyote roaming the neighborhood. And how did they find out? The very same Pry who was so unjustly accused of the crime cornered it one night in his very own barn. Bad news for the coyote, I'm afraid," he said, stepping back critically to observe his work. "But the sheep lived happily ever after."

Sonny and I shared a look, neither one of us quite sure how to respond. Then I said, "The trip wasn't entirely a bust, though. Jen thinks Cisco might have some talent as a medical alert dog."

"I don't doubt it for a minute," said Corny, who was Cisco's biggest fan. "With a nose like his, he can do anything."

It was nice to hear that kind of confidence in my dog, but before Corny launched into a rhapsody, I pointed out, "Actually, I think he was just alerting to the alcohol swab, but I have to admit it was pretty impressive. Diabetic alert dogs are really hard to train, but the girl had just tested her blood sugar and Cisco went right into his alert behavior. It turns out her blood sugar was a little high and she was trying to sneak it past her mother."

Abby came in to put an ice bucket on the walnut sideboard and overheard the last part of the conversation. "Gosh, Raine, remember Grandma Myrtle?"

"Meanest woman I ever knew," I agreed.

Sonny and Corny looked shocked, but Abby just laughed. "She wasn't really that mean," she assured them, "just a little moody. But as soon as they got her blood sugar straightened out, she was sweet as can be." She grinned. "No pun intended."

Aunt Mart came in from the kitchen with the centerpiece. "The awful thing is," she added, "the poor thing suffered for years without anybody ever thinking to check for diabetes. I remember one time she stubbed her toe and it took six months to heal. You'd think someone would've taken the hint then."

She set the centerpiece in place and beamed as she stepped back to admire the table. "Oh, look at the napkins! My, aren't we fancy?" She turned her smile on Corny, since it was clear neither Sonny nor I was responsible for the masterpiece. "Wherever did you learn to do that?"

"I worked for a caterer one summer in high school," Corny replied, pleased. I could tell he was dying to tweak the placement of the centerpiece but restrained himself out of respect to his hostess. "I'll be happy to show you some time."

I frowned, trying to remember. "So how did they ever find out Grandma Myrtle was diabetic? Wasn't there some scandal?"

"Oh my, yes," replied Aunt Mart. "She ran her car into a light pole right downtown, almost hit a pedestrian. One of Ro's deputies arrested her for DUI."

"Can you imagine," put in Abby with an exaggerated shudder, "arresting the sheriff's *mother*? That poor fellow must still be living it down."

Aunt Mart shook her head, not doing a very good job of hiding her amusement. "It was the poor boy's first day on the job, and he was terrified when he found out who he'd arrested. But really, he didn't have much of a choice. She was acting even crazier than usual, refused the roadside sobriety test, of course, so he had to take her to the hospital for a blood test. That probably saved her life. Her blood alcohol was negative, naturally; she was a Baptist, for heaven's sake. But her glucose levels were off the chart. And Abby's right, once she got her insulin regulated, she was a different person. Lived twenty more good years, too."

Aunt Mart lifted her arms to us in a shooing motion. "Now you all go on and sit down, watch the parade. You're company. Abby, honey, come help me take the cheese and crackers in. Raine, go see what the boys want to drink."

But I was thinking, with a kind of sinking feeling in the pit of my stomach, about a mosquito bite that wouldn't heal after three months, crazy mood swings, a near-miss DUI, and a trashcan filled with alcohol swabs and hypodermics. Finally I remembered what I had been trying to think of yesterday at Jen Toliver's kennel. It had been Dallas Cisco had alerted to with the same kind of behavior he'd shown to Jen's daughter when she walked in the room. And as far as I knew, junkies did not use alcohol swabs.

Crap, I thought. Dallas was not an addict. She was diabetic. And I sent her into the wilderness alone.

I was aware of my aunt waiting for a reply, and I said, "Yes, ma'am. I just need to make a quick phone call first."

Corny stepped up with, "I'll do it, Miz Bleckley." And I cast him a grateful look as I fumbled my phone out of my pocket and hurried from the room.

Abby called after me good-naturedly, "If you're calling that handsome fella of yours, tell him I said hello!"

I tossed her a backward wave over my shoulder just as I found Dallas's number on my phone and punched dial. It went to voice mail, which could mean that she had turned her phone off, was out of range, or didn't want to talk to me. Hoping it wasn't the latter—although after the way I'd behaved I wouldn't blame her—I put on my chirpiest voice and said, "Hi! It's Raine Stockton. Listen, I'm sorry to be so late getting back to you. Thanksgiving and all, you know. Anyway, I was just wondering what you decided to do about the camping trip. Call me back and let me know, okay? I mean," I added on sudden inspiration, "if you decided to stick around my aunt would love to have you come have Thanksgiving dinner with the family." And I gave only a small wince for Aunt Mart's sake, because she *would* have invited her if she'd had the chance. I said, "So call me." And I disconnected.

I stood in the hallway, gazing worriedly at the phone for a minute, and then typed out a text. She might be out of cell-phone range and still be able to receive a text. *Got your messages,* I said. *Where are you?*

I waited for a reply, but none came. I scrolled through my contact list for Lonzo's number, but he had never called me on this phone. I kept scrolling until I found Adrian.

"Hey, Raine." Marshall came around the corner, smiling pleasantly, just as I hit "dial." "I hear Mischief and Magic are going to be movie stars. We're all waiting to hear about it."

I barely glanced at him as the phone started to ring on the other end. "Kind of in the middle of something here," I muttered and walked away. I could feel, rather than see, Marshall's frowning gaze follow me.

Adrian answered on the eighth ring. He sounded half-asleep and annoyed. "Yeah?"

"Adrian," I said quickly, "this is Raine Stockton. You know, with the dogs?"

There was a silence, as though he was trying to place me. "We're not working today," he said after a moment. "It's a holiday."

"I know," I rushed on. "I'm sorry. It's just that I'm trying to get in touch with Dallas and I hoped you might know where she is."

"Dallas?" I thought I heard a smothered yawn. "She's not here. I think she went somewhere. Camping maybe. Yeah, that's it. One of the crew drove her up to the waterfall yesterday. I don't think she's due back on set until Monday. And," he added, sounding more awake now, "you're not due back at all. What's this about?"

"Nothing," I assured him. "It's just...nothing. Happy Thanksgiving."

I disconnected, wondering what, if anything, to do now. And as I stood there staring at the phone, it suddenly beeped in my hand, startling me. With relief I read the text from Dallas, *Beautiful up here. Thnx for the tip.*

I typed back quickly, *Everything okay?*

In a moment the phone chimed again. *Sure. Why? Something wrong?*

I hesitated. Was something wrong? Something aside from the fact that I was feeling guilty for having misjudged a person I barely knew, that is. Dallas was an experienced wilderness camper in better shape than I was who was perfectly capable of taking care of herself. My suspicion about her medical condition was just that—a suspicion. Absolutely no good could come from my interference. So naturally I typed back, *Did you pack insulin?*

A long time passed without a reply. Then, *What are you talking about?*

I replied simply, *I know about the diabetes.*

Again there was a long delay. I held my breath.

She replied, *No one knows. Don't say anything. I'll explain later. Promise.*

Marshall said behind me, "Is something wrong? Anything I can help with?"

I hesitated, not knowing how to reply—either to his question, or to Dallas. As I stood staring at my phone, the screen lit up with another text from Dallas.

Insulin in cooler. I'm fine. Thanks for worrying. Back Sunday. Our secret. Please.

I typed back, *OK. Have a good time. Happy Thanksgiving.* I turned to Marshall and forced a thin smile. "No," I said. "Nothing's wrong." I pocketed my phone and moved past him toward the kitchen. "Excuse me, I've got to help Aunt Mart with the drinks."

When I entered the family room a few minutes later with a tray of apple cider and iced tea, Corny was playing a game of *Sorry!* at the table in the corner with the kids, and Sonny and Abby were chatting on the sofa with Majesty, queen of the ball, curled up between them so that neither would have to stretch to pet her. Uncle Ro and Marshall were, rather predictably, talking business. They stopped abruptly when I came in, and Uncle Ro gave me a big smile. "Thank you, Rainbow," he said when I handed him a glass of iced tea.

I put the tray with the rest of the glasses on the coffee table so that people could help themselves and snared some apple cider for myself. "So I guess you heard Buck is moving to Asheville," I said casually, because that was exactly what they had been talking about when I came in.

Marshall said nothing, and Uncle Ro sipped his tea, watching Santa, all decked out in his holiday best, float down Fifth Avenue on the big screen television over the fireplace. "It's probably best," he said. "Not a good idea to have the previous sheriff stay on when the new man takes over. It can cause confusion in the office, divided loyalties, that kind of thing."

Especially, I thought but did not say, *when the new sheriff only won the election by default when the incumbent dropped out and doesn't know anything about how things are done in this county...*But I was trying to keep things civil for Thanksgiving.

It was a good thing I made the effort because Marshall's reply was, "Oh, I don't think that would've been a problem in this case, not with the restructuring. I tried to tell Buck that, but I guess he had personal reasons for leaving."

"Marshall's really going to bring the office into the twenty-first century, Raine," Uncle Ro told me, looking as pleased as though he had personally arranged for the change. The sheriff's office always had been and always would be his baby. "You should hear some of his ideas."

But I was caught on what Marshall had said before. I looked at him. "Wait," I said. "You tried to get Buck to stay?"

He nodded. "I was counting on him to take the Chief Investigator's job. Now it looks like I'm going to have to hire from the outside."

"How about that?" said Uncle Ro. "We've never had a dedicated investigator before." He sipped his tea and said to Marshall, "So who are you looking at for second-in-command?"

"I've been talking to Jolene Smith. It'll mean shuffling some paperwork until her contract with Homeland Security is up, but I think we can work something out."

I said, staring at Marshall, "You offered Buck a job and he turned it down?"

He nodded a little ruefully. "I even told him I was going to the commissioners to try to get him more money, but I guess there are a lot more opportunities in Asheville. And of course he's got his wife to think of." He lifted his glass toward the television. "Look, the dog show is starting." He grinned. "My money is on the golden retriever."

I smiled back, hoping that would make up for all the rotten things I'd been thinking about him this week. "The beagle's going to win."

But it turned out I was wrong about that, too.

Chapter Fourteen

The holidays are probably a busy time of year for boarding kennels in the city, as everyone packs up for Grandma's house and, unfortunately for the family pet, leaves Fido behind. But here in Hanover County, Grandma's house is generally just over the next ridge, so Thanksgiving and Christmas are among the slowest times at Dog Daze. I don't mind this quite as much as I might, especially since Miles pointed out that it wouldn't be unreasonable to raise our rates on holiday weekends. Knowing that I would at least be able to make payroll took the sting out of having only five boarders for the weekend. And it gave me a second chance to earn at least part of my so-called expert witness fee.

At 9:00 the next morning I checked in with Corny, who was still raving about Aunt Mart's cranberry dressing and how sweet she was to include him in the Thanksgiving plans and how much he'd enjoyed meeting my cousins, and how cute the kids were. When he took a breath, I told him I was going to pay a surprise visit to Kate Greene, Rambo's former owner, who only lived ten miles away in the next town. Hopefully I'd get a chance to see how Rambo had lived on an ordinary day when he was at her home, and whether there was anything in his environment that could cause him to abruptly forget his training and bite a child.

I called Miles as I walked to the car, a delighted Cisco bouncing along beside me. We'd all video-chatted Thanksgiving evening—Miles, his mother, Melanie, and me—but I hadn't yet had a chance to tell him the results of my inspection of Jen Tolliver's service dog training operation.

"So anyway," I summarized, strapping Cisco into his canine seat belt in the backseat of the SUV, "it looks like Sonny is on the wrong side of the dog bite case. I was too," I admitted. "I shouldn't have been so quick to rush to judgment about the service dog trainer. I'm just on my way to interview the owner of the dog, and then I'm done."

"I'm going to take a wild guess Sonny won't put you on the stand," Miles said.

"It depends on what I find out today," I said, "but so far it's not looking good. I still get paid for my time, though." Then I frowned a little, because I wasn't entirely sure what would happen if the case didn't go to court at all. Dreams of expensive dog beds and interactive canine puzzle toys wrapped in red and green paw print paper evaporated like so many popped balloons in my head.

"On the other hand," I added, trying to cheer myself up, "I was right about Dallas the first time, which makes me, what—one for two?"

"I'll give you half a point on that one," Miles replied. "But who's counting?" I had told him yesterday about reaching the conclusion that the hypodermics I'd found in Dallas's trash belonged to a diabetic not an addict, and my theory that her diabetes was the cause of her bizarre mood swings. He hadn't been nearly as impressed as I was. "I still think she sounds like a flake."

"Flake is better than addict," I pointed out. I snapped the clip on the seat belt and closed the sliding door. "So what are you doing today?"

"Taking the girls out on the boat," he replied, "having lunch at the yacht club, sitting around the pool. You?"

My lips turned downward dryly as I climbed into the driver's seat. "Well, after Carlos finishes my massage, I planned on a seaweed wrap and blow-out. Then I'm going to have little stars painted on my nails and…"

Miles interrupted with a chuckle. "All that could be yours, sweetheart. And I'll throw in lunch at the yacht club for free."

I said, "Bye, Miles."

"Love you, baby."

"You too."

I put the key in the ignition and glanced in the rearview mirror. I was surprised to see a pickup pulling in behind me. The truck was all tricked out with spoilers, fog lights, and custom wheels, waxed and polished within an inch of its life. It reminded me of the kind of vehicle a country-western star would drive. Who knew? With all the celebrities in town, maybe I wasn't that far off. I took the key out of the ignition and got out of the driver's seat.

The man who got out was wearing sunglasses and a scruffy blond beard, acid-wash jeans, and a plaid flannel jacket. His boots, which I couldn't help noticing because they looked relatively new, must've cost five hundred dollars. He came toward me with a pleasant smile and a hand extended. "Raine Stockton? I'm Jess Littleton. I think you know my sister, Sarah—I mean, Dallas. Dallas McKenzie. From the movie?"

I shook his hand, trying to remember whether Dallas had ever mentioned him. I was sure she hadn't mentioned him coming to visit. "Sure," I said. "I know her."

"I drove in yesterday to surprise her for Thanksgiving," he said, "and found the set shut down for the day and Dallas nowhere to be found." He swept off his sunglasses and rubbed his jaw ruefully. "Serves me right, I guess, for trying to surprise her. I called her cell but no answer. I was starting to get worried but went back to the set this morning and the guy at the gate told me she had the weekend off. Said something about camping. He didn't know where she'd gone but said you might. He gave me the name of your business. I hope you don't mind me just coming out like this, but your address was on your website."

I said, a little worried, "She didn't answer her phone?" She might be out of range, but she had gotten my texts yesterday.

He said, "She probably just turned it off to save the battery." His handsome brow knit slightly and he studied me, as though trying to decide whether to say more. "It's just that—not many people know this, so don't repeat it—but she's insulin-dependent, you know. Not a real problem, I mean, she manages it well, but I can't help worrying about her when she's out away from civilization like this."

I *knew* I shouldn't have let her go up there alone. If even her brother was worried about her…I said uneasily, "I could call the forest service, have somebody check on her."

He shook his head with a half-laugh. "God, no. She'd kill me. But if you know where she went, I'd like to try to hike up and meet her. Is it far from here?"

I said, "No, not far." I hesitated, thinking with regret about the afternoon I'd planned to spend working on Cisco's contact points on the seesaw. He loved to take that particular piece of agility equipment at full-bound and send it bouncing when he flew off—a habit that was not only frustrating, since it had cost us more than one win, but dangerous as well. "I have something to do this morning," I said, "but if you can wait a couple of hours, I can take you to the trailhead."

"I wouldn't want to put you out. Dallas and I, we're pretty trail-savvy. I picked up a trail map at the little store in town," he said, taking a folded map out of his jacket pocket. "Maybe you could just point it out to me?"

That seemed like a good plan to me, and to tell the truth I was more than a little relieved to turn over responsibility for Dallas to someone who actually was supposed to be responsible for her. I gave him my standard speech about wilderness trail safety, although the truth was, as trails went, this one was fairly hazard free. There were a few sharp drop offs, but they were easy to see; a blind turn or two, and a shallow stream that would ruin his fancy boots before he was across it. But there were no 90-degree climbs or boulders to scale, and the snakes and bears had long since found a better place to be for the winter. I gave him directions to the waterfall, marked the trail on the map with a red pen from my purse, and said, "There are no official campgrounds up there, although there're a couple of trail shelters in case of bad weather. If I were Dallas, I would have set up camp at the first shelter, by the stream. It's not more than an hour hike, fairly easy. A lot of people do it as a day trip."

He looked a little less enthusiastic than he had a moment ago, probably thinking about his new boots. "Okay, thanks, I'll give it a try. Maybe I can reach her by phone once I get to the waterfall." He folded the map back into his pocket. "Just seems a shame to drive all the way from Texas and miss her."

"Take some water and protein bars," I advised him. I rummaged around in my purse until I found one of my cards. "And listen, give me a call if you don't find her, okay?"

He glanced at the card before dropping it in his pocket. "Sure thing. Thanks again."

I watched him drive off, then got in the car and put the key in the ignition. But I hesitated before turning it. What if the poor guy hiked all the way up the trail only to find Dallas had decided to come down early, and they missed each other? Or, more likely, what if she had planned this whole thing to have some alone time with her secret lover and didn't want to be disturbed? Then I, once again, would be accused of being a busybody and a troublemaker. So I picked up my phone and texted her: *Your brother is hiking up the trail to meet you. Should be there before noon.*

Duty done, I gave myself a short, congratulatory nod and tossed the phone into the console before I started the engine. And to tell the truth, I didn't think about either one of them the rest of the day.

Kate Greene—who, according to the painted sign on the mailbox was now Kate Greene-York—lived at the end of a short dirt drive in a single-story frame house surrounded by a chain-link fence. Cisco sat up alertly in the backseat the minute we pulled in front of the gate. There was a sign on that gate that read "Beware of Dog" which I thought must be left over from the time Rambo had lived here. Maybe, when she was a single woman, Kate Greene had thought that the sign, in combination with the mere appearance of the big shepherd, would be enough to ward off potential evildoers.

I got out of the car and looked around cautiously before opening the gate and starting across the winter-brown, bare-patched yard. There was no garage and I didn't see any cars parked anywhere, so the chances were good that no one was at home and I'd wasted a trip. The element of surprise does come with risks.

I picked my way around the clutter on the front porch—cardboard boxes, bicycle parts, rusty tools, some plastic tables with a couple of dead plants—and I knocked on the door. There were no lights on inside, and no sound of movement. I waited and knocked again. And waited some more. Apparently, no one was home. Served me right.

I turned to leave and spotted a dog crate pushed up against the rail in a corner, a pile of old moving pads stacked on top. It was rusty and sagging and the fleece mat inside was grimy, but that was not what caught my eye. There was a red service dog vest inside, just like the ones Heroes of Hope issued. I picked my way over to the crate and took the vest out to examine it.

A roar of furious barking caused me to whirl in time to see a large black and tan dog racing around the corner, teeth bared, tail arced, ears forward. Instinct kicked in as I flung up my hand, palm out, and shouted in my biggest voice, "*Halt!*"

That sometimes works, sometimes doesn't. This time it startled the dog long enough to keep him from charging up the steps. And it gave me a chance to duck down and grab a broken garden stake from amidst a tangle of twine and old nursery pots. It didn't offer much of a defense, but that was okay; I didn't intend to use it as a weapon.

Cisco, alerted by the excitement, started to bark inside the car and the dog spun around to charge the fence. He flung himself, paws up, against the chain-link, and I was glad I had latched the gate when I came in. I dashed down the steps, and when the dog saw me I threw the stick as hard as I could—not at him, but past him. That was just enough of a distraction to get me safely on the other side of the gate before the big beast threw himself against the chain-link again.

Cisco was barking and lunging against the seat restraint when I climbed behind the wheel, and I gave him a firm, "Cisco, quiet!" when I slammed the door. He couldn't resist a few more token barks and one dissatisfied whine, then settled down with the pride of a job well done. For my part, it took a few deep breaths before I was steady enough to start the car, but I definitely felt I'd earned my money that day.

And I'd found out what I wanted to know.

"I'm not sure I understand," Sonny said when I called her from my kitchen phone later than evening. "We have over a dozen sworn affidavits from people who say they witnessed the dog bite, but now you're saying the dog didn't bite the little boy?"

"Not exactly," I replied. "I'm saying *Rambo* didn't bite the little boy."

It was canine dinnertime at my house, which meant the smoky dark sky was streaked with stripes of fuchsia through the window, flames danced behind the glass door of the cast iron stove in the corner of my big country kitchen, and my three dogs, each holding a perfect sit in front of his or her placemat, watched me with absolute, unbroken concentration as I prepared their meals. I have exploited this picture on social media time and time again, believe me. The chances of all three of my dogs holding that perfect sit for more than two seconds under any other circumstances were pretty much nil.

"To most people," I explained, cracking an egg over the kibble in Mischief's bowl, "all GSD's look the same—tan with a black saddle, pointy ears, long, low bodies. But Rambo isn't a pure German Shepherd. His coat is much lighter, and his black markings are on his feet and head. Where the vest is worn, there's no black at all. But those were definitely black dog hairs I saw on that vest this afternoon. And it was a German Shepherd, with black markings, who charged me."

"And it was a Heroes of Hope vest?" she asked.

"Absolutely." I put Mischief's bowl aside and scooped kibble into Magic's. "It had the logo on it. Obviously, it was the one that was issued to Rambo. They're supposed to turn the vests in with the dog, but I guess these people didn't."

"I don't know, Raine," she said, still sounding skeptical. "Even if we had the vest as evidence, there's no way to prove that the black dog hairs on it belong to Kate Greene's dog, or that they were put there the night of the biting. We don't even know that she had another dog beside Rambo back then."

"Easiest thing in the world to find out," I replied, stirring a raw egg into Magic's kibble. I saw Magic's eyes flicker when I put the spoon in the sink, but otherwise she didn't move a muscle. "Vet records, rabies tag, microchip...they all require a current address. I'll bet you anything the new dog came with the new husband, and Jen said they were married last year."

"I've been through all the documents from the first attorney, and there's absolutely no mention of Greene owning any dog besides Rambo," Sonny said.

"That's because the first investigator probably made an appointment," I replied. I propped the phone between my shoulder and ear while I took the big bowl that contained Cisco's food from the refrigerator. His ears tilted up. "They would have made sure the dog was nowhere to be found when he got there. They knew they were in the wrong for putting a service dog vest on an animal who wasn't qualified to wear it, and from the look of their place they couldn't afford a lawsuit. Easier to let the service dog provider take the blame—and pay the price."

Sonny was thoughtful for a moment. "It's not that it's not a good theory," she said, "or that I dislike it. But we still have absolutely no proof."

"What if we did?" Cisco licked a long string of drool from his lips as he watched me scoop a mixture of oatmeal, pureed veggies and ground turkey into his bowl.

"I hope you don't mean security cameras," she said. "There might be some in the parking lot outside the ball field, but I'm sure they don't keep recordings from that far back."

I opened the refrigerator door to return the container of dog food, and Cisco shifted his feet impatiently, urging me to hurry. I gave him a warning look. If one of them broke their stay, everyone's dinner would be delayed. He knew that.

"I don't mean security footage," I said. I bumped the refrigerator door closed with my hip and picked up Mischief's and Magic's bowls. "I mean the newspaper." I placed a dog dish in front of each Aussie, and no one moved a muscle, not even Cisco. So far so good. I went back for the last bowl. "They take tons of pictures at every game. I'm not saying the dog would have been on the front page, but it's possible he's in the background of a shot somewhere. I mean, the whole point of this newspaper is to get people to buy it because there's a picture of themselves or their kid or their dog in it." I placed the last bowl in front of Cisco. No one moved.

Sonny murmured, "That's true. And even if the picture didn't make print, there's a good chance they keep all the old photos they didn't use. Everything is digitized these days."

I said, "Release!" And three dogs dived into their dinners like racehorses breaking through a gate.

I reached for my smartphone from the kitchen counter, intending to look up the newspaper archives from the summer. "I know there was a picture of all the principals in the dog bite incident in the paper the week after it happened," I said. "Wouldn't it be something if the photo showed the wrong dog?"

"That it would," Sonny agreed.

My screen showed two text messages. One was from Melanie, half an hour ago, and the other was from Dallas, sent only a few minutes after I'd texted her about her brother and subsequently tossed my phone in the car console while I drove to Kate Greene's. I opened the one from Dallas.

It read: *I don't have a brother.*

My throat went dry. "Sonny," I said hoarsely. "I have to go."

CHAPTER FIFTEEN

At six o'clock the next morning, Cisco and I were on our way to Overlook Falls. It was still pitch black and as cold as the inside of a tomb, but I couldn't have stayed in bed another minute. It was probably nothing. I was probably overreacting. Dallas was probably brewing coffee over a campfire or safe and snug back in her cabin at the production compound by now. But I couldn't relax until I knew for sure.

I had tried to call her at least a dozen times, and sent as many texts. I'd even called the sheriff's department, and they'd taken a report over the phone which, even as I gave it, sounded groundless. The deputy who took the report said there was nothing they could do unless she failed to show up for work and was officially declared missing. If Buck had been there, he would have done something.

I thought about calling the forest service, but I knew they couldn't send anyone out to search until daylight. And when they did, the person they'd send would be me.

I was probably being foolish. It was probably nothing. But why had the man lied to me about being her brother? Why had he been willing to climb over an hour up a wilderness trail to find her? Why did I have such a bad, bad feeling about this?

My high beams sliced a path through the blackness for almost twenty minutes before I saw my first car, and it was another ten minutes before the sky began to fade to a murky dark gray. Naked tree limbs were silhouetted like boney fingers against the pale shape of the mountains when at last the sun began to rise. This wasn't the first time Cisco and I had hiked up a mountainside in the cold and the dark to find someone who might be in trouble. But it was the first time that trouble was because of me.

On the other hand, it was probably nothing.

I parked at the end of the gravel road halfway to the falls, the same place I'd parked the first time I met Dallas, when they'd been filming her fall from the cliff. I snapped on Cisco's vest and shrugged into my backpack under a colorless sky, then hooked Cisco's tracking lead to his collar. He knew what he was here for and his tail swished wildly with excitement. As far as Cisco is concerned, there's no difference between a tracking class, a tracking trial, and a real search. They all are the most fun he's ever had, and they all end with treats. He watched my face, waiting for my command with bright eager eyes.

I squatted down and brushed my hand over the leaf-strewn ground. "Cisco, track," I said.

We were off.

Cisco led the way with his nose to the ground and his tail waving, while I tried to keep from tripping over deadfalls and getting tangled in his line. The cold morning damp clung to the back of my neck and turned my feet into blocks of ice, even through my leather hiking boots. The boots were three years old and had seen a lot of wear, but I was trying to wait until I could afford Gortex to replace them. It occurred to me that might be something Miles would like to give me for Christmas.

An anemic sun had cleared the tops of the bare trees by the time we reached the waterfall. The rush and tumble of all that water made the air seem colder than it was, and my misery was compounded by the steady convection breeze that rose from the falls. I cheered myself with the thought that it would grow warmer as we climbed higher, but I still wished I'd worn my wool socks.

Up until this point Cisco had stayed strictly on the trail, which was not surprising. But just before I started to pull in his lead in preparation for approaching the falls, he suddenly lifted his head and turned toward the brush on the side of the trail. I saw it too—a piece of crumpled paper caught in the twigs of a bare bush. Cisco trotted over to check it out, sniffed around for a minute, and then sat, his eyes fixed on the paper, and barked.

I am constantly amazed by a dog's ability to generalize and specialize and by the ease with which he seems to know when each is appropriate. Cisco's most recent scent training had involved rubbing alcohol, and he had been frequently rewarded for alerting to that scent alone. But he had no trouble figuring out we were no longer playing that game, that now he was tracking a human, and that he would only be rewarded for alerting to the presence of a strong concentration of human scent. That could mean anything from a sudden shift in wind bringing in scent particles from a hundred yards away, to an injured victim lying in the woods only a few feet off the trail. But somehow Cisco knew each was equally important.

I jogged up to him with praise and a liver treat at the ready, scanning the vicinity for signs of anyone nearby, but saw nothing. I ruffled Cisco's ears and spent a few moments in a brisk game of tug with his favorite rope toy before going to retrieve the paper. While Cisco entertained himself with the toy at the side of trail, I carefully disentangled the crumpled paper, which was damp with dew and the fog of the waterfall, from the brush and unfolded it. Another smaller piece of paper fell out when I did so, as though the two had been wadded up together and tossed aside. I felt my throat clutch a little as I examined them.

The paper was a page torn from the script of *Deadfall.* It made sense that Dallas might have taken pages with her to study while she was camping; every morning the production staff came around with rewritten scenes and changes to the script. The second, smaller paper was my business card. And both of them were smeared in what appeared to me to be dried blood.

We reached the shelter a little before 8:00 a.m. "Shelter" is perhaps a grand term for what is merely a three-sided wooden structure that really isn't large enough to unroll a sleeping bag inside. The Boy Scouts had built them along the most popular trails in the 1970s, and the forest service maintained them when they had the manpower. This one was built against a bank where the trail widened, and was designed to protect hikers from rain storms and offer some relief from the wind, which could be brutal on the mountainside in the wintertime. There was a bubbling stream a few dozen feet away, and a southern exposure, which meant it would get plenty of sun in the winter. People often set up camp there for just those reasons; I had done so myself, and I noticed as I approached that it looked as though Dallas had as well.

The stone-ringed fire pit still gave off the odor of fresh smoke. There was a small folding camp chair overturned beside it, and a bear bag hanging from a tree. At least Dallas hadn't broken camp. She may have hiked farther up the mountain, or just gone down to the stream, but apparently she was still on the mountain. All this I noticed before Cisco, nose to the ground, suddenly swiveled his head again and raced to the end of his twenty-foot lead, causing me to run to keep up. He stopped abruptly a few feet past the campfire, sat, and barked.

Even though he hadn't told me anything I didn't already know—that this was a place where humans were—you don't get a good tracking dog by ignoring his successes. So I made a huge fuss over him with treats and his toy before turning to call out, "Hello! Dallas, are you here? It's Raine Stockton!"

It wasn't until then that I saw what actually caused Cisco to alert in the first place. Not the smell of a campfire, or the concentration of human scent around it. Not even the scent of the alcohol swabs which I thought must be somewhere in Dallas's camping gear. In fact, I almost stepped on the object, half-hidden in the carpet of dead leaves and scrub grass, which had caught Cisco's attention. I bent to pick it up then stopped, fingers outstretched, before touching it. It was a folding camp knife, the kind you might use to cut rope or clear a small campsite, its six-inch blade locked and open. Even from that distance I could see that blade was dark with blood.

CHAPTER SIXTEEN

Cisco's second alert was a few dozen yards up the trail, where an embankment dropped off sharply to a long decline. I had found one of Dallas's gloves outside the shelter and let Cisco sniff it before giving the command to track, thus narrowing his search from general human scent to that of a specific human. After some crisscrossing and back-tracking, he led me to the edge of the ravine. I could see a sleeping bag tangled in the undergrowth less than twenty feet below, and when I climbed down to it, I saw that it, too, was dark with blood. A lot of blood. I left it where it was and climbed back up. The police were already on their way.

Cisco and I searched for Dallas until they got there, at which time we were summarily dismissed to wait at the car. I was not okay with that, but one of the deputies who responded was Jolene, with her dog Nike, and within a couple of hours two blood-hound teams arrived from the prison. Cisco was better than Nike at wilderness search, but there was a possibility that whoever had used the knife was still on the mountain, and Nike was better than Cisco at tracking fugitives. The bloodhounds were better than both of them. Of course, I wouldn't have given up so easily had I believed there was anything left for Cisco to find. But I had seen how much blood soaked that sleeping bag. Cisco was not a cadaver dog.

Five hours later, Cisco and I still sat on the open tailgate of my SUV, surrounded by sheriff's department vehicles and the crackle of radios. The SBI had sent a mobile crime scene unit, which was parked at the more accessible trailhead near the lodge, along with a couple of investigators. I had already told one of them everything I knew. They had told me nothing.

Jolene took Nike off the search to rest her in the back of the K-9 unit. I volunteered to take her place, but was told to stay where I was. I was in no hurry to leave; not until I got some answers, anyway.

After a while, Jolene came over to me. She said without preamble, "This man who came to your house. You say you've never seen him before?"

I shook my head.

"Describe him."

"I already did," I replied. "Twice. Once to Mike…" He had been the first deputy to arrive on the scene. "And once to that SBI guy."

She reached into the pocket of her windbreaker and pulled out a sheet of paper, which she unfolded and showed to me. "Did he look anything like this?"

It was an enlarged copy of a Texas driver's license, and there was no doubt the photo was of the man who'd come to my house yesterday looking for Dallas. The only problem was, the name on the license was not Jess Littleton. It was Brett Thornton.

I said, "That's him." I looked at her. "But that's not the name he gave me. Where did you get this?"

She chose not to answer my question, which did not surprise me. Clearly, she had gotten it from the DMV. The real question was why.

She said, "And you gave him your business card?"

"I already told you that. I turned it over to Mike, along with the page from the script. I found them about fifty feet past the waterfall, on the side of the trail in the brush. They both had blood on them."

"Why?" she asked. "Why did you give him your card?"

"Because I was worried about Dallas. I told him to call me if he didn't find her. She was diabetic. He seemed worried about her too."

She said, "There was no insulin in her backpack. No other diabetic supplies, either."

Dallas's backpack had been inside the shelter, but I hadn't thought to search it. I was too busy searching for her.

I said, "That's strange. She told me she had packed insulin."

"When did you talk to her?"

"I didn't talk to her. We texted back and forth on Thanksgiving, about noon I guess."

"Don't erase those texts," Jolene advised. "We might need to see them. And you'll need to come by the office and give a statement before you go home."

She started to turn, and I sprang down from the back of the SUV. Cisco, not having been given orders to the contrary, did the same. "Wait a minute! That's it? What about the search? Cisco and I can go back out once you've secured the scene. We can help!"

She said, "We're turning this over to the SBI. We'll give whatever support we can on the search, but Deke's recalling most of us to regular duty."

I stared at her. I'd forgotten that Deke was acting sheriff. The only thing he knew how to do was keep a duty roster, and heaven forbid anything should happen to throw that out of whack.

I said, "That's crazy. You can't just—"

"Look, Stockton." There might have been just the smallest flicker of compassion in her gaze. "You saw the sleeping bag. That was dried blood, at least twelve hours old, and the temperature dropped into the twenties last night. We're not going to find her, at least not alive. Nobody could've lost the amount of blood that was on that sleeping bag and survive, especially when you factor in exposure. We're not even searching the trail anymore. We're searching the bottom of the ridge. Whether she wandered off, injured, or whether someone tossed her over, it's most likely a body we're going to find. We've got the whole state looking for Thornton. There's nothing you can do."

I knew that. I'd known that from the moment I'd found the knife. I felt sick. "Who is he? This Thornton person? Why would he go to so much trouble to..." But I couldn't finish.

Jolene must have seen my distress, because this time she answered my question. "He's Dallas McKenzie's ex- husband. Evidently, he followed her when he heard the film was being shot here. He's the one she had the fight with at the diner. Apparently he has a history of domestic violence and was arrested for it more than once. Hospital records confirm spousal abuse."

I stared at her. If she had told me that, if *Dallas* had told me that, I never would have sent a stranger up the trail after her. I remembered that night in the pizza parlor, when Dallas showed me all her broken bones, and I wondered how many of them were really work related. I remembered the fresh bruises on her arm.

I said dully. "He was the man in the pickup truck who swerved to try to hit her that day." I hadn't even recognized the truck when it pulled into my driveway, but then why should I have? If only I'd known…

Maybe Jolene read my mind and felt some culpability for her own silence in the matter, because she went on to explain, "Miss McKenzie suspected her ex of the vandalism on the set, and of switching the guns the day of the accident. She thought he was stalking her, said he'd done it before on other sets where she was filming. We were able to verify that, and it looks as though he was issued a set pass for at least one of those days. We tracked him down at the Holiday Inn and sent a deputy out to interview him right after the first incident. He didn't deny being on the set and said he had business with the director.

But since there was no restraining order, and no proof against him on the vandalism charges, there was nothing more we could do." The slight note of bitterness in her voice was unmistakable. Had they been able to do more, Dallas might still be alive.

And if I hadn't sent the killer right to her...

I sat down abruptly on the back edge of the vehicle again. Cisco, sensing my distress, put his paws in my lap. I dropped my hand to his neck. "I heard her yelling at somebody on the phone when I went by her place on Tuesday afternoon. It might've been him. But I didn't know." My voice fell to a broken half-whisper as the full impact of what I had done swept over me. "I didn't know."

"Do you remember what you heard her say on the phone?" Jolene asked.

I cleared my throat, and tried to focus. "Not really. Something about not taking anymore, or having enough...She said 'we had a deal.' She was really upset. She threw a lamp and broke it."

She nodded. "We found her phone in the stream, crushed. We probably won't be able to get anything from it. I'd like to know who that phone conversation was with. But that's the SBI's problem now."

"I should have asked her," I said tiredly. "I could tell she was upset. I should have stayed and talked to her instead of storming out. She texted me. She said she wanted to talk to me. I blew her off. I thought... It doesn't matter what I thought. I was wrong."

It was not Jolene's style to offer meaningless platitudes, and even if it had been, in this case there was nothing she could say. She glanced around. "I'll get some of these units moved so you can get your vehicle out of here. You'll want to go out the way you came in. I hear the media has already started to set up camp at the trailhead near the lodge."

I cleared my throat. "I'd like to stay until you find her."

She looked at me with frank dark eyes. "That might be months."

I knew she was right.

I got up and closed the cargo door, then turned back to Jolene as something occurred to me. "What about her gun?" I said.

"What about it?"

"Is it still in custody after the shooting, or did you give it back to her?"

I think she was starting to see what I was getting at. "We took it in, told her she could pick it up the next day. If I recall, she did."

"Was it in her backpack?" I asked.

"No." Her expression was thoughtful. "No one has reported finding it. Are you thinking the knife might not have been the murder weapon? We didn't find any shell casings."

I answered, "I just know that no experienced camper would go into the wilderness alone without a gun, and Dallas was already paranoid enough to have her hand on her gun the night Mitch confronted us at dinner. She acted like she knew how to use it. So how did she let herself be stabbed to death in broad daylight?"

Jolene did not have an answer for that. Or if she did, she kept it to herself.

We both looked around at a sudden commotion beyond us; the spinning of gravel, the screech of brakes, and Seth Rosenstein got out of his black Mercedes, not bothering to close the car door behind him. He lunged toward the police tape that sealed off the trail. A deputy tried to stop him and Rosenstein began yelling at him. Jolene strode toward him. I grabbed Cisco's leash, which had fallen to the ground, and followed.

"I will *not* stay back!" he shouted. "I demand to speak with someone in charge. Do you know how I heard one of my cast members was missing, possibly even dead? On the *news*! What is the matter with you people? Let me pass!"

Jolene said, "Mr. Rosenstein, you need to calm down." She had a strong voice, with the kind of steady authority that made even a man like Rosenstein look around. "I'm Deputy Jolene Smith," she reminded him. "We met the other day."

He looked her over behind the amber-tinted glasses. "Are you in charge?"

"I can answer your questions," she told him. She nodded toward his car, only a few feet away. "Let's get out of the officers' way."

He hesitated, then followed her to his car, demanding, "Where is Dallas? Tell me what you know."

Clearly he was a man who was accustomed to being in charge.

I intended to follow at a distance, not wanting to intrude but unwilling to miss what was said, either. Cisco had other ideas. As Jolene and Rosenstein reached the open door of his vehicle, Cisco suddenly bounded forward. He was still on his long tracking leash—it was the only one I'd brought—and the fabric spun through my fingers like fishing line with a marlin on the other end. Rosenstein took a startled step backwards as Cisco raced past him and bounced up to put his front paws on the white leather driver's seat. By this time, I had enough control of the lead to prevent him from jumping in the car with all four feet, and I gave a dismayed cry of "Cisco!" just before I reached him. But before I could grab him, Cisco backed out of the car of his own accord, sat, and gave a single sharp bark.

Rosenstein glared at me, and Jolene said irritably, "Control your dog, Stockton."

I had no idea what Cisco had alerted to, but I was taking no chances. I dug into my pocket for a liver treat, rubbed his head enthusiastically, and told him, "Good find!"

I glanced up at Rosenstein. "Has Dallas been in your car recently?"

Jolene regarded me with more interest, and I explained, "The last scent object I gave Cisco was Dallas's glove. He has a good tracking memory. One time he found a slipper belonging to a missing child a week after he'd been shown its mate."

Rosenstein looked at me with growing incredulity. "Who the hell are you?"

Before I could remind him that I actually worked for him, Jolene said, "She's a member of the search team."

Coming from her, that was practically a compliment.

Jolene added, "Answer the question, sir. Was Miss McKenzie in this vehicle recently?"

"No, of course not," he returned angrily. "No one has seen her since Wednesday. Isn't that more or less the point? Now will you for God's sake tell me what's going on?"

Cisco looked up at me, probably wanting another treat. I stroked his ear and said nothing.

Jolene said, "Did you know Miss McKenzie well?"

"I've known her since we were kids," he replied shortly. "She's worked on four or five projects with me."

"Did you know about her plans to come up here camping this weekend?"

"Everybody did. It's not like it was a secret. Dallas does things like this all the time. She calls them 'meditative retreats.'"

"How did she get here?" Jolene asked. "There was no car when we arrived."

Rosenstein gave a brief shake of his head. "Dallas doesn't have a car out here. Lonzo usually drives her. He probably dropped her off Thursday morning. I don't know how long she intended to stay."

I said, "Did everybody have the weekend off, or just Dallas?"

He looked at me as though debating whether I was worth responding to. Then he said dismissively, "Of course not. Most of the actors and the tech crew had Thursday off, and a lot of the production staff. But everything else was business as usual."

Jolene said, "What about you, sir? Were you at the production lot Thursday and Friday?"

"Off and on." His tone was clipped. "I have an office at my rental house. When we're not filming, a lot of my work is done there."

"And when was Miss McKenzie expected back on the set?"

"She'd finished her scenes. I told her to be back on the set Monday morning in case we needed reshoots. Listen, if something has happened to Dallas, you need to tell me, and you need to tell me now."

Jolene said, "It's beginning to look as though Miss McKenzie has met with foul play. Can you tell me when was the last time you heard from her?"

He stared at her. "Foul play? What are you talking about, foul play?"

With a succinctness that had become her trademark, Jolene explained the morning's findings, including the fact that I had found the knife and the bloodied sleeping bag and called it in. When she finished speaking, he sagged against the car door, his expression stunned.

"When did you last hear from her?" Jolene repeated.

It seemed to take him a moment to process the question. "Yesterday," he said. "Yesterday morning. She texted me a picture of mountains."

"What time was that?"

"I don't know," he replied distractedly. "I'd have to check my phone."

Jolene said, "We'll need to see that text."

"Yes, of course."

He pulled out his phone and brought up the text. Jolene looked at it and showed it to me.

The picture was of foggy morning clouds layered over blue and purple mountains, the kind tourists love to take of the Smokies. There was no message, just the photo. The time stamp said 10:45.

"It looks like the view from her campsite," I said, returning the phone to Jolene. Which meant that at 10:45 yesterday morning Dallas was still at her campsite, enjoying the view, having no idea that her killer was even then hiking up the trail to find her. I felt sick.

Jolene said, "Please don't erase any communications you've had with Miss McKenzie since she left the set Wednesday. We may need to see them." She returned his phone to him.

Rosenstein put the phone in his pocket, then frowned, turning to me. "What made you come up here to look for her? How did you even know she was here?"

I had no choice but to tell the truth. "I'm the one who told her about the trail," I said. "And yesterday, when that man Thornton came to me claiming to be her brother and wanting to surprise her Thanksgiving…"

He tensed. "Wait a minute. You talked to him? You told him where she was?" His voice rose in anger. "You sent Dallas's crazy ex up into the mountains after her? Do you have any idea how many times he's tried to kill her?"

He looked as though he would lunge for me, and Cisco got to his feet, alarmed. Jolene stepped smoothly between us. "We are aware of a number of complaints against the man," she said. "He is definitely a person of interest in this case."

Now he turned his incredulity and outrage on her. "A person of…" The rest was lost in a puff of breath, and he dragged a hand across his face. "My God, what have you idiots done? What have you *done?*"

Jolene said, "We'll want to talk to you further, Mr. Rosenstein, along with everyone else Miss McKenzie worked with. But right now I need you to leave the scene so we can get back to work. Do you have a card?"

He looked at her for a moment as though he might argue. Then he got into the driver's seat and stretched across to open the glove box. He took out a business card and a pen. "This is my cell phone," he told her, writing on the card. "I'm writing the address of my rental house on the lake, and my assistant's cell. If you can't reach me, he'll know where I am."

He got out of the car and handed the card to Jolene. "But I'm not leaving until I know you've got that bastard in custody. I'll be at the production compound."

Cisco's eyes were fixed on a small scrap of paper that had fallen on the ground when Rosenstein got out of the car, apparently dislodged from the floorboard. Mine were too. I tightened Cisco's leash and kept him close.

Jolene took the card. "We'll be in touch as soon as we know anything further."

He got back in the car and slammed the door without another word.

When he was gone, I bent down and picked up the small paper that had fallen from the car. Only it wasn't a paper at all. It was an alcohol swab. And it was still damp.

Now I knew what had caused Cisco to alert. What I didn't know was why Rosenstein had lied.

CHAPTER SEVENTEEN

"They picked up Thornton a few miles outside of Waynesville," I told Miles wearily on the phone that night. "They brought him back to Hanover County for questioning."

I was curled up on the sofa beneath a comfy old quilt with Cisco warming my feet and Mischief and Magic warming themselves before the fire. A mug of tea cooled on the end table at my side, which I hadn't even tasted. I think I'd made it because tea is supposed to make everything better, although when I think back I can't recall a single instance when it's done so.

"He claims he's innocent, of course," I went on. "He says he didn't even go all the way up the trail, and he never saw her at all."

I knew this because I had been at the sheriff's office giving my statement when Thornton was brought in. He was handcuffed, outraged, and escorted by two deputies. He happened to see the desk where I was sitting while we waited for a copy of my statement to print out for me to sign, and he looked at me with blazing eyes. "Did you do this?"

he demanded of me. "You did, didn't you? You crazy bitch! You set me up! First you send me on a wild goose chase up the damn mountain and then you call the cops! Did she put you up to this? Did she?" He actually jerked against his restraints as though to lunge at me, but a deputy's firm hand on his shoulder brought him back into line.

I didn't see the point in repeating any of this to Miles, but I understood why Dallas had been afraid of Thornton. Still…

"The thing is," I went on, "Dallas sent Rosenstein a text at 10:45 yesterday morning, and Thornton claims he was back at his hotel by 11:00. If that checks out…well, it's a thirty-minute drive from the trailhead, not to mention the hour's hike down the mountain. There's no way he could have killed her after 10:45 and gotten back to the Holiday Inn by 11:00."

"Sure there is," Miles said. "Just because a text was sent from the victim's phone doesn't mean she sent it."

"Right," I murmured, sitting up a little straighter. I must be really tired; I hadn't even thought of that. "He could have sent the text himself after he killed her just to give himself an alibi."

"Maybe," Miles agreed. "I guess the police searched the motel room."

"Yeah." I was abruptly defeated again. "That's the other thing that doesn't make sense. They didn't find anything, or at least not anything they're sharing with me." In fact, the only reason I knew as much as I did was because I still had a few friends left in the sheriff's office, and Mike, the deputy who'd taken my statement, was one of them. "No bloody clothes, anyway, or anything obvious like that. No blood in his car, either, and if he even touched that sleeping bag there's no way he could've avoided getting blood on him. The SBI has a forensic team going over the car and the room and searching the dumpster for evidence he might've thrown away." I sighed. "No fingerprints on the knife, either, but he was probably wearing gloves. I was. It was cold yesterday."

Miles said, "You say the fellow's name was Thornton? Brett Thornton?"

"That's right."

He was silent for a moment. "I thought so. That's the name of the man who filed all those lawsuits to stop the production of the movie these past ten years," Miles said. "The man who claims to have written the original book."

I sat up straighter. "Dallas's ex-husband?"

"Looks like it."

"That's weird," I said. "I mean, that Rosenstein would hire the ex-wife of the man who's been trying to ruin him, even if she was an old friend."

"Maybe that's why he stopped filing suits," Miles suggested. "Maybe Dallas influenced him somehow, and in exchange, Rosenstein gave her the job."

"Maybe," I said thoughtfully. "Maybe that's the deal she was talking about on the phone. "But Jolene said Dallas had filed multiple complaints against Thornton for domestic violence. Rosenstein said he'd tried to kill her more than once. That doesn't sound like someone you'd want to make a deal with."

"I don't know, honey. The dynamic between victims and their abusers is complicated. Maybe she thought the only way she could stay safe was to give him what he wanted."

"Maybe he came to town to renegotiate whatever deal she made with him. He was on the set, and he claimed he had business with the director. Maybe he tried to threaten Rosenstein somehow, and that's why Dallas was so angry on the phone."

"Could be. At any rate, it's starting to sound as though Thornton should have been the one to fear for his life. He certainly had enough enemies."

"Yeah," I agreed. "And if Dallas was scared enough of him to carry a gun even when she was thousands of miles away from where he was supposed to be…"

"On the other hand," said Miles, who had the most annoying habit of seeing both sides of a situation, "lots of women carry guns, especially if they've been previous victims of violence."

He was right, of course. I had a handgun, which I mostly carried on hikes or wilderness searches in case of snakes. "They never found her gun," I said. "At least they hadn't by the time I left the sheriff's office. They searched pretty much the whole production compound."

I was thoughtful. "You know what doesn't make sense?"

"Only one thing?"

"If Thornton has been here all week," I said, "and if he was able to get on the set and even get Dallas's gun to switch it out for the prop one…"

"Which you said he denied," Miles reminded me.

"The point is," I went on, choosing to ignore the interruption, "he had plenty of opportunities to kill Dallas without hiking up a mountain to find her. I mean, nobody was really sure where she was. Even I was just guessing. It just seems like a lot of trouble with no guarantee. I sure would like to talk to him."

"I'm not sure what good that would do," Miles said. "The man appears to be a fairly expert liar."

"I'll tell you what else I don't understand," I went on, mostly to myself. "Why Seth Rosenstein would lie about Dallas being in his car. If he's the one who drove her to the campsite, why not just say so? Someone is bound to have seen them."

"A question I'm sure the authorities have already asked and answered," Miles assured me.

"I guess. It's just…" I rubbed my forehead wearily. "I feel responsible, you know? Dallas wouldn't have even been up there without me, and then I sent a killer in after her. The least I owe her is to try to find out the truth."

One of the best things about Miles is that he knows when to say nothing. So he took a moment before replying, "And I know for a fact that if there's anybody in the world who could do that, it would be you. You have an amazing ability to look at all the facts and reach the most sensible conclusion.

In fact, you probably have one of the most logical minds know."

I was immediately suspicious. His next words proved I was right to be.

"Which is why," he said, "I'm confident you've already figured out the best thing for you to do is to stay out of the SBI's way on this one. They have a reputation for being pretty good at their job."

I bristled. "I'm not going to get in anybody's way."

"Of course not. You're too smart for that. And you know too much about how these things work to try to interrogate a prisoner who has already proven to be violent and who may be guilty of murder. Or to confront a powerful director who already blames you for his girlfriend's death."

I tried to keep my tone neutral. "I'm really tired, Miles. I'm going to bed."

"Sleep tight, sugar," he said gently. "It wasn't your fault."

I sighed, enormously grateful for the thought, even if I couldn't make myself believe it. "I love you, Miles."

"Me, too, baby."

For once, I didn't mind being called baby.

CHAPTER EIGHTEEN

Idreamed about bacon, possibly because I had been too dispirited the night before to eat and had gone to bed hungry. At least that was what I thought until I was abruptly awakened the next morning by a weight bouncing on my bed and a girlish voice crying, "Morning, Raine! Surprise!"

I struggled upright from beneath the mountain of covers. "Melanie!"

I hugged her hard, and Cisco began his happy bark as Pepper scrabbled across the hardwood floors. Before I knew it both dogs were on the bed, and I was almost too delighted to care. Almost.

I sent the two tussling goldens back to the floor where they belonged and exclaimed to Melanie, "What are you doing here? What time is it? You're not supposed to be home until tonight!"

She grinned at me. "Pepper and I slept on an air mattress in the back of the SUV. It was great. Dad said breakfast will be ready in ten minutes, so hurry!"

The bacon I had dreamed about was real. So were the pancakes and fluffy scrambled eggs and hash browns that accompanied it. And so was the man who prepared them, the same one who hugged me so hard I thought my ribs would crack when I raced into the kitchen less than five minutes after Melanie woke me up.

"I can't believe you drove all night," I said, stepping back to look at him in wonder. "I seriously can't believe it."

To which he replied, taking my face in his hands, "I can't believe you thought I wouldn't." And, with a quick glance over his shoulder to note that Melanie was busy letting the dogs out, he bent to give me a kiss that was, I sincerely hoped, only a hint of things to come.

When I had eaten more pancakes than was wise by any standard and was debating whether to make Cisco's dreams come true with the last piece of bacon on my plate, I said one more time, "I can't believe you drove all night." I leaned back in my chair and cradled my coffee mug against my chest. "That's crazy."

"It wasn't all night," he said, tossing a scrap of pancake to Pepper, who caught it expertly. Cisco cast a quick glance toward his canine friend, then fixed his eyes on me, licking his lips. "Besides, Mel has lots to do to get ready for school tomorrow."

"Not that much," she objected, bright eyed. "I figured since you've been too busy making the movie to finish scouting the trail for the tracking trial, we could do that today. And Pepper could get her first tracking lesson!"

It seemed like a few years, rather than a few days, since I had stumbled into this whole mess while innocently scouting the trail. I sipped my coffee and glanced at Miles. I said, "I don't think we can do that today, Mel. The trail is going to be closed off for a while."

"Right," she said, nodding sagely. "The murder." I shouldn't have been surprised. After all, it had been all over the news. "So are we on the case? Any leads? Pepper and I can help."

"There is no case," Miles told her firmly. "And if there were, neither one of you would be on it. That's what we have trained law enforcement officers for. Am I right, Raine?"

I replied carefully, "You should always listen to your father, Melanie."

That didn't fool Miles for a minute. Or Melanie.

She said, "Well, I'm *going* to be a trained law enforcement officer. I don't know how I'm ever going to learn anything if I'm not allowed to get some experience." She changed the subject, as she was smart enough to do when she knew she was on the losing side of an argument, by turning to me and informing me, "Dad's going to take me to the sheriff office's junior gun safety course this spring. I could go by myself," she added confidently, "but you have to be accompanied by an adult. Hey, maybe you could go, Raine!"

"I could," I agreed, surprised. "I didn't even know there was such a thing."

"It's one of Marshall's new public education programs," Miles said. "Good idea, huh?"

"Yeah," I agreed, and hoped the smile that followed wasn't too slow. I wondered why no one had thought of it before. Maybe Uncle Ro was right—Marshall *was* bringing the sheriff's office into the twenty-first century.

"Cool," Melanie said, swinging her feet beneath the table. She looked, bright eyed, from one to the other of us. "That'll be fun. But what're we going to do *today?*"

"Actually," said her dad, "Raine and I have someplace to go this morning. Why don't you hang out with Corny for a couple of hours?"

Needless to say, I was surprised. Not only was this the first I'd heard of any plans we had together, but I'd actually made some plans of my own. It was not a fight I wanted to have in front of Melanie, however, so I picked up the piece of bacon on my plate and bit into it. Cisco watched me with eyes that could melt the coldest heart, but around here you have to do more than make big eyes to earn something as valuable as bacon.

Melanie objected, "Aw, *Dad*, it's the last day of vacation! Besides, the kennel is closed on Sunday, nothing fun is going on."

"Make your own fun," Miles challenged her, and Melanie rolled her eyes. He bent a meaningful look on her. "Didn't I hear something about a special holiday project you wanted Corny to help you with?"

"Oh, yeah." She grew thoughtful. "I hope he has a glue gun."

I thought the chances of that were pretty good, since Corny was a self-proclaimed master of arts and crafts.

Melanie pushed her chair back. "May I be excused from the table?"

"You may," Miles replied. "Take your dishes to the sink."

Melanie hurried to do as he instructed, but before departing, she had a final shot. "By the way, you're not fooling me. I know you're trying to get rid of me so you can get up to some more of that mushy stuff with Raine."

Miles regarded her soberly. "Some day soon," he told her, "maybe not today, maybe not tomorrow, but soon—you are going to beg me to stay out of your personal business. I will remember this moment."

I tried not to laugh as she gave us both a carefree wave and left by the back door, Pepper trotting by her side as she crossed the yard to the kennel.

Cisco, who had waited long enough for the last bite of bacon to magically leap from my fingers into his mouth, got up, backed three steps in a perfectly straight line, spun around twice, sat, and raised both his paws. I grinned and tossed him the bacon. He gulped it down without even tasting it.

Miles got up to take his plate to the sink. I said, "Miles, you know I enjoy the mushy stuff as much as the next girl…"

"Glad to hear it."

I picked up my own plate and orange juice glass. "And I'm really, really happy you drove back early, honestly. It's just that I wasn't expecting you, and I kind of had some stuff planned today."

"I'm sure you did." He turned from the sink to take my dishes. "I did a little more research last night," he said. "That book Thornton wrote? The one he claims Rosenstein stole in order to make this movie? It turns out it was never published."

I was confused. "But then how...?"

"He claims the manuscript went missing after the divorce, and shortly thereafter Rosenstein registered a screenplay that followed his book virtually word for word...or scene by scene, as it were."

"Dallas," I said. "She gave the manuscript to Seth Rosenstein and he plagiarized it?"

"That's the most likely explanation," Miles agreed, placing the dishes in the dishwasher, "at least in Thornton's mind. And even worse, Rosenstein— or I should say, his production company—also holds the book rights and the merchandising rights associated with the movie, which means Thornton can't even publish the book he wrote. I'm not sure that's a motive for murder, but it sure doesn't make Thornton look any less guilty."

"Yeah," I agreed thoughtfully. "Only guilty of what? Maybe he killed Dallas for revenge, or because he's a crazy wifebeater, but his real problem was Rosenstein. Why didn't he go after him with something more effective than a lawsuit?"

"Good question," Miles said. He closed and locked the dishwasher and dried his hands as he turned to me. "So," he said, "where to first? To talk to Thornton at the jail, or Rosenstein at work?"

I just stood there looking at him for the longest time, and I couldn't stop a smile. In almost every way, Miles and I are polar opposites, and there are moments that I honestly wonder why we ever got together. But this was not one of those moments.

"The jail," I said. "I'll get my purse."

CHAPTER NINETEEN

The Hanover County Detention Center is located in the courthouse complex, a short walk down the sidewalk from the sheriff's office. Visitors check in with the jailer during visiting hours, but to see a prisoner outside those hours you need permission from the sheriff. I didn't think Deke would give me any trouble. All he had to do was make a phone call.

There were news trucks in the parking lot and more than one unfamiliar face milling around on the courthouse steps when Miles and I got out of his SUV. Cisco, who was as familiar with Miles's vehicle as he was with mine, had jumped in the moment I'd opened the passenger door, scrambled over the console and into the backseat, where he sat looking so charming that I didn't have the heart to drag him out. So he had come along for the ride, and now waited patiently while Miles and I went into the sheriff's office.

Annabelle, the day receptionist, looked particularly harried, so I didn't waste time with chitchat. She made a phone call when I told her we needed to see Deke, and I was surprised when, a moment later, Jolene came to the front.

"The acting sheriff is in a meeting," she told me. "If you want to wait for Sheriff Lawson, he's on his way in from Asheville to deal with the press. Is there something I can do for you?"

Her eyes flickered briefly to Miles, and he nodded pleasantly to her. "Deputy Smith," he said, by way of greeting. "Nice to see you again. We were hoping to talk to one of your prisoners. I'm sure you can guess which one."

She didn't seem even a fraction as annoyed with him as she would have been with me had I made the same request. It might have been because of his natural charm, or because of his status in the community, or because he looked particularly fine today in his scuffed jeans and leather jacket. But I think it was mostly because he wasn't me.

Jolene said, "If you mean Mr. Thornton, I'm afraid he's no longer an inmate at the Hanover County Detention Center."

I was disappointed. "Did the SBI take custody? Was he transferred?"

She shook her head. "We had to cut him loose. His alibi checked out. Security cameras showed him at the hotel at 11:00 a.m., just as he claimed, and with evidence that Miss McKenzie was alive at 10:45, the timeline doesn't work."

"But he could have sent that text himself," I objected, "after she was dead! That doesn't prove anything!"

"It proves we didn't have enough evidence to hold him," Jolene replied. "Particularly without a body."

Miles said, "When did you release him?"

"About fifteen minutes after his lawyer arrived this morning."

"Damn it," I whispered, my frustration mounting. "It was him, it had to be! I can't believe you let him go!"

Miles touched my back in a light, soothing gesture—but also in a warning. As he was always saying, you catch more flies with honey.

Jolene said, "I didn't say he wasn't a suspect. I said we didn't have enough evidence to hold him. And I also said," she reminded me, "that this isn't a sheriff's office matter. The SBI has it fully in hand."

I demanded tightly, "Where is he? If he's material to this case he wouldn't be allowed to leave the state, and you've got to know where to contact him. So where is he?"

She looked at me as though she couldn't believe I'd even asked. "It's against policy to—"

"A woman is dead because you followed policy!" I snapped, loudly enough that Annabelle looked up from her desk and a couple of heads in the waiting room turned toward me. Miles's fingers tightened a little against my spine, but I ignored him. "If you had told me that first day I saw you on the set that Dallas's ex-husband was stalking her I never would have told a stranger where to find her! If you hadn't been so damn close-mouthed about everything, if you hadn't refused to answer every single question I asked, I never would have let her go up that mountain alone and Dallas would be alive today! We could have stopped this if you had just *talked* to me!"

Jolene looked at me for a moment, her jaw knotted and her dark eyes unfathomable. Then she turned to Annabelle and said calmly, "I'm going on patrol."

She started to push past us, then stopped and glanced at Miles. "Do you mind me asking, sir, what you wanted to see Mr. Thornton about?"

I wanted to signal Miles to say nothing, just out of spite, but of course that would have been pointless. He said, "Actually, I was curious about the lawsuits he filed against Mr. Rosenstein accusing him of—among other things—plagiarizing his book for *Deadfall*." I could tell by the slight frown that flickered across Jolene's eyes that she hadn't known about that. "Specifically," Miles added, "I wondered why he stopped filing them, and whether he'd reached some kind of out-of-court settlement with Rosenstein that allowed the production to go on unimpeded. Do you think," he added earnestly, "something might have gone wrong with their agreement, and that's what brought Thornton to town?"

"Are you suggesting some kind of payoff?" Jolene said, looking thoughtful.

"Could be," Miles said. "Miss McKenzie might even have brokered it, and Thornton could have blamed her when it fell apart. After all, he did accuse her of stealing his manuscript and giving it to Rosenstein."

I could tell this, too, was a surprise to Jolene, although she covered it well. She said, "I appreciate your interest, Mr. Young, but we try not to encourage civilian involvement in criminal cases."

He smiled. "I understand."

She added, "I'm sure the SBI is investigating every avenue." She didn't sound sure at all.

He replied politely, "I'm sure they are." He glanced at me. "We should go, Raine."

I glared back at him, but didn't say anything until we were outside. "You, she listens to," I said, scowling. "Me, she tells to shut up."

He tucked his fingers into his jacket pockets, striding easily beside me. "That's because I'm nice."

"It's because you're a man."

"No doubt."

"And rich."

"That too."

"Anyway, I don't see what good any of that did," I said. "We still don't know where Thornton is."

"No," he agreed. "But at least the police have a reason to question him again. And frankly, I think they'll have a lot more luck getting answers than you would have. Besides, Rosenstein's the one you really need to talk to if you want to know what was going on between him and Thornton. If anything."

I held out my hand for the car keys. "I have a set pass," I said. "I'll drive."

He tossed the keys to me amenably and got in on the passenger side of the car. Cisco greeted us both with a panting grin, and Miles turned to cluck Cisco under the chin before fastening his seat belt.

I adjusted the seat and the rearview mirror, casting Miles a suspicious look. "So why the interest, all of a sudden? I thought you wanted me to stay out of this."

"I do," he assured me. "But since there's no chance of you actually doing that, I feel a lot better if I can keep an eye on you while you're not staying out of it. Besides," he added before I could make the inevitable snarky reply, "I'm curious. There's something a little too convenient about the way this all went down, not to mention the way you got caught up in the middle of it."

I glanced at him as I buckled my seat belt. "What do you mean?"

But he wasn't willing to share his speculation with me. "Let's just talk to Rosenstein. He's the movie man."

But when I arrived at the gate to the production lot and showed my set pass, the security guard Gary—who remembered me from the dogs—informed me that Mr. Rosenstein hadn't come in today. He noticed Cisco in the backseat and commented, "Hey, you got a new dog!" I didn't bother correcting him. There's something about having a dog around—especially a golden retriever—that makes people friendlier and less guarded than they might otherwise be. I was counting on that, and I was right.

"I guess you heard what happened," Gary added somberly. "Everybody's pretty upset, what with the police and all, and the set is dark. You're not on the schedule for the day," he added unnecessarily, and with a touch of regret, "so I can't let you in."

"That's okay," I said. "I really just wanted to talk to Mr. Rosenstein. I know he and Dallas were close. I guess he's at the lake house."

Gary chose to neither confirm nor deny. He pointed to a cleared spot on the side of the drive. "You can turn around over there."

"Sure thing." I put the car in gear and then hesitated. "Gary, do you happen to know how Dallas got to the trailhead? I mean, did she drive herself or…"

He shook his head. "Nah. I was on duty that day. The only thing that was available was one of the equipment vans, so one of the drivers took her. The police have already talked to him."

I smiled my thanks and turned the car around.

"So Rosenstein didn't take Dallas to the trailhead," I said when we were on the road again. "But he did lie about her being in his car. I figured Lonzo might have driven her, using Rosenstein's car, and that's how the alcohol swab got there."

"I think you might have to write that off as a coincidence," Miles said. "It could have fallen out of a first aid kit or he could have cut himself shaving or any number of things. It doesn't prove Dallas was in his car. In fact, it might prove just the opposite."

I glanced at him. "How so?"

"You said it was still damp," he pointed out, "and the scent was strong enough to attract Cisco. But you're talking about alcohol, here. Those things dry out in a matter of hours. If it belonged to Dallas, it would have been days old—and dry."

Which of course explained why Jolene had not been very interested when I turned over the "evidence" to her. I murmured, "Yeah, I guess." But I was thinking about the diabetic supplies that had been missing from the campsite, and wondering why someone would take those and nothing else. I said, "Dallas seemed worried that I would tell someone about her diabetes," I said. "She said no one else knew."

"I guess she could have lost her job if she lied about it," Miles said. "But with Rosenstein being her friend, probably not. If word got out though, she wouldn't have been able to get another job."

"Because of the insurance," I remembered.

"Possibly," Miles agreed. "But like I said, it would be a lot more serious if we were talking about one of the principals—writer, director, leading cast members. Stunt people are replaceable."

"That's true," I said thoughtfully. "So why didn't Rosenstein just replace her? I mean, according to Lonzo it was one thing after the other with her, and nobody else in the industry would give her a job. He had a lot at stake with this movie. Why would he risk it all just to give an old friend a break?"

"Because he was sleeping with her?" suggested Miles.

"Or because she was the one blackmailing him over the script," I said, "not Thornton, and maybe he was tired of it. Or maybe the two of them were in it together somehow. Maybe it was Rosenstein Dallas was so angry at on the phone that day, when I heard her yelling about having a 'deal.' Maybe he was trying to get out of the deal, and she wasn't having it."

"He was the one who fired the gun with the real bullet on the set, wasn't he?" Miles said, frowning.

"Right." I slowed down to make the turn onto the winding country road that led to the lake, and I looked at him again. "It could've been a warning. Or maybe he just had bad aim."

Miles was silent for a time. "Any chance of getting you to turn around and go home?"

I shook my head. "I don't know how this all fits together. Maybe Thornton killed her, maybe he didn't. But I think Seth Rosenstein was on that mountain with Dallas. And if she wasn't in his car, then something of hers was, and recently. I just need to give Cisco a chance to find it."

At the sound of his name, Cisco, who had been snoozing in the backseat, sat up and looked around, panting with excitement.

Miles said, "It won't hold up in court."

That wasn't the point, and he knew it. I said quietly, "I just need to know, Miles. I need to know whether I'm the reason Dallas is dead."

He didn't say anything else.

The drive to the lake is about forty-five minutes from town, which makes it something of a problem for fire and police service. Fortunately, most of the dwellings there are summer cabins that are only occupied a few weeks a year. There are a couple of nice houses along the shoreline, though none as nice as the Hamilton place, but they, too, are only used in the summer. The narrow, winding road that encircled the lake was completely empty.

A discrete wooden plaque at the end of a leaf-strewn drive announced simply "Hamilton." I turned the car into the drive and began a slight upward climb toward the house that I could see silhouetted behind the bare branches of trees. Leaves crunched under the tires, and Cisco panted in my ear. Somehow dogs can always tell when they near their destination.

The first thing I saw was a closed wrought iron gate across the drive. It was mounted on stone posts, but the fence that was adjacent to it was a purely decorative, three-foot-tall split rail one. It was an instant later that I noticed a tricked out black pickup truck parked beside the driveway, in the woods next to the fence. I stepped on the brake. "That looks like Thornton's truck," I said. "Texas plates."

Miles said, "That's a key-card entry system. See if there's a buzzer."

I rolled down the window and found the buzzer. I pushed it and waited. Nothing happened. I pushed again.

"Maybe he's not here," Miles said.

"Or maybe it's broken," I suggested.

"Or maybe he doesn't want any visitors."

I put the car in park and turned off the ignition. "I guess we'll just have to walk to the front door and find out."

Miles didn't bother to argue. He knew me too well by now.

I let Cisco out of the backseat and walked him to the side of the gate. Miles stepped over the low fence and extended his hands to help me. I dropped Cisco's leash and said, "Cisco, over." He sailed over the split rail while I braced my hands on Miles's shoulders and let him swing me over. That kind of help I can always use.

The house was in sight, visible beyond a curve of the drive perhaps fifty feet away. It was a stately white clapboard, two story with a deep wraparound porch and tall, green-shuttered Charleston windows with forever views of the mountains across a sparkling lake...or so it was depicted in the magazine where I'd seen it featured. The front of the house, where we approached, was mostly white pavement lined with now-dormant flower beds; the lush landscaping and architectural features would be in the back, overlooking the lake.

The morning was still and bright, with a chill breeze coming off the lake. The smell of old woodsmoke lingered in the air, probably from last night's hearth fire. I let Cisco sniff his way up the drive on a loose leash, and the only sound was that of our footsteps and his snuffling.

Miles said, "I don't think anyone's home."

"Then where's the driver of the truck?"

"Probably looking for Rosenstein, just like we are. And listen to me." He turned a look on me that said he wasn't kidding. I had one of those looks too, but I used it a lot more often than he did. So when Miles looked at me like that, I paid attention. "If we do run into Thornton, we're going to turn around and go straight back to the car. Talking to him in jail is one thing, but getting into an argument with the man out here in the woods is another. He's dangerous, and he already blames you for a night in jail. Stay as far away from him as you can get. Do we understand each other?"

For once, we were in agreement. I could still see the fury in Thornton's eyes when he'd yelled at me last night. It had terrified me, and he'd been in handcuffs then. "Don't worry," I said. "The man's a nut job, and I've got Cisco to think about."

He started to say something, and then stopped dead, raising his hand as though to halt my forward motion as well. The gesture was unnecessary. I had seen it the same time he did, and more importantly, so had Cisco. Lying at the bottom of the steps about twenty feet away, crumpled in a bloody heap, was the figure of a man.

Miles ran toward him and so did I, with Cisco scrambling forward at the end of his leash. Miles reached him before I did, dropped to one knee, and checked for a pulse. "He's been shot," he called back to me, and took out his phone.

I had a blurry impression of the scene: the front door gaping open like a wound, blood on the steps, blood smeared on the white railing, the newel post. I couldn't see the man's face. Cisco pulled me toward the house with the same kind of mad determination he showed when he was at the other end of the tracking leash and his find was in sight. I had to use both hands to hold onto the leash, and I shouted, "Cisco, halt!"

To my shock, he did. Abruptly, he stopped a few feet away from the steps, sat, and barked. He had made his find.

Dallas McKenzie came out of the open front door and stood at the top of the steps about six feet away. She held a handgun in a shooter's stance, and it was pointed right at us.

CHAPTER TWENTY

"**D**amn it," Dallas said lowly. "It had to be you." Cisco barked, confident in his find. All I could do was tighten the leash by another loop. My throat was dry, my lips numb with shock. "Dallas," was all I could manage to say.

Miles stood slowly, hands raised palm-up to his shoulders. "I've already called the police," he said. His voice was remarkably calm. "They're on their way."

"I'll be gone before they get here," she said. "Move away from him."

I didn't think Miles had had time to dial 911, but even if he had, she was right. Help was at least half an hour away at top speed. I fastened my eyes on him, willing him to obey her.

Dallas pointed the gun at Miles. "Get over there." She jerked her head toward me. "No sudden moves."

Miles said, "He's still alive. If you let us help him, there's a chance you won't even face charges. You could say it was self-defense."

"It *was* self defense!" she cried. "I've been defending myself from men all my life!"

In the movies, that would have been the moment, while she was upset and distracted, when Miles rushed her in an attempt to disarm her. I thanked God he was too smart for that.

Dallas regained control in an instant, her face hardening. "I said move," she told Miles.

Carefully, not taking his eyes off her, Miles moved to stand beside me. Dallas came to the top of the steps. Cisco whined and stretched his head forward, tugging a little at the leash. Dallas came slowly down the stairs, the gun unwavering.

"I don't want to hurt you," she told me steadily. "Or your dog. But I will put a bullet through your boyfriend's skull if either one of you tries to stop me. Do you understand?"

I swallowed hard. "We won't. We won't stop you."

I thought she meant we shouldn't stop her from trying to leave. But instead she went over to the crumpled figure on the ground, planted her foot on his shoulder, and shoved, rolling him over face-up. The face was that of Seth Rosenstein.

He groaned and she lowered the gun abruptly, pointing it deliberately at his head. I screamed, "Dallas, don't!" I lurched instinctively toward her. Miles grabbed my arm. Cisco barked and leapt to the end of his leash. Dallas swung the gun toward us.

"I warned you!" she screamed.

"Okay!" I cried. I pulled Cisco close with one hand, and I flung the other up in a pacifying gesture. My breath came shallowly. "Okay, it's okay, we won't move, just…Dallas, talk to me. What happened? I thought—we all thought—you were dead!"

She looked back at Rosenstein, who was gray faced and motionless on the ground. His white sweatshirt was bright with blood over the abdomen, his hands were smeared with it where he'd clutched the wound. She said, "It was Seth's idea. A way to get rid of Brett once and for all. The law couldn't stop him. I couldn't hide from him. He always found me. But if I were dead, he couldn't find me. If I were dead, he'd leave me alone. It was supposed to be a stunt gone wrong, it happens all the time. There was this scene coming up where I was pushed off a dock. If I didn't come back up, if there was no body, everyone would think I was dead, it would be over. But then Brett showed up here, that day in the diner, and then he tried to run me down, you saw him. And then he kept calling me, all day, saying he wanted to work something out and that things were going to get bad if I didn't cooperate, so that night I took one of the studio cars and went to his hotel."

She stopped, her eyes going vague for a minute, her breathing rapid. Cisco whined and shifted his weight. I glanced quickly at Miles and he returned a short, almost imperceptible shake of his head.

She was rambling, but as long as she was talking, she wasn't pointing the gun at the man who lay bleeding on the ground. I said, "Is that who you were with when the sheriff's deputy stopped you for speeding?"

She came back to herself, focusing on me. "I thought if I could talk to him, find out what he wanted...but he was waiting for me when I got there, and he pushed me into the passenger seat and started driving, real crazy-like, trying to scare me, and he did scare me. I think he really might have killed us both if the cops hadn't stopped him. I wanted to say something, to signal the deputy somehow, but my insulin was low and I was feeling loopy. I couldn't think. Brett told the officer I'd had too much to drink, and he let us go."

It was cold, and my ungloved fingers were growing numb on Cisco's leash. But there was a fine sheen of sweat on Dallas's face, and when she removed one hand briefly from the stock of the gun to swipe the back of her arm across her forehead, I saw her hand was shaking. I thought her insulin might be low now, too. Hadn't I read something about stress affecting a diabetic's blood sugar levels somehow?

Miles glanced at me, and I knew he had noticed her unsteadiness too. It wouldn't be long before she lost focus completely and dropped the gun. Or Rosenstein would be dead.

Miles said, "Where is Thornton?"

"I didn't kill him!" she cried. "I didn't! He came here...damn it, why did he have to change the plan? Why did he make him come here? Why did *you* have to come here? It would have worked, everything would have been fine, I would have been safe. But now...now I don't know what to *do*!"

Her voice, and her manner, was taking on a note of hysteria. I didn't know whether that was a good thing or a bad one. So I tried, once again, to pull her focus. "What would have worked?" I said. But then, somewhere in the back of my mind, pieces began to fall together, and I started to answer my own question. Something Corny and Melanie had said about one of Rosenstein's early films. All the things that hadn't made sense about the accidents on the set. Something Miles had said about a *Rockford Files* plot.

"You set him up," I said slowly, thinking out loud. "You wanted to make a scene that day at the diner. You wanted to make sure people remembered Thornton. You vandalized the set the next day, you switched the guns, knowing that Thornton had a set pass. And every time there was an investigation you pointed the police in his direction."

"I told you, it was Seth's idea," she said. She lifted her hand from the gun again, this time to touch her forehead, where a yellow bruise surrounded the fine line of stitches there. "But he hurt me. He wasn't supposed to hurt me. He promised he wouldn't." Her voice fell a little. "He always promises."

I said, "You went to nursing school. You know how to take blood. You must've been planning this since that night we went to dinner, and you asked me about camping. It was all scripted, from the very beginning, to make it look like your ex-husband murdered you while you were alone in the wilderness, camping. You saved your blood, just like in the vampire movie, and you poured it all over the sleeping bag to make it look like you'd been stabbed to death."

Miles shot a quick look at me, but I could tell by Dallas's expression that I was right. "But how could you have known Thornton would follow you to the campsite? How could you be sure he'd come to me, and I'd give him directions?"

"That was just good luck," Dallas admitted. She licked her lips, which were dry and cracked with the cold. "The plan was for Seth to plant the bloody knife in Brett's truck and leave some blood on the steering wheel and other places to make it look like he'd had blood on his hands. We knew he'd be the first one the police looked at, after all the complaints against him. All we had to do was supply the evidence. But when you texted to say someone who claimed to be my brother was coming for me, it was even better."

She frowned faintly. "Only he didn't come after me. He was too damn lazy. He got just past the falls, I guess, and turned around and went back to the hotel. But he threw your business card away, and it was a good thing I found it, because it placed him at the scene. I thought that would be enough, with the page from the script, and a little blood. Maybe it would have been. But he didn't come after me. He had an alibi. They let him go."

Miles said quietly, "Is Thornton dead? Did you kill him?"

What he really wanted to know was whether or not there was anyone else, with or without a weapon, on the premises, who was likely to ambush us or distract Dallas. I wanted to know that too. Seth Rosenstein was very still on the ground. I couldn't tell if he was breathing.

Dallas said, "Seth was so mad. He doesn't like it when people don't do what he says. He hates to change the plan. He said I'd screwed everything up. He was so mad." Her voice sounded small, weak. And the barrel of the gun, which was still pointed at us, wavered a little. And then her lips tightened, almost defiantly, and her shoulders straightened. "He said it was all my fault, but it wasn't. I stayed with the plan. I fixed the campsite and planted the knife and threw the sleeping bag over the cliff like we planned, and I texted Seth a photo when I was done, just like we'd planned, so he knew when to come get me. He picked me up and brought me here and everything should have been fine, I should have been on my way to Switzerland the next morning...but Brett had an alibi. It wasn't my fault."

Cisco's head suddenly swiveled to his right. I saw it too, a slight flicker of movement near the corner of the house. Was it Thornton? Was he coming for us?

I tightened the leash, edging closer to Miles. His heat, his solid, living form, calmed me and made me feel stronger than I was. Miles had noticed the direction of Cisco's gaze, and he had a better view of the house than I did. Cisco, ears pointed in the same direction as his eyes, started a low growl. Miles spoke over it, and Dallas didn't seem to notice.

He said, "We know it wasn't your fault. We can help you. We can tell the police what we know. Rosenstein used you. He wanted Thornton out of the way just as much as you did, maybe more. He had millions at stake, he couldn't afford to lose this film."

"It was all about the movie for him," Dallas said, her jaw tightening. "I loved him, I would have done anything for him, but all he cared about was the movie. He was supposed to take care of me. He promised to take care of me!"

I could feel Cisco's muscles tightening in preparation to lunge, and I tightened the leash. *Stay, Cisco, stay,* I begged silently. I heard another low rumble in his throat.

Miles said, "Rosenstein threatened to invoke the health clause in your contract if you didn't cooperate, didn't he? And if that became public, you'd never work again."

Once again she lifted her hand to blot her damp face. She looked hurt, puzzled, and maybe a little confused. "He didn't have to do that. I wanted to help him. I wanted to help *us.* I gave Brett everything I had, fifty thousand dollars, and I promised to give him half of what I earned on this film. He was going to leave us alone. Everything would have been fine. But that wasn't enough for Seth. He's the one who called Brett out here, said he had a proposition for him. But all the time he had this plan, to set Brett up for my murder and send him to prison for life."

Cisco's head snapped around as something else caught his attention from the house, this time to the left. Dallas noticed and started to look that way, but Miles spoke quickly. "That makes sense," he said. "It was a good plan."

She gave a single harsh, angry shake of her head. "We could have *made* it work! I tried to tell Seth that, tried to tell him that as long as Brett thought I was dead we could make anything work, I would be safe from him and nothing else mattered!" She drew in a quick sharp breath that was almost like a gasp, as though even acknowledging the truth was physically painful for her. "But that's not what he wanted. Seth didn't care what happened to me. All he cared about was the movie. He just wanted Brett out of the way."

Miles said again, very carefully, "Where is he? Where is Thornton?"

Dallas replied simply, "He's dead. Seth called him, told him to meet him here this morning. He brought him *here*. Where I was! Seth brought him here, and he didn't tell me and then he shot him dead, point blank. There in the house, by the fireplace. He used my gun." She looked at Seth Rosenstein on the ground, her face curiously expressionless. "He didn't care what happened to me at all. He said he had a new plan. He said we'd tell the police about the scam, about how I'd faked my death to get away from Brett and that Brett had broken in here and that I'd shot him in self-defense. He said I probably wouldn't do time. He said the trial would be great publicity for the film. And that's when I realized he'd been lying to me all this time, he was never going to send me to Switzerland, we were never going to have a life together. He'd made the whole thing up just to trick me into helping him get Brett off his back. Just so he could have his movie."

She took a shaky breath. She was losing focus, I could see it in her eyes. She might be on the verge of collapse. Or she might be about to lose control entirely.

She said, "I couldn't believe it. I couldn't believe I'd been such a fool. I starting screaming at him, tried to get the gun away…we fought, the gun went off. I should have killed him," she added, gazing down at him dispassionately. "Don't you think he deserves to die?"

That was when I saw two figures detach themselves from the shadows of the house and begin to move toward us at a rapid pace. My heart lurched to my throat. Cisco started to bark. Dallas swung the gun toward him and cried, "What is *wrong* with him? What's he barking at?"

She started to turn toward the direction in which Cisco was looking, but I stopped her with an urgent, "It's your blood sugar! He can tell when it's too high or too low. He's trying to warn you."

I dropped to one knee, wrapping my arms around Cisco to calm him. She stared at us. "I've heard about that," she said uncertainly. "He can do that?"

I said, breathing hard, "Dallas, put the gun down. You can't do this, you know you can't. You're too sick. Let us help you."

Those last few seconds seemed to go on forever. She looked at me, and I held her gaze. Cisco whimpered, trying not to bark. I didn't breathe.

Dallas whispered, "I'm so tired." She lowered the gun slowly to her side.

The two sheriff's deputies, approaching from behind, reached her then. She didn't even struggle when one of them took the weapon from her hand, and the look in her eyes, when her gaze met mine, was simple relief.

We watched as the ambulance took Seth Rosenstein away. Emergency Rescue arrived a few minutes later with EMTs to check Dallas out, but I heard someone say she had begun to stabilize as soon as she got her insulin injection.

"They'll probably take her to the hospital to be checked out," Jolene told us. "We'll interview her there as soon as the docs give us the all-clear. She hasn't been making much sense up to now."

This was as forthcoming as Jolene had ever been about an active case—or anything, really—and I figured it was out of respect for Miles. I took advantage of her cooperative mood and said, "Will you arrest her?"

Jolene glanced around. The place was swarming with SBI agents and sheriff's deputies; crime scene tape roped off the entire approach to the house. Deke was there, full of self-importance but mostly looking for something to do. Buck had not yet arrived.

Jolene shrugged. "Not up to me. But if it were… she had the murder weapon in her hand, along with motive and opportunity. It doesn't look good for her."

Miles said, "How did you get here so fast? In fact, how did you get here at all? I didn't have time to call 911."

Jolene said, "Rosenstein reported a shooting at 9:55 a.m. The SBI had asked us to keep an eye on Thornton so we had deputies in the vicinity already. Officers arrived within ten minutes, but reported a hostage situation and advised caution."

It took me a moment to realize that the hostages she referred to were Miles, Cisco, and me. I looked over at Dallas, who was sitting on the back of the rescue truck with a blood pressure cuff on her arm and two deputies and an EMT hovering over her. "Can I talk to her?" I asked.

Jolene shook her head. "No. You both are witnesses and she's a suspect. I just came over to tell you that you can go. We have your statements, and we'll be in touch if we need anything else."

I drew a breath to object, but Miles spoke over me. "Thank you, Deputy."

Jolene looked as though she wanted to say something else, but then changed her mind. She gave Miles a polite nod of her head and walked away.

Miles put his arm around my shoulders. "Come on, sugar. I'd really like to get out of here before they bring the body out."

I looked up at him helplessly. I didn't know what to say. I settled for, "I'm glad you were here, Miles."

He smiled his reassurance and squeezed my shoulders, but the smile turned into concern. "You okay, baby? How do you feel?"

I looked over my shoulder at Dallas, who had been lied to, controlled, and abused by two men and whose life now, through very little fault of her own, was in ruins. Cisco leaned companionably against my knee, looking around with interest at all that was going on. Miles cradled my shoulders. Surrounded by the warmth of my two guys, I was secure, protected. And loved.

I smiled back at Miles. "Lucky," I said. "I feel really lucky."

CHAPTER TWENTY-ONE

A week went by, and another, and the reporters and satellite trucks went home. So did the production company. With the film's director in the hospital and the executives in California scrambling to find someone to replace him, the shooting schedule came to a halt. Mischief and Magic might never see themselves on the big screen after all. I had a feeling they wouldn't care.

I heard Seth Rosenstein had surgery in Asheville and was transferred to a fancy private hospital in Atlanta to recuperate. He was expected to make a full recovery. I also heard that Dallas had been released on her own recognizance after the shooting was ruled "accidental." I guess she went back to California, or Texas; I never knew for sure. To tell the truth, I was pretty busy the next few weeks with Dog Daze, and the big tracking club event, and the holidays coming up. My brush with Hollywood had left a sour taste in my mouth, and I didn't go out of my way to remind myself of all the violence and chaos it had brought into our peaceful mountain community.

A few days after the tracking test—which was a huge success, by the way, and netted the club almost $500—Sonny and I met at Miss Meg's for lunch, where she presented me with a check and an update on the dog bite case. Of course, delighted visions of stockings overflowing with dog biscuits danced in my head when I saw the check, but I hesitated when Sonny informed me that she was not, after all, taking the case to trial.

I tried not to let my disappointment show as I pushed the check back across the table to her. "But if you're not getting paid…"

She laughed and pushed the check back to me. "Don't worry, everyone is getting paid. We settled with Kate Greene's homeowner's insurance. Once she realized her insurance covered the damages, she let herself be persuaded to tell the truth about what happened, saving everyone the cost of a jury trial."

I grinned and retrieved my check. "So I was right? The paper had pictures of the dog at the ball game?"

"Actually," Sonny admitted, "that's the bad news. They didn't. But the good news is that neither Kate Greene nor her new husband knew that. You were right about the German Shepherd being her husband's dog. He had tried to take the dog to a game before but had been turned away at the gate. So this time he decided to sneak him in wearing Rambo's vest. He still swears up and down this was the first time his dog has ever bitten anybody."

I shook my head. "That's one time too many," I said bitterly. "That little boy is going to be afraid of dogs the rest of his life, and even if it *wasn't* a real service dog wearing the vest, how many people are going to know that? It still gives service dogs a bad name."

Sonny nodded soberly and sipped her coffee. "Of course, I'd prefer to have it all brought out in open court, but that just wasn't in the best interest of my client. I did, however, call in a favor from the editor of the local paper, and he's agreed to do an article and tie it into a feature about what *real* service dogs do. And at least Jen Tolliver's name is cleared."

I raised my coffee cup in a toast to that.

Sonny glanced up over my shoulder and swallowed her coffee. "Good afternoon, Deputy," she said.

I turned to see Jolene standing behind me wearing her usual inscrutable expression and holding a mug of coffee. I said uncertainly, "Hi, Jolene."

She replied, "Ladies." And she just stood there.

Sonny glanced at me, clearly puzzled, and gestured to the empty chair at the head of our table. "Will you join us?"

To my everlasting surprise, Jolene did.

A moment of awkward silence passed while we all sipped our coffee and tried to think of something to say. Then Sonny glanced at her watch and said, "Actually, I'm afraid I have to be going. I've got the check, Raine."

But I waved her on. "My treat," I said, and grinned. "After all, I'm rich."

We watched as Hero gathered up Sonny's purse and briefcase and stood ready until she was on her feet. When they were gone, I nibbled at the remaining French fries on my plate, waiting for Jolene to say something. Eventually she did.

"I thought you might like an update on the Thornton murder case," she said.

To say I was taken aback would be an understatement. I answered, "Okay."

She sipped her coffee. "We've been in touch with law enforcement in Texas and in California," she said. "It looks like Thornton wasn't the only one who got his kicks by beating up on women. Rosenstein was just more subtle about it. Two of his exes are ready to come forward with testimony of psychological abuse and physical threats, and at least three actresses claim they were threatened or intimidated into performing sexual acts for him. Dallas McKenzie claims that when she was fourteen he broke her arm and that twice when she went to the emergency room with injuries supposedly sustained from her husband, they were actually inflicted by Rosenstein."

I put down my uneaten French fry, my appetite gone. "That's sick." I couldn't think of another word for it.

Jolene nodded soberly. "McKenzie is one of those women who came from a home where physical violence was the norm. It was all she'd ever known. She went from one abuser to another, maybe because she didn't know how to stop it, maybe because in some weird way she was addicted to it, the same way she was addicted to the rush she got from doing all those crazy stunts. Who knows? But at some point she decided she was better off with Rosenstein than with Thornton, and that's when the real trouble started."

I said, "Are you talking about the stolen manuscript?"

"Apparently, McKenzie promised Rosenstein the book to get in his good graces, but when Thornton found out, he refused to sell the movie rights to Rosenstein. So Rosenstein stole the story, wrote his own screenplay, and registered all the rights. Since Thornton's original work wasn't copyrighted, he never had the evidence to prove plagiarism, only enough to make accusations and scare away investors. McKenzie tried to pay him off, but he broke their deal, kept making threats to shut down the production. I guess that's when Rosenstein had enough and came up with that crazy scheme to frame Thornton for Dallas's murder."

She sipped her coffee. "Anyway, with everything that's coming out, it looks like Rosenstein's decided a trial isn't in his best interest. He's claiming Thornton broke into his house and he shot him in self-defense. McKenzie is backing him up."

I objected, "But she told us…"

"Doesn't matter what she told you. She was in the middle of a diabetic incident and claims she doesn't even remember what she said. It would be hearsay anyway."

That made me enormously sad. After everything that had happened, she still was under Seth Rosenstein's spell. I asked, "What will happen to her?"

"So far, no charges have been brought," Jolene said. "They probably won't be. Rosenstein's shooting was ruled accidental. Maybe he bargained with her to back him up on the Thornton shooting by promising not to bring charges against her. By the time all the lawyers are finished, both of them will probably get off scot-free."

The waitress stopped by to top off Jolene's coffee and mine, and Jolene waited until she was gone to add, "Anyway, I thought you'd want to know."

I had to ask. "Why? You never tell me anything. Why now?"

She hesitated. "I thought about what you said. A little town like this, I guess law enforcement depends more on the cooperation of its citizens than it does on following policy. Maybe it wouldn't hurt to share what we know when we can. Maybe it might even do some good. Anyhow, it looks like I'm going be here for a while, so I might as well start getting used to doing things your way."

She lifted her coffee cup, not quite meeting my eyes, and I knew that was as close to an apology as I'd ever get from her. That was good enough. I smiled. "I heard you're up for Chief Deputy. Congratulations."

She didn't say anything for a moment. Then she took her phone from her pocket and scrolled a few pages. I thought that was her way of dismissing me, but I hadn't finished my coffee or my French fries, so I picked up my cup, determined to take my time enjoying both. At first I didn't understand when she turned the phone around to show me a picture of a beautiful little boy of about four or five with cocoa skin and almond eyes and an impish gap-toothed grin.

"His name is Wilson," she said. "He's my son."

I was too shocked to even respond. The glint of pleasure in her eyes told me she had gotten exactly the reaction she wanted.

"He's been living with my mom in Raleigh," she said. She looked at the picture one more time, her expression softening briefly, before she put the phone away. "That's why I wanted this job, to be close to him. But with it being the middle of an election year, and with things the way they were between Sheriff Lawson and me..." She gave a small, almost imperceptible shrug of her shoulders, as though trying to rid herself of an uncomfortable burden. "I didn't know how long I'd be here. Now, though... looks like I've got four years, anyway. Wilson is coming home for Christmas. To stay."

I found my voice at last. "Wow," I managed. "That's great. Really. I mean, seriously. More than great."

She smiled a little at my discomfiture, and picked up her coffee cup again. "I guess you heard Sheriff Lawson decided to stay on as Chief Investigator."

Shock Number Two. "No," I said. "I hadn't." I'd really been trying to mind my own business lately.

She nodded. "He'll be working mostly outside the office, pretty much independent of the rest of us. I guess things didn't work out for him in Asheville."

"What about Wyn?" I asked. "Will she be going back on the force too?"

Jolene shrugged. "Not that I heard of. Talk around the office is she's staying in Asheville awhile longer."

I didn't really know what to make of that.

"Anyway," Jolene said, "Looks like it's all going to work out." She finished off her coffee and stood. "Well, I've got to get back to work. You have a good day now, Stockton."

You know something? I thought I would.

The Saturday after school was dismissed for the winter break, Melanie, Miles, and I went to the local Christmas tree farm and hauled a six-foot spruce back to my house. Miles set it up in a corner of the living room by the window while I passed down boxes of ornaments to Melanie from the attic. Pepper, Cisco, Mischief, and Magic scampered around inspecting each box, dragging out strands of tinsel and ropes of lights. The house was filled with giggles and squeals and play-barking and yes, even the occasional crash. It was perfect.

Miles's mother was coming the following weekend to spend the holidays. We were all having Christmas dinner at Aunt Mart's, and Sunday brunch at Miles's house after church. Miles was having an eighteen-foot Douglas fir shipped in from Asheville because, he claimed, he couldn't find one locally that was big enough to do justice to his foyer. He was also, not surprisingly, having it professionally decorated by men with ladders. Miles enjoys acting like a regular guy, but that doesn't stop him from taking advantage of the best that money can buy when the opportunity presents itself.

We built a fire in the fireplace and put a pan of gingerbread in the oven, and Miles made a non-alcoholic eggnog that tasted like the best milkshake I'd ever had. He assigned himself the job of arranging the lights on the tree while Melanie and I sat on the floor around the coffee table, placing hangers on ornaments under the watchful eyes of four alert canines. Someone had found a holiday music channel on the television. I was reminded, over and over again, why this was my favorite time of year. And how glad I was that Miles had decided not to go to Peru.

Melanie chatted on and on about school and Christmas shopping and taking Pepper to the pet store in Asheville to have her picture taken with Santa. And then, out of nowhere, she said, "So, Raine. Are you going to marry my dad or what?"

I didn't have to raise my eyes to know that Miles, across the room, had heard the question and was looking at us. I focused my attention on threading a wire hanger through the loop of a glitter ball, my heart suddenly beating faster. I waited until I could speak without betraying my nervousness before I answered.

"Yeah," I said, as casually as I possibly could. "I think I will." I looked over at Miles and added, "Maybe not right now, but…yeah."

Melanie replied easily, "Cool." She held up her ornament for inspection. "Pepper can be the flower girl."

Miles lifted his cup of eggnog to me, eyes twinkling, and smiled. "Sounds like a plan," he said.

I smiled back. "Sure does," I answered.

It was going to be a great Christmas.

ALSO IN THE RAINE STOCKTON DOG MYSTERY SERIES

Smoky Mountain Tracks
Rapid Fire
Gun Shy
Bone Yard
Silent Night
The Dead Season
All That Glitters: A Raine and
Cisco Christmas short story
High in Trial
Double Dog Dare
Home of the Brave
Dog Days
Land of the Free

ABOUT THE AUTHOR

Donna Ball is the author of over a hundred novels under several different pseudonyms in a variety of genres that include romance, mystery, suspense, paranormal, western adventure, historical and women's fiction. Recent popular series include the Ladybug Farm series, The Hummingbird House series, The Dogleg Island Mystery series, and the Raine Stockton Dog Mystery series. Donna is an avid dog lover and her dogs have won numerous titles for agility, obedience and canine musical freestyle. She lives in a restored Victorian Barn in the heart of the Blue Ridge mountains with a variety of four-footed companions. You can contact her at www.donnaball.net.